Joyce Holms was born and educated in Glasgow. She has worked in a range of jobs, from teaching window-dressing and managing a hotel on the Island of Arran to working for an Edinburgh detective agency and running a B & B establishment in the Highlands. She lives in Edinburgh and her interests include hillwalking and garden design. She is married with two grown-up children.

MR BIG

When one of the better-known drug barons in Edinburgh, Chick Mathieson, is killed, lawyer Tam Buchanan finds himself reluctantly drawn into the dodgy dealings of the city's underworld. Freddie McAuslan, the young man arrested for Mathieson's murder, has recently done time for a crime that was almost certainly committed by Mathieson himself, and Buchanan is convinced of his innocence. Aided by Fizz and her grandpa, who is in Edinburgh for an operation on his famous clicking knees, he sets out to prove it . . .

Books by Joyce Holms
Published by The House of Ulverscroft:

FOREIGN BODY
BIG VIBES

JOYCE HOLMS

◆

MR BIG

9 901208471

Complete and Unabridged

ULVERSCROFT
Leicester

First published in Great Britain in 2000 by
Headline Book Publishing
London

First Large Print Edition
published 2002
by arrangement with
Headline Book Publishing
a division of
Hodder Headline Plc
London

British Library CIP Data

Holms, Joyce
    Mr Big.—Large print ed.—
    Ulverscroft large print series: mystery
    1. Edinburgh (Scotland)—Fiction
    2. Detective and mystery stories 3. Large type books
    I. Title
    823.9'14 [F]

    ISBN 0–7089–4611–9

Published by
F. A. Thorpe (Publishing)
Anstey, Leicestershire
Set by Words & Graphics Ltd.
Anstey, Leicestershire
Printed and bound in Great Britain by
T. J. International Ltd., Padstow, Cornwall

This book is printed on acid-free paper

For John

Prologue

Glendinning had only recently moved from his winter to his summer residence.

His constitution in recent years had not been robust, due in part — as his medical adviser enjoyed reminding him — to a certain lack of restraint in matters alcoholic. Be that as it may, he had considered it only prudent to postpone his removal until the end of May. As local parlance had it, 'Ne'er cast a cloot till May be oot', and at this latitude, however balmy the days, the nights were frequently rather nippy.

His summer quarters at the Carleton Highland Hotel, however, were cosy enough and he enjoyed being in the centre of things, particularly during the Edinburgh Festival when proximity to the theatres, the restaurants, and the hustle and bustle of Princes Street was of enormous value to him. The only drawback in residing so close to the city centre was the noise pollution. He had, to a certain extent, become used to it over the years but there were still nights — like tonight, for instance — when thoughtless people made sleep difficult.

1

He had been drifting in and out of slumber for several minutes now, while a peculiarly harrowing sound competed with the effects of his copious nightcap. For some of that time — whether minutes or seconds, he could not have said — the noise had blended with his dreams, turning them into nightmares. Finally he started awake, sweating and wide-eyed, only to realise that the noise was not a dream and could not be banished by casting off his blanket and sitting up.

Somewhere in the darkness around him, somewhere close at hand, a man was being murdered. The noises Glendinning had half blotted from his mind had been hysterical gibbering intermixed with racking sobs, muffled cries, scuffling, pleading and finally an appalling sound — a wheezing, gasping, gargling sound: the sound of someone choking or being strangled to death.

Glendinning's mind refused, at first, to accept that he was awake. Still somewhat the worse for drink, his eyes focused only gradually on the orange glow of streetlights around him, and he recognised the warm draught of air on his neck as coming from the air shaft of the hotel behind his back. Above his head, the arc of the North Bridge blotted out the stars, and at either edge the sky was filled with swirling pigeons, disturbed from their roosts by the stark-naked, wriggling, gargling figure that was swinging like a hooked fish from the parapet.

Quick thinking was not Glendinning's forte. It was some minutes before it occurred to him that he was in the wrong place at the wrong time. The naked body had stopped jerking by then and there was, in the sky, a faint paling that told him dawn was not far away. Moving with the dogged precision of the very old or the very drunk, he gathered up his blanket, his plastic carrier bag, and his half-can of Guinness, and headed for his winter quarters in a disused wash house behind Fleshmarket Close.

1

'*Grapes*, next! Have you nothing better to waste your money on? D'you think they're not feeding me in here?'

Fizz snapped off a sprig and filled her mouth with fruit. 'Nobody's forcing you to eat them if you — '

'You don't need to yell at me! I'm not as deaf as all that!'

'If you don't want them I'll eat them myself.'

'You can take them away with you,' said her grampa, charming as ever. 'And while you're about it, you can get rid of these books you brought me yesterday. There's not a word of sense in any of them.'

'You didn't like *The House with the Green Shutters?*' Fizz yelled.

'Och, but I read that years ago. And this other one — the one about the soldier coming home from the American Civil War — what he needs is a good slap round the head to teach him to stop whingeing and just get on with things! I couldn't be doing with it.'

'I'll see if I can get you any George

MacDonald Fraser. You always liked his — '

Grampa hitched himself round in his wheelchair to glare at her. 'You don't need to be getting me any such thing. I'm not feeling like reading and, in any case, I won't be in here long enough to get through a book. Just leave it be.'

Fizz drew a sigh. 'Grampa, you'd better face it. You'll be in here for at least another week. You heard the doctor say he wanted to keep an eye on you for a while before letting you go back to the farm. If you start tramping up the hill with those knees of yours — '

'My knees are fine. And who says I'll be tramping up hills anyway?' Grampa's already bristly eyebrows jutted angrily. 'The lambing's over and Geordie Grant can do the hard work for the rest of the summer. There's no need for me to be stuck in this madhouse for another week. I told them that. That doctor is nothing but a laddie. Not a year out of medical school, by the look of him, and that scared of making a mistake he'd keep me in here for a month if I let him.'

He shot a glance at Fizz, expecting some sort of dissent, but her throat was too sore with shouting to encourage her to waste her breath. Taking this as a sign of agreement Grampa nodded briskly to himself.

'I need to be back in Am Bealach to see

6

what they're doing,' he growled, one choleric eye still keeping watch on Fizz's lips in case she said something and he missed hearing it. 'Geordie's willing enough, but he knows no more about sheep farming than your Auntie Duff, and the pair of them will cause havoc if I'm not there to put them right. No. I'm going to phone Geordie and get him to drive down and pick me up at the weekend. I can do my convalescing at Am Bealach.'

'Like hell you will, you old bastard,' Fizz muttered, while she tried to think of some way of diverting him from such a crazy ploy. Am Bealach was a two-hour drive away, and two hours in the antique Am Bealach Triumph Herald would do his rheumaticky knees no good at all.

'Speak up, lassie!'

'I said, that's a pity because Buchanan was planning to come in and visit you on Sunday.'

'Tam?' Grampa reared up as though he was hearing the skirl of the pipes at Lucknow. 'Did he say that? I got a card from him but he never said he'd be in to see me.'

'Well, that's what he told me,' Fizz lied. 'He's been commuting to Dundee all week for some sort of tribunal but he'll be clear by tomorrow lunchtime. I checked his diary.'

The chances were that Buchanan would want to see Grampa anyway. The two of them

7

had been quite pally since Buchanan's holiday on the farm last year, and had he been in town during visiting hours he'd probably have already made a point of dropping by. Of course, he might have a golf date on Sunday but, hell, he'd just have to cancel it.

'What day is this . . . Thursday? Aye, well, I was hoping to see Tam while I was here, I'll not deny it. He was telling me on the phone a while back that he got a great pair of waders from his parents last Christmas. Tungsten studs. We'll need to be having him up for a weekend's fishing before the best of the season's past.' Grampa lifted his liver-spotted hands and folded his dressing gown tighter across his chest. 'I wonder would he like to be running me home and maybe staying for a few days?'

'Well, you could ask him,' Fizz said brightly, confident that Buchanan would do no such thing. Swiftly changing the subject, she reached across and lifted Grampa's newspaper off the top of his locker. 'You've got on well with the crossword today.'

'Don't you be doing that last clue,' Grampa snapped, making an unsuccessful grab for the paper. 'It'll come to me later.'

'I'm just looking. It's twenty-five across, is it? 'Franco-German agreements on board.' '

That had to be 'ouija', Fizz thought, notwithstanding the fact that Grampa had an 'e' in it. She dithered about telling him that he'd made a mistake in 17 down, which should have been 'paralysis' not 'paralysed', but decided to let him sweat it out. It would keep him out of mischief.

She started to say, 'Well, I must be going,' and then stopped, her eye caught by a news item next to the crossword. 'Blimey, I know that guy!'

'What? I wish you'd open your mouth when you talk, lassie!'

Fizz went on scanning the item. 'This guy McAuslan . . . the one they've arrested for murder . . . I know him!'

Grampa reclaimed the paper, donned his specs, and gave the story a cursory glance. 'Chick Mathieson. I remember reading something about him recently. That's right — it was in *Scotland on Sunday*. Hanging from the bridge at the end of Princes Street. He was mixed up in all sorts of dirty business, wasn't he?'

'Allegedly.'

A militant light appeared in Grampa's hooded eyes and his jaws sunk in as though a suction pump had been applied to his rear. 'Well, just you keep your nose out of this, d'ye hear me? It's not the sort of company you should be getting yourself mixed up with. How do you come to know this chappie who's murdered him?'

'Allegedly.' Fizz wished she didn't have to yell everything. The visitors at the next bed were more interested in her conversation with Grampa than they were in chatting with their own relatives. 'He was one of old Mr Buchanan's clients. Tam's father, I mean. I've been helping him research his memoirs since last summer and I remember this was one of his cases. He was the instructing solicitor a few years back when McAuslan was put away for manslaughter. McAuslan was supposed to have caused the death of someone involved with drug dealing. Maybe deliberately.'

And that, Fizz reflected, was *not* one of the cases old Mr Buchanan was likely to be including in his memoirs. He had been curiously unwilling to discuss it when Fizz first unearthed the file, and only later had it emerged that he was still furious at losing the case. He was convinced that McAuslan was wholly innocent of the charges against him and, although Fizz could never get him to name names, she reckoned that the old boy had his own suspicions as to who had really committed the crime. And now . . . here was McAuslan out of jail and immediately in trouble again. Made you think.

'Well, it's none of your business,' Grampa grunted, fixing her with what he clearly imagined to be a petrifying stare. 'You don't have time to be poking your nose into things like that. Just because your exams are over for this session I don't want to see you sitting back all summer and never opening a book. If you're working full time for Tam all through the holidays you'll need to get on with your reading in the evenings. Just you take a tumble to yourself, my lady, and start putting your studies first.'

'I'm twenty-eight years old, Grampa,' Fizz yelled. 'I don't need to be nagged to study! I study harder than anyone else in my year and I — '

She hauled in a breath of disinfected air and shut her mouth with a snap. Nothing she did was ever going to be good enough for Grampa so there was no point in arguing with him.

'Well, see you do that, then,' he returned, undeterred. 'It's all very well doing your part-time job in Tam's practice — and I don't know how he puts up with you! — but I don't like the way it gets you mixed up with all sorts of criminal types. You've more to do than waste your time ferreting around in other people's affairs the way you do. I wish to God you could just mind your own business like other folk.'

Fizz gave him her sweetest smile. 'I'm a reformed character, Grampa. After that business with the wee boy last Christmas I swore I'd never get involved in anything like that again. Too much hassle. Buchanan has people he can call on to make investigations.'

Grampa said nothing, but said it with an air that implied he was unconvinced.

Fizz reached for her shoulder bag and slid to the front of her seat. 'Time I was going. I'll see you tomorrow evening, OK?'

He glowered up at her as she stood, his gaze sweeping critically from her hair to the tip of her Doc Martens. 'If you've nothing better to do.'

Fizz was conscious of a wave of covert interest coming from the visitors at the next bed. They'd be expecting her to give her grampa a parting kiss, no doubt, a pat on the shoulder at least. The thought almost made her giggle.

At the doorway she turned her head to glance back at the old devil. He was getting tucked in to the grapes.

★   ★   ★

Selina was waiting for Buchanan on the transom above the front door and dropped, purring, on to his shoulder as he crossed the threshold. This little habit of hers, abominated by unprepared visitors, always filled him with pleasure. He found it unfailingly comforting, after a hard day, to be welcomed with such impatience and with such undisguised affection. It did occasionally cross his mind that a woman could perform the same function but one had to be grateful for what one had.

There wasn't going to be time for a game of golf before the light went so he changed into his shorts and tracksuit top with the idea of going out for a bit of a run later on. It would be cooler then and there would be fewer tourists walking the tracks around Arthur's Seat.

He was just about to unpack his Chinese takeaway when the phone rang. Selina, who had been sitting virtually on top of the receiver with a hind leg over her shoulder, attending to a small matter of personal hygiene, fell untidily on to the floor and stalked off into the kitchen.

'Buchanan.'

'Tam . . . ' said his father's voice. 'Have you seen the *Scotsman*?'

'I just got in, Dad. I haven't had the chance to open — '

'Yes, well, take a look at page two: at the

bottom of the right-hand column.'

Buchanan licked black bean sauce off his free hand. 'Can't you just tell me about it?'

'It's about Freddie McAuslan — you remember Freddie?'

Buchanan was unlikely to forget Freddie, even though he'd had little to do with his case and, on top of that, it must be all of five years since the guy had been put away. 'What about him? He's not out yet, is he?'

His father made a noise that was half chuckle, half growl. 'Out and *in* again. He's just been charged with the murder of Chick Mathieson.'

Buchanan sat up and dropped his king prawns on the coffee table. 'You're joking!'

'I'm bloody not and from what I'm told there's a fair bit of evidence against him. His fingerprints on the door of Mathieson's car, some of Mathieson's possessions in his room — and of course every rookie in the CID knows he had a motive.'

Selina, alerted to the presence of king prawns, hurried back from the kitchen, her tail an exclamation mark. Buchanan gave her a small donation which she carried under the table to chew. He said, 'I can't believe it. *Freddie*? It can't be true, Dad!'

'Of course it's not bloody true! Freddie's nothing but a daft laddie. He's too daft even to realise what everyone else realised five years ago — that he was set up to take the rap for Mathieson, and he certainly hasn't got the balls to kill him for it. It's taken him all this time to remember that he has a solicitor and phone the office.'

'Who's been looking after him up till now?'

'Paul Swan. He was the duty solicitor when they charged him, but apparently he and Freddie didn't hit it off.'

Buchanan reached for his paper and tried one-handedly to unfold it to page two. 'So what's happening? Who are you going to instruct?'

'Not me, Tam. You. I thought Lawrence Grassick might be worth — '

'Just a minute, Dad.' Buchanan abandoned his fight with the newspaper and swallowed a king prawn unchewed. 'You're not suggesting that I should *personally* take on this case? What about Alan? It's much more his kettle of fish and I'm sure he remembers Freddie much better than I do.'

'Tam . . . ' Buchanan noticed the hesitancy in his father's voice, 'I want you to do this, son. Alan's a good solicitor but . . . I hate to say it . . . but he lacks imagination. Maybe I'm not too long-suited in that area myself, but you are.'

There was a short silence but Buchanan

15

had a feeling there was more to come and he was right.

'I took it bad when Freddie was put away. He didn't deserve that. Not any more than he deserved all the other shit that life has dealt him — you know what I'm talking about. He's one of life's victims and I always felt we'd failed him — me and that cretin advocate I instructed. I'd like to see him get a break just this once and you're the only man I know who'd put any time or effort into saving him.'

There was no arguing with that view of things. To anyone else Freddie was just a cheap hood, a weak-minded recidivist who'd been in and out of remand homes, detention centres and HM prisons since he was old enough to lift a car radio. Most advocates — even Lawrence Grassick, if the truth were told — would be tempted to make a token attempt at defending him, take their fee and run. And there were plenty of people who'd say that maybe he deserved no better.

'Dad . . . it's been pretty hectic since you retired and I've got a hell of a lot on my plate right now. I've been away all week and — '

'Don't worry about that, Tam. I'll be happy to come into the office a couple of days a week at least. To tell you the truth I've been feeling that time's hanging heavy on my

16

hands these last few months.'

Buchanan's heart sank. It had taken years for his father finally to release his stranglehold on the practice and once he got a foot back in the door it wouldn't be so easy to eject him again. One felt sorry for the guy, of course, but, hell, everybody had to face old age eventually and when one's memory started to lose its edge that was the time to say adieu. Especially in a law practice.

'I could at least take the conveyancing off your hands, couldn't I?'

Buchanan couldn't bear it. He said, 'Dennis is handling that now, Dad — but sure, it would be a comfort to know you'd be on hand if needed.'

'You'll do it then, Tam?'

Buchanan rubbed a hand through his hair but couldn't think of any way to stall him. 'On one condition.'

'What's that?'

'That you don't mention a word of this to Fizz. You know what she's like.'

'Right,' said his father in immediate understanding. 'Absolutely. We certainly don't want Fizz to get involved in this one. I hear what you're saying, son — she'd be right in there up to her elbows if she got a sniff of it. No, no, no. This is not one for

17

Fizz. Too many very nasty characters involved, you could bet on it.'

'OK. I'm back in Dundee tomorrow for the morning but you can tell Beatrice to make an appointment for me to see Freddie in the afternoon.'

As Tam hung up the phone the doorbell rang.

'No,' he said, and closed his eyes, rather in the manner of an ostrich heading for a pile of sand. But as he walked to the door he already knew who it had to be.

Fizz swung through the doorway with a practised zigzag motion, sidestepping Selina, who thudded to the floor behind her. 'Hi,' she said. 'Thank God you're home. I need to talk to you.'

'I was just going out . . . '

'Where?'

Buchanan glanced down at his running shorts. 'Well, running obviously.'

'That's OK then,' Fizz said, making for the living room. 'I thought you meant something important.'

'It's important to *me*,' Buchanan muttered, thinking negative thoughts. 'I've been sitting around all day.'

Fizz fell on to the couch. 'Well, you can do some running on the spot while I talk to you, I don't mind.'

'You can have exactly ten minutes, Fizz, then you're out of here.'

Fizz stuck out her bottom lip and looked at him with hurt eyes but he could see her mind at work and knew she was wondering why he was in such a hurry to be rid of her. With any luck she'd assume he had found himself a girlfriend who was into running and didn't want to keep her waiting. It wasn't a likely scenario. He preferred his women languid, china-frail, and sybaritic, but she wasn't to know that.

She threw him a piteous smile. 'So . . . I suppose a quick coffee's out of the question?'

He returned her look blankly, reminding himself not to grind his teeth. 'It's included in the ten minutes, OK? So start talking.'

'I'm worried about Gramps,' she said, getting up and following him into the kitchen.

He stopped at once, smitten by the thought that he should have made a point of visiting the old boy, even though it would have meant leaving the tribunal early to make it by visiting time. 'What's wrong — '

'Don't panic, it's nothing serious. He's not going to pop his clogs or anything like that, it's just that he's threatening to discharge himself from hospital.'

Buchanan switched on the kettle and leaned his bum against the edge of the sink.

19

'But his treatment's complete anyway, isn't it? I thought you told me he'd be out by the weekend.'

'Well, that's what I thought but now it turns out they want to keep an eye on him for another week, just to make sure the inflammation doesn't flare up again, and he's spitting tacks.' She checked out his spice rack in an absent sort of way, turning round the bottles so that she could read the labels. 'He was saying this afternoon that he had plans to phone Geordie Grant, who's keeping an eye on his sheep, and have him bring the car down and pick him up.'

That sounded just like the old devil, Buchanan thought. He had to be at least eighty-two and, as Fizz frequently pointed out, they were going to have to drive a stake through his heart one of these days to be rid of him. He and Buchanan got along pretty well, largely because they were both into salmon fishing and malt whisky, but Grampa was not an easy man to live with.

'I wouldn't worry too much about him,' he said. 'Auntie Duff will see he doesn't do anything too energetic for a while.'

'Yes, but it's a two-hour drive to Am Bealach, and what if he has a relapse? The doctor at the hospital obviously thinks it would be a bad idea for him to be miles from civilisation at the moment. The nearest doctor's miles away in Killin.' Fizz clawed at her hair, twisting it back into the elastic clasp that was supposed to be keeping it under some sort of control. 'No. It would be a really bad idea. Unfortunately, he was so set on it I had to tell him you were planning to visit him on Sunday.'

Buchanan, who had started to spoon coffee into mugs, stopped and leaned both hands on the work surface. Slowly he turned his head to look at her. 'You what?'

'It was the only thing I could think of.'

'But I'm playing golf with friends on Sunday afternoon. At Muirfield.'

'It won't take you long to drive back,' Fizz pointed out brightly. 'There's a visiting hour in the evening.'

'We were planning on having dinner together — '

'Oh, well . . . forget it then,' Fizz insisted, backing down immediately now that she had him where she wanted him. 'As you say, it probably won't do Grampa any harm to drive back in the Herald. I dare say he could sit sideways in the back seat and get his legs almost straightened out. He'll be fine.'

In a sullen silence, Buchanan poured water and milk into the mugs and handed her one. Fizz said nothing to put him out of his misery and finally he muttered, 'What time's the visiting hour?'

'Six thirty till seven thirty.'

'OK. I suppose it wouldn't kill me.' He looked at his watch and then gave her a hard look. 'Is that all?'

Fizz took a sip of her coffee and ambled back into the living room with Buchanan trailing at her heels. As she approached the couch he overtook her and removed the *Scotsman* from the coffee table, pretending to glance at the headlines before dropping it casually out of sight behind a chair.

'Is that the *Scotsman*?' she said sharply, and he twitched.

'Uh . . . yes.'

'Have you read it?'

'No.'

Fizz smiled at him tenderly. 'I have.'

Buchanan gave up the ghost immediately to save time. There wasn't any point in trying to flannel his way out of it when she obviously knew the score, and there wasn't any point in appealing to her common sense either, but he did anyway.

'Fizz . . . please . . . just this once . . . don't give me a hard time about this. It's really not something you'd want to get involved in. I mean, this is not your average criminal we're dealing with here. I'm not going to get in any

22

deeper myself than I have to. I swear to God, Fizz, I only promised my father — '

Fizz held up a hand to stop him. 'I thought as much,' she said. 'Your dad was pretty sicked off about the outcome of that case. I just knew he'd want you and not Alan to handle it.'

Once she had the bit between her teeth there was absolutely no stopping her. Buchanan knew that. She didn't need his, or anyone else's permission to start nosing around, and if anything happened to her everyone, including he himself, would blame Buchanan. He threw himself into a chair and sat hunched forward with his elbows on his knees and his head in his hands. Selina snaked out from under the table and sniffed at his fingers, lifting her top half off the ground to reach them.

'Dad doesn't want you to get mixed up with this one,' he said plaintively. 'If you know anything at all about Freddie's background you know that he's heavily involved with organised crime. We're talking wide-scale drug dealing, prostitution, extortion, and every sort of violent crime imaginable. Freddie was mixed up with some seriously nasty people. Any inquiries I make are going to have to be very, very discreet and there's really no place for you in this sort of work,

Fizz. If you knew what you were getting into you'd — '

'All right, muchacho,' Fizz said equably. 'You'd better tell me what I'd be getting into. I got little more than a glance at Freddie's file so you could fill in the background for me.'

Buchanan could think of no way out other than to play for time. He stood up. 'D'you want some king prawns?' he said, and without waiting for an answer — it had been a rhetorical question anyway — went back into the kitchen for plates and forks.

'I don't understand why your dad gives a shit about that guy,' Fizz called after him. 'It seems to me he's a born criminal with no respect for other people's property and willing to do just about anything to make a fast buck. Even if he wasn't guilty of the crime he was convicted of, he was obviously guilty of just about everything else.'

'The law in this country is about justice, Fizz,' Buchanan felt he had to point out, 'not about revenge. I just hope you manage to get that clear in your mind before you get your degree.' He came back in with a loaded tray and dumped the plates and tinfoil containers on the table. They were no longer all that hot to the touch but at least there was plenty and Fizz had never been choosy as long as she wasn't paying.

'So . . . tell me about Freddie, then,' she persisted as soon as she had a minute.

Buchanan sighed. 'Freddie's a one-off.' He selected a king prawn and gave it to Selina, who was going frantic with impatience. 'If you met him you'd think him — well, you'd think him a bit simple, maybe, but basically *nice*. And he is. He's gentle, trusting, sweet-natured . . . he's a genuinely nice guy.'

'You'd have a hard job getting a jury to believe that,' Fizz remarked. 'Even if it were composed entirely of members of the Flat Earth Society.'

Buchanan shook his head. 'Wrong. A jury wouldn't know about his previous convictions and you only have to look at the guy to see that he's a complete innocent.'

He realised as he said it that it was less than two years since he had made the same assumption about Fizz and look where that had got him.

'Yeah, well,' she said, helping herself to most of the crispy noodles, 'the last jury found him guilty as hell, didn't they?'

'That's true, but they had no choice. There was a mass of evidence against him and Dad, for all he tried, never did manage to turn up anything really cogent in the way of a defence.'

'What was the charge? Culpable homicide, wasn't it?'

'Uh-huh. It started off as murder but Dad — and the advocate he instructed — managed to get it reduced. But call it what you like, the idea of Freddie beating a guy to death was — and is — totally preposterous. He'd never been done for anything like that.'

Selina went sniffing around Fizz's knees with her tail in the air and an ingratiating expression on her face but Fizz, who was no animal lover, shooed her impatiently back to Buchanan, who gave her another titbit.

'There was a witness,' Fizz remembered.

'Not to the actual attack, no. There were two witnesses who placed Freddie at the scene of the crime at around the time it was committed and there were several witnesses who claimed he'd had a noisy argument with Morgan, the guy who was beaten up, earlier that evening. But, although he was alive when they got him to hospital, Morgan never regained consciousness sufficiently to identify his attacker and no one came forward to admit to witnessing the attack.'

Fizz helped herself to more pork in black bean sauce. 'What was Freddie's version of the story?'

That wasn't going to be an easy question for Buchanan to answer without making his client look decidedly iffy. He concentrated on his food for a minute or two while he considered his answer. Finally he said, 'Freddie, at that point in his life, was engaged in drug trafficking — yes, I know how that sounds, Fizz, but bear with me. That was the only scene he knew. He grew up in one of the worst council schemes in Edinburgh. His father was Pakistani and he took off before Freddie was born. His mother was a heroin-addicted prostitute who was into shoplifting, begging, and all kinds of petty thievery to feed her habit. Any male who stuck around long enough to become a father-figure to Freddie was invariably a criminal. His mother's family were criminals, the neighbours were criminals, his school friends — and some of his teachers — were criminals. He was also, I have to say, not particularly gifted intellectually so there was really no other option open to him to earn his living.'

'There's always an option,' Fizz asserted, scraping the last dregs of black bean sauce out of the carton with a prawn cracker. 'I've been on my uppers plenty of times. I slept on a Greek beach for nine weeks once. I worked as a dishwasher in Toronto and ate the scraps off the plates. I went barefoot almost the whole time I was in Italy because my shoes were on their last legs, but I've never done anything I was ashamed of.'

Buchanan compressed his lips and looked at her kind of sideways. Shame was not an emotion that would come easy to Fizz, nor one that would cost her any sleep if it did. She certainly had her own code of practice but it didn't preclude taking liberties with the truth, manipulating people, or bamboozling those of a trusting disposition. She also had the advantage of looking like a fourteen-year-old poppet and possessing the most impossibly innocent and trusting blue eyes known to man; advantages not shared by the unfortunate Freddie.

Buchanan said, 'OK. OK. But you've got brains, Fizz. You were raised to be independent and resourceful. You can see alternatives.' He smiled. 'You're also a girl. And you know how to be cute.'

Fizz knew him too well to take that as a compliment so she merely grunted.

'Believe me,' he insisted, 'Freddie didn't choose to be bad. I doubt if he ever really appreciated what distress he might be causing other people. He just went the way of least resistance . . . and when Chick Mathieson got his talons into him he was like a lamb to the slaughter.'

'Yeah, and you don't have to tell me there's

one law for the debs and another one for the plebs.' Fizz unlaced her Docs and curled her legs up on the couch. 'Tell me about Chick Mathieson.'

Buchanan watched her preparing for a lengthy stay with growing depression and then collected up the remains of their meal and disposed of them in the kitchen. When he came back he stood at the window with his back to her, staring out at the sunset and thinking about Freddie as he had first known him eight years ago.

'Chick Mathieson,' he said after a couple of minutes. 'I never met the guy but he was pointed out to me a couple of years back and his name crops up frequently around the courts. I don't think there's much doubt but that he had his fingers in just about every branch of crime in Edinburgh and, in places like the housing scheme where Freddie grew up, he was something of a role model for the young lads. Drove a white Mercedes, dressed well, and also gave the impression of being very generous and paternalistic to those he was hoping to recruit.'

'What age was he?'

'Early fifties. Big guy. Looked like an ex-boxer to me.' Buchanan returned to his seat and allowed Selina to spring on to his knees. Her claws scratched his bare legs till he picked her up and rearranged her in a less awkward position. 'Anyway, Freddie thought he'd struck it rich when — at the age of thirteen — Mathieson took him on board. One of his mother's boyfriends had put in a good word for him, apparently, and the next thing Freddie knew, he was engaged in peddling small quantities of dope around the clubs and the university. He reckoned he was in a job for life and Mathieson promised him that, if he kept his nose clean and his lip buttoned, he would be promoted to greater things as and when he deserved it.'

'Dope,' Fizz said. 'Well, I suppose you could say that's not the worst crime in the book. Plenty of people are calling for cannabis to be legalised. But I suppose Freddie's involvement didn't stay at that level?'

'No, not for long. For the next five years he was in and out of court for cannabis dealing, most of the charges relating to bigger and bigger deals, and more recently, to other mind-altering substances including cocaine.'

He could see that Fizz was having a hard time accepting Freddie as a candidate for her sympathy. Her lip curled a fraction as she said, 'OK. So this habitual jailbird you think so much of — '

Buchanan lifted a finger. 'Not habitual, no.

Apart from his youthful misdemeanours he was never convicted of anything — not until the manslaughter charge. Mathieson looks after his cohorts. Very few of them actually come to trial. Witnesses lose their memories, evidence disappears — '

'Evidence?' Fizz said, frowning her disbelief. 'You mean police evidence? You're saying Mathieson's bribing coppers?'

'I'm saying . . . ' Buchanan pressed his lips together and stared at the wall for a second. 'I'm saying . . . it's possible that deals were done. Certain valuable items of stolen property were located, perhaps. Maybe other information of interest to the authorities was made available . . . who knows? It happens. No use pretending it doesn't. Sufficient to say, Mathieson believed that it wasn't in his own interest to let his recruits do time.'

'Yes, but if that's the case, how come Freddie was put away for twelve years? If Mathieson was into intimidating witnesses, couldn't he have leaned on the people who saw Freddie around the scene of the crime?'

'Exactly my point,' Buchanan said, sounding to his own ears as if he were in court. 'He could have, but he didn't. There's some slight evidence that one, at least, of the prosecution witnesses was the wife of one of Mathieson's own employees, but he didn't make a move to

31

prevent her giving evidence. Nor did he arrange to have Freddie represented by his own solicitor as he had done before. He kept well out of the whole scene and let Freddie stew in his own juice.'

Fizz shook her head impatiently and the wispy curls around her ears danced like gold springs. 'Why?'

'You tell me.' Buchanan twisted up a corner of his mouth and shrugged. 'If you listen to my father — and I'm not sure, in this instance, that you should — you'll be tempted to believe that Mathieson himself was the guilty party. There were rumours at the time . . . various unsubstantiated allegations, but no one would speak up in court.'

'You think they were scared?'

'Damn right they were. Violence was a way of life for Mathieson and his outfit. Anyone who stepped out of line, anyone who talked too much, any dealer found fiddling his take, Mathieson made an example of them. Whether he arranged it or whether — as rumour has it — he did the job himself, I don't know, but retribution was both swift and exceedingly debilitating.'

'Was that what happened to the guy Freddie was supposed to have beaten to death?' Fizz asked. 'Was that retribution?'

'That's what Freddie claimed. Apparently

Morgan was one of Mathieson's pushers and he was gambling with the takings.'

'Not exactly a smart cookie, this Morgan,' Fizz remarked. 'But then, I don't suppose you get many brain surgeons in that line of work.' She glanced at the paper lying on the floor beside her. 'So, it looks like Mathieson went a little over the score when he was making an example of Morgan. I imagine he'd have expected the guy to take his beating and shut up about it like the others he'd punished but then he up and died — in hospital, did you say? Right. Too late to hide the body then. So Mathieson decided to frame Freddie for it.'

'That's one possibility,' Buchanan said, unwilling to accept that it might be the only one. It was admittedly the version that seemed most probable but until there was proof one way or another he didn't like to make assumptions. He suddenly realised that he was getting cold and, putting Selina on the floor, went into his bedroom and pulled on his tracksuit trousers. While he was gone Fizz went to the loo, washed her hands and, as usual, counted the condoms in the bathroom cabinet. He knew she did it — even she couldn't open the cabinet door without letting it creak — but he kept forgetting to remove a few johnnies so that she wouldn't know how barren was his sex life. One of these days he'd lower himself to shouting through the door, 'Still four left, Fizz, same as last time!'

When he returned to the living room she was chasing Selina off the couch and curling up in her corner again as though settling down for the evening.

'That stain's come back,' she said.

Buchanan turned and stared at the skull-shaped patch of darker colour on the wall behind him. 'I know,' he said bitterly. 'It's a swine. Apparently there's a lot of oil in an avocado and it seems to have soaked into the plaster. I've painted it three times and it keeps coming back.'

'Why don't you have a decorator take a look at it?' Fizz wondered. 'It's not like you to do things like that yourself. Maybe you're harbouring a subconscious desire to be reminded of Janine.'

'Well, that's an interesting idea,' he said, pretending to consider it. 'Maybe I need to keep reminding myself to choose my fiancées more carefully in future. I could have been blinded if I hadn't ducked.'

Fizz's eyes flickered, and she made visible haste to change the subject, probably because she had just remembered that she herself had been the cause of that exciting little contretemps.

'So, what's our next move?' she said quickly. 'You haven't spoken to Freddie yet, have you?'

Dammit, she was the most provoking woman! He went and stood with his back to the fireplace so that he could glower down at her. 'You're not going to let this go, are you, Fizz? I never knew anyone in my whole life as nosy as you. Why can't you just let me get on with this my own way?'

'Because I'm better at it than you,' Fizz told him with a sunny smile.

'You think so, do you?'

'Well, I'm at least as good as you are, Buchanan, and two heads are better than one. Besides, you know you'd rather we worked together on something like this than have me ferreting around on my own.'

Buchanan examined her cherubic face with something akin to awe. 'How have you lived this long without someone strangling you?' He sat down and glared at her some more and finally said, 'OK, I suppose it's the lesser of two evils, but listen to me, Fizz. You've got to promise me you won't do any creative investigating on your own on this one. It's different from anything we've worked on before and if you got yourself kneecapped — or worse — your grampa would raise hell. I'd never hear the end of it.'

She tipped her head on one side and regarded him with pseudo-affection. 'I'm touched, compadre, I really am. I never knew you cared. OK, I promise. Brownie's honour. If anyone starts shooting at us I'll hide behind you.'

'No, Fizz,' he said, recognising a typical piece of flannelling. 'I'm not particular who you hide behind. What I want is your promise that you'll work *with* me and keep me informed of your moves before you make them.'

The two lines that constituted her blackest frown appeared between her brows. 'What are you like, for God's sake? Have The Wonderful Beatrice type it up and I'll sign it!' Then, seeing that he wasn't going to take that for an answer either, she said, 'OK. Whatever you say,' and muttered something inaudible, and probably insulting, under her breath.

Buchanan let it go at that, consoling himself with the thought that, considering what Fizz was like, he had come out of the contest pretty well.

2

Fizz was quite prepared to dislike Freddie McAuslan, no matter what Buchanan's thoughts on the matter, and her first glimpse of him did little to change her mind. He was in his late twenties and he was what Perthshire sheep farmers like Grampa would have described as a 'shilpit wee nyaff' or, in plain English, a poorly put together, sickly-looking, undernourished weakling. His bearing, as he preceded a prison officer along the corridor of the interview area, was noticeably shifty, and he had about him the air of one momentarily expecting a clip round the ear.

Buchanan shook hands with him and introduced Fizz as his assistant, and then said, 'How've you been, Freddie?'

Freddie lifted his thin shoulders and glanced at Fizz out of the corner of his eye. She thought he was probably unable to describe his feelings in any words he could utter in front of a lady. In the end he said nothing but his miserable face was comment enough. The guy had, after all, been out of jail less than three weeks and now he was facing another even longer term inside. How did Buchanan expect him to have been?

'Yes . . . right,' Buchanan said. 'Well, don't let it get you down. We're going to pull out all the stops to get you out of here.'

'I never did nuthin' to Chick Mathieson, Mr Buchanan,' Freddie said, suddenly lifting his eyes and staring hard at both of them across the table that separated them. 'I swear to God I never laid a finger on him — I wouldn't ever've done that! He was the bes' frien' I ever had — looked after me — gave me a job — an' a place to live. Honest, Mr Buchanan, I never done it. Honest.'

Fizz, seeing him properly for the first time, was astonished by the purity of his face. It was like something out of a Pre-Raphaelite painting — fine-boned, with a straight nose and sensitive lips and brown, straight-lashed eyes that looked directly into hers with what appeared to be complete openness. Against the *café au lait* of his skin his small teeth gleamed unnaturally white.

In another situation, in other clothes and with a decent haircut, you'd have taken him for an aesthete. Small, yes, delicate even, but the product of visibly good genes. Crossed with a suitably robust female, Fizz thought, he might have produced some interesting offspring.

Buchanan nodded and took some papers out of his briefcase. 'That's what we're going to prove, Freddie, but first I need you to put me in the picture. I know you've gone through everything with Mr Swanston, who dealt with you when you were arrested — I have a copy of his notes — but I'd like to hear your side of things in your own words.' He leaned back in his chair and crossed his legs. 'Suppose we start at the point when you were released from prison. The first thing you did was to contact Chick Mathieson, right?'

Freddie's open face took on a shifty look as though he expected criticism. 'I needed a job, see? An' a place to kip.'

'Sure. And Chick provided both.' Buchanan's eyes flitted to the top page of his sheaf of papers. 'He let you have a flat, in fact. In Causeyside Street. That was extremely generous of him, surely?'

'Just temp'rary,' Freddie said earnestly. 'He was gettin' me a job in London, like he promised. Coupla weeks, he said.'

'He promised you a job in London? When was that? After you came out of prison or before you went in?'

'Before. He always said he'd get his pals down there to take me on. If I done good, like.'

'That was a perk, was it?' Fizz interjected,

39

forgetting that she had promised to let Buchanan do the talking, but Freddie only looked at her blankly. 'Going to work in London: that was a big deal, was it?'

'Aye,' said Freddie, as though the answer should have been obvious to the meanest intelligence.

Buchanan shifted his position, bringing Freddie's attention back to himself. 'But in the meantime you were back on Mathieson's payroll: collecting money, dealing drugs — '

'No, Chick never had nothin' to do with the drugs, Mr Buchanan.' Freddie's eyes lifted from the table top but rose no higher than Buchanan's tie. 'That was my own scam. Honest.'

It was painfully obvious that he was lying. This was a guy who couldn't have outwitted a peahen that had been dropped on its head as a chick. Fizz didn't even try to hide her grin but Buchanan merely drew a long breath and nodded. 'So what *did* you do for him?'

Freddie's eyes searched the four corners of the interview room for inspiration. 'Just odd jobs, like. Went round with Kennedy when he done the deliveries.'

'Mm-hm.' Buchanan took another look at his notes. 'Kennedy was Chick Mathieson's . . . assistant, I see. He helped Mathieson with his wholesaling business, is that right?'

After a moment's consideration Freddie decided that this was something he could admit to. 'Aye. He delivered the stuff through the week an' then he helped Chick with collecting the money on a Friday.'

'What sort of stuff?' Fizz asked.

Buchanan turned to her with a faint smile. 'Clothes,' he said, inviting her scepticism. 'Designer labels.'

Yeah, sure, Fizz thought. Just the sort of scheme that would appeal to a thug like Mathieson: hook the suckers with the prospect of a quick profit on counterfeit goods, then threaten them into taking bigger and bigger deliveries. No chance of any bad debts either, not with Mathieson's reputation for vicious and immediate retribution.

Buchanan's finger found a place on the sheet in front of him. 'Apparently Kennedy hasn't been seen since the night Mathieson died. Any ideas where we might look for him?'

'No, I don't know nothing about that, Mr Buchanan. He was in the Cally Bar waiting for Chick when I went to get the car and that's the last I seen him. I told the police where he lived but they never found him.'

'Mm-hmm. How did they get on together, Mathieson and Kennedy? Was there any hard feeling between them?'

Freddie seemed to find this sort of question intellectually threatening. He shrugged nervously. 'I seen Chick punch him a coupla times, but it was nothing personal, like. Kennedy didn't take it bad.'

He was probably used to Chick's quaint little ways, Fizz surmised, faintly bemused by this insight into how the other half handled relationships.

'OK,' Buchanan said. 'Let's talk about what happened on Friday the thirtieth — that's a fortnight ago today — the night Chick died.'

Freddie clenched both fists on the table top and looked willing.

'You told Mr Swanston that you didn't see Mathieson that night.'

'Aye, that's right. I went to the Cally Bar, like, but he never showed.'

'But you'd have expected him to be there?' Buchanan prompted patiently.

'On a Friday night, aye. That's where he used to meet up with Kennedy an' then they'd go an' put the week's money in the night safe at the bank. Sometimes I went along with them.'

'But that night Mathieson didn't turn up. Were you concerned about that?'

Freddie seemed to be experiencing a little difficulty in remembering that far back. He shrugged. 'I thought he'd turn up later but he never. Kennedy went to look for him with a coupla other guys that came in an' he never showed again. It was near half nine when Chick phoned.'

'He phoned you at the Cally Bar? Had he ever done that before?'

'No.'

God, Fizz thought, it's like bloody drawing teeth. She wondered if a slap in the mouth would wake Freddie up a bit but doubted it. He had never learned the gentle art of conversation, had probably never been chatted to as a baby, had never associated with the sort of friends who liked to reshape the world over a nice bottle of merlot and a spot of taramasalata of a Saturday night.

'Do you remember that phone call?' Buchanan said. 'I'd like to know exactly what Mathieson said to you.'

'He just said to pick up his car — '

'Just a minute. Presumably you said, 'Hello' and he said something like, 'Hello, Freddie, is that you?' Try to remember his exact words, Freddie.'

Freddie looked vaguely insulted for a moment, as though Buchanan had called him a liar, and then tried to concentrate his mind by poking a finger in his ear and twisting it. 'He said . . . I think he said, 'Freddie? Is

Kennedy there?' an' I said, 'He went to look for you,' an' then he said . . . he swore a bit and then he said, 'OK, here's what I want you to do.' Freddie's eyes glazed slightly almost as though he were reciting something learned by heart. 'He said, 'Get the train to Dunbar and you'll find my car in the station car park. The keys will be under the rear offside wheel. Take it down the lighthouse road, leave the driver's door open, and run it over the cliff.' An' then he said there would be money in the glove compartment and the address of his pals in London. He said they'd be expectin' me an' that I wasn't to come back to Edinburgh. An' then he said it all again — what I was to do — an' then I had to say it all back to him so he knew I'd got it right an' . . . an' that's the last I ever heard from him.'

Buchanan nodded. 'You mentioned to Mr Swanston that Mathieson told you to catch the next train for London from Dunbar station.'

'Yeah, that's right. I forgot that bit. Yeah, an' not to tell anybody.'

'He didn't mention any names or give you a message for anyone?'

'No, just what I told you, Mr Buchanan. Uh . . . he said I'd be well in with his pals in London if I done what he told me.'

'Right.' Buchanan chose another sheet of

44

notes and took a minute or two to study it while Freddie watched him with anxious eyes.

Fizz, watching Freddie, wasn't finding it easy to remain impartial. It was simply too unlikely that Freddie could have come up with a story like that if it weren't true. He didn't have the savvy. There were other possibilities, of course. Someone could have fed him the story. Or maybe he wasn't as thick as he wanted them to believe. Buchanan raised his eyes from his papers and met Freddie's gaze. 'You didn't notice that the driver's door was ripped loose when the car hit the rocks on the way down?'

'It was dark,' Freddie muttered, twisting his bottom lip sideways to gnaw on it. 'I heard the splash when it hit the water, like, but I never seen the door stuck in the rocks. I wasn't thinking about fingerprints or nuthin', I just done what Chick said.' His delicate hands curled round the edges of the table and gripped. 'An' that stuff they found in my room, the key ring an' the hip flask an' that, it wasn't stealin', Mr Buchanan. I wouldn't steal from Chick — if I'd left them in the glove compartment they'd have sunk with the car anyway.'

'Yes, well . . . ' Buchanan said. 'You may have a point there, Freddie, but it's unfortunate that you were caught in possession all the same. Even if you'd stayed in London as Chick told you to — '

'But when I heard my ma had been beat up and might die — '

'Well, you know now that there was no truth in that phone call, don't you, Freddie? You realise that someone wanted you back here where the police could find you?'

Freddie ran delicate brown fingertips across the table like Yehudi Menuhin caressing a Stradivarius. 'I wondered . . . afterwards, like . . . how the hospital knew I was working at the Club Zed.'

'Who did know your address, Freddie?'

'Nobody, Mr Buchanan. I never told nobody. There wasn't nobody to tell except my ma . . . and she wouldn't have remembered anyway.'

'What about your employers at the club?' Fizz had to ask. 'Didn't they advise you not to go back to Edinburgh?'

'There's nobody at the club all day 'cept me and the cleaners, miss, an' the doctor . . . the guy who phoned, like . . . he said I'd better catch the next train.'

That struck Fizz as decidedly iffy. 'Well, somebody knew where you were and precisely what you were doing,' she said, barely hiding her exasperation. 'Whoever it was that topped Mathieson deliberately brought you back here to take the rap.'

Freddie had no response whatever to offer other than an expression of profound despair.

'OK, Freddie,' Buchanan said, reorganising his sheaf of papers, 'let's go back to the time before Mathieson was killed. Did you have any suspicion that he was worried about anything? Were the police bothering him?'

Freddie stared at him blankly.

'How did he seem to you?' Buchanan persisted. 'Was he jittery, do you remember? Worried, maybe? Bad-tempered? Was he behaving normally?'

'He was fine.' Freddie lifted his shoulders. 'Didn't look any different.' He thought about it for a minute and then added. 'He was real happy.'

Buchanan looked up from his papers. 'Happier than usual?'

'Yeah,' said Freddie, concentrating on some picture visible only to him. 'I seen him one mornin' — the day before he died. He was gettin' into his car an' he was talking to Kennedy and laughin'. Real happy, he looked.'

'You don't know why? Kennedy didn't mention anything to you?'

Freddie shook his head with a half-smile. 'Chick didn't like people who ask questions. I just keep my nose clean an' do what Chick tells me. That's the way to get on in this business. That's what Chick says.' He subsided into a thoughtful silence and then substituted, 'Said.'

Fizz tried to catch Buchanan's eye but he wasn't having any.

'Chick's dead, Freddie,' he said. 'Nothing you say can harm him now. If there's anything you know that might help your case now is the time to tell me about it.'

Freddie looked uncertain. He wasn't certain about a whole lot, it seemed to Fizz. If there was a brain inside that beautifully shaped skull he didn't believe in wearing it out.

'See . . . ' he said hesitantly. 'I could be gettin' somebody into trouble . . . '

'It's you that's in trouble, Freddie,' Fizz couldn't help pointing out. 'You're facing another long sentence — probably a life sentence this time — for something that somebody else did! Nobody's moving a muscle to save *your* arse, are they? So stop worrying about other people and look after yourself. If you know something you'd better tell us.'

There was a long silence while Freddie digested this advice. He was now definitely missing his security blanket. 'But I don't think I know nuthin', see? Chick had lots of scams goin' but I don't know what they were. All I know is him an' Kennedy an' the clothes business. Nobody told me nuthin' an' I never asked.'

Buchanan studied him briefly and then nodded. 'Well, we'll leave it at that for the moment, Freddie,' he said, sweeping his papers into his briefcase and tucking his pen into his breast pocket. 'But I want you to think very hard about what we were discussing just now. Think about who might have wanted to kill Chick because, whoever that was, he's willing to let you take the rap for him. You don't want to let him get away with that, do you, Freddie?'

'No.' Freddie knew the answer to that one at least. 'I don't want to do time again, Mr Buchanan.'

Buchanan smiled his quietly confident smile and leaned across the table to give Freddie a light punch on the shoulder. 'OK. We'll talk again soon.'

Leaving matters up in the air like this was by no means satisfactory to Fizz and she lost no time in apprising Buchanan of her displeasure.

'You should have leaned on him a bit harder,' she told him as they emerged from the prison. 'He doesn't even have the savvy to

49

realise that his main function in Chick Mathieson's organisation was as a professional fall guy. You'd have thought that one spell in the slammer would have been enough to open his eyes.'

Buchanan held the door for her and got stuck there, holding it, while a column of offenders' visitors filed through behind her. When he caught up with her he said, 'You have to take things slowly with Freddie. He needs time to think. I told you he wasn't particularly brainy.'

'Particularly brainy?' Fizz hooted. 'If the guy had two more neurons he'd be a halfwit — but that's where *we* come in, surely? We have to do his thinking for him.'

'And we will, Fizz, we will,' Buchanan said in his God-give-me-patience voice. 'But I don't want to get off on the wrong foot with him. If I push him too hard right from the beginning he'll simply dig his heels in and we'll get nothing more out of him. You saw what he's like. He doesn't question authority. He's been told too often that he doesn't have the brains for it. But if someone he trusts tells him to keep his mouth shut that's exactly what he does.'

Fizz waited while he unlocked the Saab and then threw her shoulder bag into the back seat and got in. 'It's not going to be easy, helping someone who won't even confide in you.'

'Give it time, Fizz. A few more meetings, a few more days in a cell. It won't be long before he starts to realise that, in this situation, I'm the guy he should be trusting, and then we'll get some answers to our questions.'

Fizz regarded his austere profile while he wasn't looking and thought he was probably right. People trusted Buchanan as a matter of course, but then he worked at being trustworthy. He lived by an unhealthily rigid moral code that harked back to the Middle Ages and caused him no end of angst but, in the end, it marked him somehow as a dependable sort of bloke. She'd seen the most unlikely people take one look at him and start weeping on his shoulder so it wouldn't be all that surprising if Freddie did likewise.

She thought about Freddie for a minute or two while Buchanan backed out of the parking space. Her natural reaction to someone as overtly innocent as Freddie was one of cynicism and suspicion. Could he really be all that witless? He had to have known what grief he was causing people by peddling drugs. He saw his customers, he must have seen what the stuff did to them, he was probably aware of the depths they had to sink to for the sake of getting a fix, yet he chose to continue to live off their need. Could be Buchanan was right and Freddie didn't have the bottle to tell Mathieson where to stick his job, but maybe Buchanan was wrong and Freddie's apparent lack of comprehension might turn out to be nothing but a piece of very clever camouflage.

The CID appeared to be satisfied that they had the right man — either that or they were so keen to get a result that they were willing to stitch Freddie up like a patchwork quilt. But then, stranger things had happened.

'OK,' she said. 'What next? You think we should try to locate this Kennedy character? He's our only lead at the moment.'

Buchanan took his time about formulating a reply but she could see his grip tighten on the wheel so she wasn't at all surprised when he finally said, very calmly, 'I'm not entirely sure that's the best place to begin this investigation.'

'You have a better idea?'

'I'd have thought you'd want to suss out Mathieson's wife first. In my experience you'd get a better reaction from her if you approach her right at the start instead of letting her find out you've been asking questions behind her back.' He slowed to wave a stymied Mondeo into the stream of traffic ahead of him and flicked Fizz an enquiring glance. 'That's something that will have to be done and, to be honest, I'd really like to leave it to you. I'm not good with emotional women.'

'Where does she live?' Fizz asked, momentarily diverted.

'At the top of Comiston Road. You could give her a ring to ask if she'd see you and then, even if she refuses, she can't claim she didn't know we were making inquiries.'

Fizz supposed there was some justification for taking that stance. This was the first time she'd been involved with an official pre-trial investigation and she could see that the niceties would have to be observed.

'Well, OK,' she said. 'I don't mind doing that but I think you should also be making an effort to establish where we can suss out Kennedy. He's the guy most likely to know who wanted his boss out of the way. At least he could tell us why Mathieson was so goddamn happy just before he died.'

Buchanan kept his face blank but the muscles at the side of his mouth were clenched tight. Quite clearly, the thought of Fizz and Kennedy getting together was doing his head in.

'To be honest,' he said, very calmly, 'I'm

not sure that a direct approach would be appropriate in that quarter, Fizz. It could be Kennedy who's behind this business and if we start — '

'Well, obviously,' Fizz interrupted, 'I'm not suggesting we kick his door down and start demanding to know where he was on the night of Friday the thirtieth. What I'm saying is that we should simply — '

'No, Fizz, I don't think that's a — '

'Oh, stop it!' Fizz exclaimed, irritated beyond measure. 'Kennedy's the guy we have to talk to. Why do you have to argue about it?'

'I don't deny that Kennedy's an important lead, Fizz,' Buchanan said patiently, 'but my immediate concern is with your choice of the term 'we'. To be honest with you, the idea of you and Kennedy having a little chat brings me out in a cold sweat. I don't even want to do it myself.'

'But you'll force yourself, huh?' Fizz said, staring at him nastily. 'I suppose you're planning to do all the real interviewing in this case and give me full responsibility for the *vitally* important job of soothing distraught ladies. Is that it? Well, I don't think so, Buchanan. I really don't think so.'

He pretended to be watching the traffic.

54

His expression didn't change but he wasn't fooling Fizz any. She waited till they had made the turn into the Haymarket and then said, 'There are ways of getting next to people and gently picking their brains.'

'Not in this instance, Fizz.' He threw her a hard look and then lifted a hand from the wheel to massage his temples. 'These are not amateur criminals we're dealing with. They're not going to be fooled by someone like you turning up on their doorsteps pretending to be the Daz doorstep challenge or the Avon lady or whatever. This time we play it cool. OK?'

'And how do we do that?'

Buchanan's long, spatulate fingers drummed a tattoo on the wheel as he waited for the lights to change. 'We could try to locate Kennedy — though, frankly, if the CID haven't been able to locate him by this time we might find that difficult — but as for trying to question him — definitely not. Not even indirectly. Even with Mathieson out of the way, the chances of getting anything worthwhile out of Kennedy are probably nil and, at this stage in the game, it's better to look as if we're doing no more than preparing our case. So, for the moment we *play it cool*.'

Working with Buchanan, Fizz thought for

the hundredth time, was like having a cannon ball chained to each ankle and what made it infinitely more frustrating was the suspicion that, just occasionally, he knew what he was doing.

3

Chick Mathieson's house was on the south side of Edinburgh where the ground started to rise towards the Pentland Hills. From that height there was a wide view across the city to the Firth of Forth, and at eight o'clock on a fine summer evening that view was magnificent. Arthur's Seat crouched like a big cat, right in the heart of the Old Town, and Fizz could pick out the castle on its crag, the dome of St Giles' Cathedral and the Grecian columns of the Acropolis on Calton Hill.

Closer at hand, the street lay empty: the only sound was the distant *tuck* of tennis ball on racket and that had to be carrying from the courts on the main road, a quarter of a mile away. The gardens of the two other houses in the area were immaculately tended, each of them a blaze of early summer colour, a perfection of paved pathways and neat edgings, a miniature Kew. You could tell by the details that this locale was for the rich and influential. There were post boxes at every other corner, speed bumps every hundred yards, and cherry trees lining the pavements. If anyone dropped a cigarette packet in the gutter there'd probably be a police car and six coppers on the spot in seconds. The Neighbourhood Watch around these parts had to be a Rolex.

Mathieson might not have been too choosy about the way he made his money but he sure as hell knew how to spend it. The house he had chosen was fairly modern but economy had obviously not been a factor in its construction. It occupied a corner site, separated from its only neighbour by a decorative screen of trees and shrubs. The garage housed a blue Toyota and, as she climbed the steps to the front door, Fizz spotted a red Cherokee Jeep parked further down the garden.

Her ring was answered by a woman much younger than she had expected: a tall redhead in her late thirties or early forties. Everything about her said 'money': the heavy gold bracelet, the three diamond rings, the carefully careless hairstyle, the silk knit top and designer jeans. She'd had an eye job that had left her looking permanently surprised and if those were her own teeth she was awfully lucky. No amount of money, however, could alter the fact that although her features were individually quite pleasant, they added up to a rather coarse and unappealing whole.

'Miss . . . ?' she said, and her eyes zipped

all over Fizz in a fraction of a second, finishing up, faintly shocked, on her face. 'Miss Fitzpatrick?'

Fizz was familiar with the reaction. A lot of people thought, at first glance, that she was a kid in her very early teens. If it had bothered her unduly she could, she supposed, have cut her hair and worn high heels and maybe even changed the shape of her baby-face with make-up. But she couldn't afford to keep her hair short, and high heels did her ankles in and, anyway, what the hell? Sometimes it came in handy.

Mathieson's widow pulled herself together. 'Do come in.'

Fizz followed her, making the usual apologies for intruding, into a lounge the size of Waverley Station. It contained three couches and three armchairs, a piano, a bureau and a whole raft of occasional tables and cabinets and pouffes and standard lamps, groups of paintings and huge displays of fresh flowers, etc., but it still had a roomy feel to it. It was very far from the environment she'd have chosen for herself if she'd had the kind of money Chick Mathieson must have had but quite a lot of people would have considered it very close to heaven.

Fizz walked over to the wall-wide picture

window and took in the view. 'What a lovely house.'

Catriona Mathieson heaved an audible sigh but by the time Fizz turned to look at her there was no expression on her face.

'Yes. It's a nice place to live,' she said with little sign of enthusiasm, and waved a hand invitingly at the grouping of couches. 'Sit down, Miss Fitzpatrick, and tell me how I can help you. You said on the telephone that you were making inquiries into my husband's death.' She was very calm, very matter-of-fact, but she was having to work at it.

'Yes. We're acting for Freddie McAuslan.' Fizz sat down and took her notebook out of her shoulder bag. 'I hope it won't distress you to speak about these things for a few minutes.'

'No. Not if it'll help you come to the truth. I want to see someone punished for the murder of my husband . . . well, naturally I do, but . . . if Freddie McAuslan's innocent I'd be only too happy to see you prove it.' She reached across to a side table for a pack of cigarettes and lit one, turning her head aside to avoid blowing the smoke in Fizz's face. 'Nothing would be gained by jailing the wrong man.'

Fizz gave her an encouraging little nod. Catriona was saying all the right things but her eyes were wary. 'Did you know Freddie?'

'I met him once or twice. He came to the house sometimes with parcels for Chick. I doubt if I ever exchanged more than a couple of words with the chap but he always came across as pretty inoffensive. I have to say I was quite shocked when the police told me he was responsible for Chick's death.'

In the silence after she finished speaking Fizz became aware of music playing somewhere upstairs; salsa music. Not exactly what you'd expect in a house of mourning, but maybe Catriona had simply been trying to cheer herself up. There were no children in the family, that much she had been able to discover earlier, so it was probably pretty dismal rattling around on your own in a place this size.

She said, 'Did you meet any of your husband's other employees?'

Catriona looked at the end of her cigarette and then smiled an acid little smile. 'You're not referring to his shop staff, I take it? You mean the people he employed to do the dirty work.' She made a puffing sound in her nose that was supposed to indicate derisive laughter. 'I appear to be the only person in Edinburgh who didn't know about the drugs and the massage parlours and the resetting and all the rest of the degradation they're

61

saying he was into. Funny, isn't it? Eight years I'd been married to that man and I never suspected how low he would stoop.'

Fizz tried to look as if she were anything but the nasty sceptical person life had made her. It was, after all, just possible that Catriona could be that blind. 'How did you think he made his money?'

'As far as I was concerned the real gold mine was the shop in Dalry Road,' Catriona said, still pinning that unnatural smile to her lips. 'Just second-hand cameras, videos, guitars . . . odds and ends, but he said he was making a fortune. He had a garage and a row of lockups, and I understood there were also some flats around the city that he said were rented out to students and suchlike.' She lifted one shoulder wearily. 'He always had some new project on the go, always seemed to be selling one business and buying another.'

'But you never suspected that he was doing anything illegal?'

'Well . . . that's another matter.' She stood up and walked over to a small walnut cocktail cabinet at the fireplace. 'I'm going to have a drink. Would you like something? There are soft drinks if you prefer them.'

Fizz plumped for a G&T and Catriona did the same, carrying hers back to her seat and curling up her long legs without a thought for the silk tapestry upholstery. She evidently was in no hurry to be rid of her visitor and, Fizz surmised, might even be glad of some company.

'Yes . . . ' she said, harking back to Fizz's last question. 'I suppose I knew that Chick wasn't exactly the most principled of businessmen but I never suspected anything on this scale. Fiddling his tax returns, yes. Possibly even buying goods that could have 'fallen off the back of a lorry', but never . . . never for a minute would I have believed that he was a well-recognised channel for stolen goods.' She took two decent-sized mouthfuls of G&T. 'I've told the police all I know so you may as well hear it too. I don't think they really believe that I could be so naïve but it's true. Chick never *ever* discussed anything like that with me and I honestly never thought there was anything going on that I should be worried about. It's floored me, I don't mind telling you.'

'The police don't have anything against your husband, Mrs Mathieson,' Fizz told her. 'I mean, they don't have any proof.'

'Oh, I know that. They were very careful to point that out but, nonetheless, they left me in no doubt that it's all true. They've had their eye on him for years, that's what they told me, so it would all have come out sooner or later. Now I'm going to have to suffer the story being plastered all over the tabloids. God, I could kill the man!'

She took a second to realise what she'd said and then tried to drown the echo of her words by topping up their half-empty glasses. There was a lot more gin in Fizz's second helping than there'd been in the first one but she wasn't worried. She had learned in a hard school and suspected her capacity would rival Catriona's any day of the week.

'You should go away for a while,' she said, edging the conversation on to a slightly more chummy basis. 'Just throw some things into a bag and grab a cruise in the Bahamas or do some shopping in New York.'

Catriona sniggered. She had lost some of the cool refinement she had displayed at the front door and her cheeks had become slightly flushed. 'They didn't tell you, then? About my wonderful husband's estate? No? What a lovely surprise *that* was, on top of everything else!'

She downed some more booze while Fizz waited politely and then she said, 'Virtually cleaned out his bank account before he died, apparently. Not that there was such a hell of a lot in it, as it turns out, but now they tell me that every damn asset he had was in hock — including the family home! Even the bloody shop is rented!' Something like a sob escaped her and Fizz saw her hand shaking as she raised the glass to her lips again. 'The accountant tried to explain it to me but I . . . I suppose I wasn't taking it in properly. Something about 'robbing Peter to pay Paul'. He was getting loans on one piece of property and using the money to pay the interest on another.'

Fizz glanced down at her notebook in case rampant disbelief was written all over her face. If Mathieson was the Mr Big he was reputed to be there was no way he'd be as short of money as that. It was improbable that he was even down to his last million. More likely he had salted away the better part of his income and another woman somewhere stood to inherit it. No doubt the police would suspect some such scenario and if Catriona didn't she was even dumber than Fizz suspected she was.

'It takes a clever man to play that sort of game and get away with it,' she remarked.

'And Chick wasn't as clever as he thought he was,' Catriona said bitterly. 'Not by a long shot. He was lucky. He was tough. And, yes OK, he made some good deals, but it wasn't brains that helped him get to the top of his particular profession.'

'What particular talent was it then?' Fizz

prompted, draining her glass hastily as Catriona headed back to the cocktail cabinet.

'Don't ask me what his talent was. I didn't even know what his *occupation* was till last week.' Catriona stood facing the window but not looking at it, with both glasses in her hands and the low beams of the setting sun slanting in on her face. 'Maybe he was good at scaring people. He scared *me* sometimes when he got into one of his rages. You didn't cross him, I can tell you that. He only hit me once — way back when we were first married — and I took good care he wouldn't have cause to hit me again.'

'Why stay with a man you were scared of?' Fizz had to ask. This was an enigma that had engaged her in the past. OK, women were the weaker sex, but a guy had to fall asleep eventually and blunt instruments were not all that hard to find, right?

Catriona stared into her glass for a minute. She was noticeably flushed now but still more or less in command of the situation. 'Why stay? Well, for all this,' she said flatly, and rolled wide eyes at the opulence around her. Then she added, 'It worked. It wasn't the greatest love story ever written but it worked. Chick did his own thing, I had my horse and my dogs and my cheque accounts, we lived high, spent a lot of money, and if Chick had his little fling on the side it didn't particularly bother me. What's sauce for the goose is sauce for the gander.'

Fizz looked down at her notebook. She'd written nothing in it but that didn't matter. All the important facts were lodged in her brain. She said, 'So what now? What happens to Chick's business interests?'

'God knows. It could be months before they get it all straightened out and by the time they've paid all his debts there'll be damn little left for the grieving widow, that I *can* tell you.' She finished lighting a cigarette and then waved it in a wide gesture that encompassed the room and the garden and the panorama beyond. 'All this is history. The cars. The cottage in Skye. The villa in Marbella. I don't know the figures but, the way the accountants are talking, I'll be lucky if I inherit a penny. Oh . . . ' a pause to drag a mouthful of smoke deep into her lungs, 'I'll still have some money in my own name, but all the rest is up in smoke.'

She blew a long stream of tobacco smoke towards the ceiling to illustrate her point and then turned a determined and somewhat desperate grin on Fizz. 'New horizons, right? A whole new beginning. Sounds exciting, doesn't it? Today is the first day of the rest of my life.'

Fizz rather thought she might be talking more sense than she knew. She could find that money wasn't really the be-all and end-all of everything. The lifestyle she'd enjoyed with her violent husband had cost her plenty — probably a lot more than she was admitting — and it seemed to Fizz eminently probable that she would be happier having a goal in life.

Catriona began suddenly to look as if she realised she was talking too much. She looked thoughtfully at her glass, probably calculating how many she'd had, and then said, 'I hope you're not driving? Maybe I shouldn't have — '

'No, I'm fine. Honestly. I use public transport.'

'Still . . . it wasn't very smart of me to ply you with gin like that.' The phrase 'a kid like you' wasn't actually uttered but it was implied. 'Would a coffee be a good idea?'

Fizz was willing to go for anything that would keep Catriona talking.

Left alone, she took the opportunity to give the room a close inspection but it was as unproductive as a stage set. Everything was so aggressively tidy that it was hard to believe that someone actually lived here, watched telly, read books or newspapers, nibbled biscuits, wrote letters. It was a room made for looking at. Period.

She was standing close to the window, trying to pick out the roof of her flat in the High Street and inhaling the scent from a vase of tall cream roses beside her, when she caught sight of a corner of pasteboard protruding from between the blooms. Quickly easing it out she found it was a gift tag bearing the words, 'Chin up, my darling! Back on 20th. Sam.'

She was tempted, just for a moment, to pocket it but, realising it might be missed, she poked it into its original position, zapped back to her seat, and was sitting there, innocently scribbling in her notebook when Catriona returned.

'There's something else I wanted to ask you, Mrs Mathieson,' she said when they had settled down with their mugs.

'Oh, Catriona, for God's sake. Call me Catriona.'

'OK, if you'll call me Fizz. Tell me, Catriona, what was your husband's state of mind just before he died? Was he depressed about anything?'

'Absolutely not.' Catriona didn't even need to think about it. 'He was as happy as a sandboy — dashing around all over the place, full of enthusiasm like he always was when he had some new project on the go. In fact he was happier than I'd seen him for a long time.'

'You mean, he'd been a little down lately but cheered up prior to his death?'

'Yes . . . I suppose.' Catriona hesitated. 'Yes, that's probably true. I think something had been getting him down for a while but he forgot about it in the excitement of whatever ploy it was that he was up to.'

'You don't know what that project was?'

Catriona was sipping her coffee so she answered only with a shake of the head, to which she added, after a second, 'He was never specific about things like that. If he looked like making a huge profit he might say things like, 'How do you fancy buying a place in Hawaii?' or something like that, but I wasn't supposed to ask for any details.'

'Did he drop any hints about his latest deal? Like whether there was a lot of money involved?'

'No . . . he didn't mention it to me at all but I could tell there was something going down. I could always tell. He was totally hyper for a couple of days, dashing around in his car with one of his pals. I hardly saw him.'

'One of his pals?' Fizz said, veiling her acute interest by leaning forward and placing her mug on the coffee table. 'Do you know who that was exactly?'

'Not a clue.' Catriona stuck a cigarette between her collagen-plump lips and left it there, unlit, while she thought back. Then she said vaguely, 'Probably not one of his usual accomplices. Somebody different.'

'What makes you think that?'

'I heard him getting the guy's phone number from Directory Enquiries.'

'What name did he ask for?'

'He didn't ask for a name. He asked for the number of Green ... Greenside ... no, Green*field* House.' Catriona applied her lighter to the cigarette and drew the smoke deep into her lungs. 'I was just passing through the hallway to let the dogs out so that's all I caught but, on my way back, he was saying, 'We'll take my car, then. I'll meet you outside the park gates at half eight.' Then, a minute later, he came into the lounge and asked me for my car keys to swap the cars over because he was going out early in the morning.'

'That was within a few days of his death?'

Catriona took another nicotine hit. 'That was the evening of the day before he died.'

'You can be sure of that?' Fizz asked, and Catriona nodded firmly.

'Absolutely.'

'And you never thought to find out who lives at Greenfield House?'

'I'd forgotten all about it till you asked me.' She stubbed out her cigarette and sat looking at it for a few seconds, then slid forward in her chair. 'Will you do it or shall I?'

'Maybe I should do it,' Fizz said. 'Just in case it's someone who might recognise your voice. Better if you keep a low profile till we find out what we're dealing with here. We'd better dial 141 as well, to withhold the number.'

They went out into the hallway and Catriona picked up the phone from the hall table and dialled Directory Enquiries.

'Don't you have a phone book?' Fizz asked, shocked at the extravagance, but Catriona just muttered, 'God knows where it is,' and handed her the receiver.

She watched tensely as Fizz got the number of Greenfield House and dialled it. When a man's voice answered she leaned close to listen and Fizz obligingly held the phone a little way from her ear.

'Hello. Is that Greenfield House?'

'Yes.'

'Could I speak to the owner, please?'

'Sorry?'

'Could I speak to the owner?'

'Which owner's that?'

Fizz and Catriona swapped confused looks. 'Are you the owner?' Fizz persevered.

'This is Greenfield House. There are lots of owners. Sheltered housing.' There was a short silence. Then, 'Are you talking about the Variety Club?'

Fizz had no idea what he was asking her. Sheltered housing meant, she supposed, something like an old folks' home. Not, in short, the sort of place you'd look for one of Chick Mathieson's criminal contacts. No explanation was forthcoming from Catriona so all she could do was to claim she'd dialled the wrong number and ring off.

'You're sure it was Greenfield House that your husband asked for?' she asked Catriona, who was looking half disappointed, half relieved. 'You couldn't have made a mistake, could you?'

'I'm pretty damn sure I didn't.' She stalked irritably back into the lounge, her fancy trainers squeaking on the parquet floor. 'But it beats me why he would be phoning someone in a sheltered housing development. What was that about a variety club?'

Fizz shook her head confusedly, wishing she'd taken time to enquire. 'He could have been phoning another Greenfield House entirely,' she suggested. 'It's probably not an unusual name. It could have been in another city, even.'

'That's possible, I guess,' Catriona said

unwillingly, 'but I'm pretty sure he didn't leave the house unreasonably early the next morning. I'd have remembered that. So, if he was meeting someone at eight thirty he didn't have far to travel.'

'Right.' Fizz thought about that for a while and began to wonder if she had given up on the sheltered housing place too easily. Maybe it would be worthwhile giving it a closer look. There was no reason why a geriatric couldn't be a crook and, anyway, sheltered housing didn't necessarily mean gerries. Maybe there were younger people there who, for physical or mental reasons, needed ongoing support.

Catriona combed her hair back with her fingers and heaved a sigh. 'I suppose this is something I really ought to pass on to the police. God. I'd hoped I'd seen the last of the snide bastards. That po-faced detective inspector gets on my tits.'

'No hurry,' Fizz said nonchalantly. 'Time enough when we've discovered whether it's significant or not. We can pursue it through our own channels and if it's worth passing on to the CID I'll let you know.' Somewhere in the house a clock started to chime and she realised it was getting dark. 'I should go,' she said, grabbing her things together. 'I didn't mean to take up so much of your time but what you've told me tonight has been really helpful. If you should come across any more information that might help us I hope you'll give me a ring.'

'Well, I'll certainly think about what you've told me, Fizz,' Catriona said, lifting her shoulders a little hopelessly, 'but I really don't have a clue about what Chick was doing. Not that week or any other.'

'Still, you'll be going through his papers and things like that. You never know what you'll find hidden in his sock drawer.'

A flash of amusement was there in Catriona's eyes and gone in an instant but it was enough to confirm Fizz's suspicion that Chick's widow would be shedding few tears for him as she emptied his wardrobe for Oxfam.

4

Buchanan had passed by Greenfield House once or twice before but had not had occasion to pay it any professional attention. Flats in the complex never came on to the Edinburgh property market since, as he had been able to tell Fizz right away, it was owned by the Variety Club of Great Britain and they had their own procedure for allocating any accommodation that fell vacant.

It was in a good residential area surrounded by imposing Victorian villas, and his impression, formed some ten years ago when it was newly built, had been of a fairly up-market development. On closer inspection, he found that it had changed very little. Behind the high stone wall that gave it privacy the garden was immaculately tended, with long undulating lawns bordered with shrubbery and flowering perennials. Partly screened by trees, a curved row of garages faced on to a circular turning area. The building itself was an X-shaped three-storeyed construction, cleverly designed to give each of its twenty-odd flatlets a modicum of privacy combined with easy access to a communal lounge.

Fizz got out of the car and stood looking around her with her hands on her hips.

'Well, I've seen worse,' she said grudgingly. 'If I ever get so decrepit that I can't exist on my own you can shunt me into a fancy place like this. I won't argue.'

Buchanan considered telling her he hoped to God he wouldn't know her in her old age. She was impossible enough now; what she would be like in her dotage defied prediction.

He said, 'I've seen a few of these places and this is about as nice as they get. Quiet part of town, half an hour from Princes Street, views of Blackford Hill and the Pentlands, and probably highly subsidised by the Variety Club. I wonder what the flats are like inside.'

'Hopefully we are about to find out,' Fizz said, glancing at him sideways. 'But, frankly, I'm not wildly turned on by your cunning plan. If we claim to be looking for a fictitious resident we're going to look suspicious right away. It's practically a cliché. Nobody but an innocent like you would think to make that excuse.'

'Doubtless you now have an alternative suggestion?' Buchanan enquired politely. 'One that does not entail lying yourself black in the face?'

'Well, yes and no.'

'Meaning, yes, you have an idea and no, it *does* entail lying yourself black in the face?'

'Forget what your mummy told you, Buchanan,' Fizz said. 'It wouldn't be the end of civilisation as we know it if you were to tell one little porkie-pie.'

'Let's not go through all this again, Fizz.' Buchanan knew already that he was going to nip this new plan of Fizz's smartly in the bud. He'd had sufficient trouble in the past through allowing her creative imagination full rein, but squashing her idea at the outset was the quickest way to make her dig her heels in, so he said, 'If you have a suggestion to make regarding how we approach this matter let's have it.'

'Well, it's a retirement complex, isn't it? Why don't I make enquiries about getting Grampa in there?'

Buchanan cracked a smile. 'I suspect Grampa would plump for euthanasia.'

'I think you're right,' Fizz agreed, visibly sobered by the thought of Grampa's reaction to any such suggestion. 'However, he doesn't need to know about it. After all, we haven't a hope in hell of getting him in there without an Equity card, but the beauty of it is that if anyone should get suspicious and think to check up on me, I really *do* have an old codger in the background who might be looking for what Greenfield House has to offer.'

Buchanan wasn't enchanted at the prospect of stretching the truth even slightly but he had to admit to himself that this option had a better chance of success than his own plan. 'OK,' he said. 'But you do the talking.'

'Actually, I'd probably have a better chance of success if I went in on my own,' Fizz said, her eyes wide and innocent. 'With two of us there — '

'No chance.' Buchanan locked the car with a finality that put paid to any argument.

'Right. OK,' she said with a very ill grace. 'If you absolutely have to hold my hand every step of the way, so be it. I suppose I could introduce you as my boyfriend.'

'I'm not being your boyfriend,' Buchanan returned with a vehemence which Fizz pretended to regard as deeply offensive. 'I don't see why you should have to introduce me at all but, if you feel impelled to identify me, I'm a friend, OK? Just a friend. And don't mention my name — or yours — unless it becomes necessary.'

'I live to obey, O golden one,' she said placatingly, peering at him through a fringe of golden ringlets which the breeze had liberated from her hair toggle. 'But don't crowd me. The concierge, or whatever they have, will be less on his guard if you're not breathing down his neck so try and stay in the background as much as you can.'

That suited Buchanan just fine. He was under no delusions about Fizz's superiority to himself in matters requiring a degree of duplicity. In recent years he had come to comprehend that her talent was largely a matter of approach. She appeared to have an inborn aptitude for spotting a sucker's weak spot and going for it, a skill she had, no doubt, honed to a fine edge during the years she had wandered the world living largely off her wits. Then, as now, of course, her juvenile appearance and expression of dove-like innocence constituted a secret weapon of devastating effectiveness, as Buchanan himself could testify.

He heard her say something that sounded like 'Hi!' and turned to find her addressing a thin, red-haired woman in a wheelchair. The red hair was conspicuously not natural and none too abundant, and it clashed outrageously with a pink satin shirt and a yellow tartan lap rug.

'You have a kind of lost look about you,' cried the vision in tones that reminded Buchanan of Alastair Sim in his role as headmistress of St Trinian's. She had apparently just rolled down the ramp from the entrance but now executed a nifty three-point turn and approached at speed. 'What number are you looking for?'

'We're not looking for a number, actually,' Fizz confided, her smile a radiant amalgam of welcome, deference and an immense willingness to chat. 'We're just window shopping. Wondering if this is the sort of place my grampa would like to move into.'

The lady's heavily made-up eyes widened coquettishly, including Buchanan in their catchment area. 'But, angel, you do know that this is a Variety Club complex, don't you?' she asked, in a voice pitched to carry to the back row of the gallery. 'Does your grandfather have an Equity card?'

Fizz appeared to hesitate before deciding, for once, that the truth would serve her best in the long run. 'No ... I didn't realise ... would he need one?'

'I fear so, poppet. Besides, there are no vacancies at all at the moment — there very rarely are, you know.'

'That's too bad.' Fizz looked utterly struck down. 'It looks such a lovely place. I'm sure he'd have been happy here. He's in hospital just now — and, of course, he would prefer to go back to his own home — but I did think, when we noticed this place, that he'd have seen the advantages of having other people around him.'

'I'm sure he would. Yes, I'm sure he would because, of course, there *are* advantages, especially when one gets a little older.' She glanced around her as though she hadn't taken any particular note of her surroundings for some time. The breeze ruffled her hair, exposing an inch of white roots and areas of pink, shiny scalp. 'Yes. It's very pleasant at this time of year and we're a cheery bunch, you know. We have our little concerts and our whist drives and our Scrabble tournaments. The occasional barbecue on the lawn. Visits to the theatre and the cinema.'

'Sounds wonderful,' Fizz said, propping her behind against the car as though settling in for a long visit. 'Does the Variety Club arrange your entertainment for you?'

'No, no. We have our little Social Committee to see to that. We're quite independent.'

'But you said the Variety Club owns the complex?' Buchanan put in.

'Yes, dear boy, they own the grounds and the communal parts of the building and each of us owns our own little flat. It's terribly convenient.'

Fizz drifted a look across the front of the building where a tall bay window projected at ground level. 'I'd love to see inside,' she said. 'Would that be possible, do you think?'

'But of course it would,' replied the old dear without a moment's hesitation. 'I'll show you myself if you're interested. It's not often I have visitors these days.' The wheels of her chair spat gravel as she spun it around. 'The name's Helen, by the way, Helen Marshall, but nobody bothers with surnames here.'

Her eyes darted to each of their faces in turn as she spoke her name, clearly in the hope of spotting some glint of recognition, but Buchanan was unable to oblige.

Fizz, however, screwed up her face and said, 'Now why is that name so familiar to me?'

Helen donned a look of becoming modesty. 'You may have seen me on TV. I had a long run as the mother in *This Man Kincaid* and then played Fenella in the adaptation of *The Rowan Tree*. Rather a long time ago now but still within living memory.'

'Of course,' said Fizz warmly, she who almost never watched TV and had, over and above that, been out of the UK almost constantly for most of her adult life. 'I should have recognised you. *This Man Kincaid* was one of my all-time favourites.'

'How sweet of you to say so, dear. It was one of my favourite series too, I have to say.

Such fun playing opposite Jenny Hargreaves and Simon Lamont.'

She rambled on happily while Buchanan and Fizz followed her up the ramp and into the vestibule, which was a hexagonal area with four short corridors opening off it. It was immediately obvious that an effort had been made to avoid any resemblance to an institution and with some success, given the limitations. The carpeting and soft furnishings were expensive, as were the framed prints on the walls, and every windowsill was lined with pots of pelargoniums in varying shades of pink. At one side was a sliding window that opened on to a reception office, currently empty.

Helen whisked ahead and, without waiting for Buchanan to open it for her, charged through a swing door into what was evidently the communal lounge. This was the room with the bay window and it was bathed with mellow, late afternoon light.

'This is largely where we live, work and have our being — well, those of us who still have a spark of life left in us. There are always some who like to seal themselves up in their wee flats and only socialise on special occasions like Christmas.' She trundled the length of the room and negotiated a passage through a group of armchairs and a piano to look out of the window. 'Everyone's outside today, enjoying the sunshine.'

Buchanan followed her and saw several groups of people sitting around in the garden, chatting, reading, knitting; a couple of ladies practising putting. It all looked too idyllic to be true. He said, 'It must be nice to have so much company.'

Helen kept her eyes on the garden as she answered. 'Sometimes it is, my dear. Yes, I dare say it is, on the whole, but all human life is here, you know, in microcosm. We have our little wars, our allegiances, our no-go areas, our cliques. It's not Utopia, but where is? Sometimes I think it would be a better world without people.' She spun round suddenly and, with a bright smile, took off towards the door. 'I'll show you the television lounge and then, if you like, you can take a peek at the flat we keep for visitors — not that it's used much. All the flats are exactly the same: the only difference is the outlook. Mine has a view of the — '

Two paces ahead of her, the swing door burst open. A man wearing a tight polo shirt and a grim expression stood there, blocking their way. He was a good twenty years too young to be a resident and there was something about his broken nose and aggressive stance that failed to inspire

Buchanan's confidence.

'Helen!' he said, projecting intense exasperation. 'The physiotherapist is here. Had you forgotten your appointment?'

'What are you talking about, Boston?' Helen poked her head forward, and stared at him as though he had run mad. 'It's not Monday, is it?'

'It's Saturday, Helen.' He bent down and laid a hand on her shoulder, gripping it lightly as he looked steadily into her eyes. 'She arranged to come early this time — remember? — because she's taking a day off next Monday.'

Helen stared her astonishment at him for a second more and then muttered, 'The physiotherapist . . . yes, of course. I'd quite forgotten.' She backed up her chair a little and his hand dropped from her shoulder. 'I'll just show my friends out.'

Boston merely clamped his mouth shut and twirled the wheelchair round to face the door, giving it a little push to start it on its way. 'You scoot along now, Helen, and don't keep Mrs Wilson waiting any longer. I'll look after your friends for you.'

Helen sent him a last look, half indignant and half submissive, and then passed through the door that Boston was holding open. 'Bye-bye then, folks. So nice to have met you.'

Fizz turned instantly to Boston, forestalling any plans he might have had for their immediate ejection. Buchanan had seen that precise expression of utter guilelessness and naiveté before and knew it for what it was, but it worked on Boston like nerve gas.

'You must be the care attendant,' she breathed, admiration and curiosity apparently overcoming her natural shyness.

Boston, who was probably less than four inches taller than she was, actually bent down a little to answer her, as though he were speaking to a child. 'That's right, miss. Care attendant, janitor, chief cook and bottle washer, that's me.' He almost smiled.

'It must be quite a responsibility — running this place.' She made a gesture towards the bay window, which effectively turned him round a little, giving her the opportunity to move between him and the door. 'Are you in complete charge of everything?'

He nodded, gazing at her with avuncular condescension. 'That's right. No boss breathing down my neck but there's plenty to keep me busy so, if you don't mind — '

'I was really disappointed to learn that only Equity members are allowed to stay here,' Fizz confided, treating Boston to the faint tremble of the bottom lip that had unmanned better men than he. 'I hoped, when I saw this place, that it would be possible for my grampa to stay here — even temporarily. He's coming out of hospital this week and I'm worried sick about how I'm going to look after him.'

Buchanan, perceiving that his input was not required at this point, drifted away a few paces and pretended an interest in a signed print of Holyrood House. Fizz's objective was, clearly, simply to keep Boston talking in the hope of learning something about the residents and two of them taking part in the inquisition would make it look too heavy. Behind him he heard Boston reiterating what Helen had already told them about the allocation of vacant flats, none of which deterred Fizz one jot.

'There's very little wrong with Grampa.' A faint quiver crept into her voice. 'He's had a lot of trouble with his knee joints but the treatment seems to be working. The trouble is that he lives on a very remote farm in Perthshire and the doctors don't want him to be too far away from medical help for a week or so just in case the inflammation starts up again. I really don't know what to do.'

'You should get on to the social work department,' Boston told her.

'Oh, I've tried them. They're no use at all. Grampa would have to be on his last legs before they could do anything. I'd really love to see him settled in some sort of sheltered accommodation for a week or so.'

A pregnant pause ensued, during which Buchanan strove to work out what Fizz was leading up to. Obviously, there was no way she'd get Grampa in here for even a matter of minutes, never mind a week or two, so she had to be playing a very complicated game. God, was there ever such an unpredictable and bewildering woman?

She sighed again. 'Of course, you don't offer temporary accommodation here, but I just wondered . . . Helen said there was an apartment available for residents' guests and it just occurred to me that . . . maybe it would be possible for you to let it to Grampa. Just for a week or so till we get him fixed up.'

Boston immediately refuted this suggestion, much to Buchanan's relief because, even if Fizz had some way of forcing her grampa to comply with her wishes, it was a terrible idea. Even she couldn't possibly take it seriously. The voices behind him gradually dropped to a level that made all but the occasional word inaudible but when he tried to edge closer Fizz sent him a venomous glance that put paid to that idea.

Whatever mad scheme she had in mind, it was entirely his own fault, of course, and only brought home to him the folly of allowing her a free hand in this sort of situation. Take your eye off her for one second and she went completely out of control. The original plan she had proposed to him had been merely to get a look at the place but now, in spite of her promise to clear everything with him in advance, she appeared to have gone off on some bizarre sidetrack that beggared understanding.

'Ready?' he heard her call and, turning, saw in her face the glow of achievement that always made his heart sink.

* * *

Fizz was quite prepared for Buchanan to be a wet blanket. That was par for the course. He was so rigid in his way of thinking that anything out of the usual, anything displaying a little flair, had to be suspect. Maybe all lawyers got that way after a few years. Maybe she'd get like that herself one of these days. And pigs would fly.

Right now there was no way she was going to pass up a God-given opportunity to find out what Mathieson had been up to — and with whom — in the period leading up to his demise. As she pointed out to Buchanan on the drive home, it was a hell of a lot simpler than trying to inveigle her way into one of his massage parlours; an argument which he appeared to consider quite persuasive.

Boston himself, she was convinced, was not the criminal type. OK, he wasn't averse to making a few bob on the side, but he'd seemed quite sympathetic to her pseudo-worries and had been no more difficult to persuade than the average bloke. He hadn't even held out for more than the two hundred quid per week that Fizz had offered him, which she had fully expected him to do. Just as well, really, considering the way Buchanan had bilked at being forced to underwrite the cash. Of course, it was all profit to Boston, who was not daft enough to pass the money on to the Variety Club.

Now the only hurdle to cross was Grampa's resistance.

She invested some of her own money in a bottle of Highland Park, one of Grampa's favourite malts, and slipped it to him when the nurses weren't looking.

'What's this?' He looked into the paper bag and then glared back at her. 'What are you thinking of, lassie? You know what a stramash they'd make if they found this in my locker. Or if they smelled it on my breath.'

'With a bit of luck you could be out of here tomorrow and drinking it in comfort.'

Grampa beetled his brows. 'What are you talking about? It was you who was trying to keep me shut up in this hellhole for another week.'

'Yes, but I've had an idea. I've thought of how you could get out of here and still be handy to the hospital for a while in case anything goes wrong.'

'I don't want to hear another word! I've seen enough of your ideas in operation, lassie. Just leave me alone to make my own arrangements. I'll wait till after tomorrow, but when I've had a word with Tam I'll get Geordie to run me home. No need for you to be taking a hand in things.'

Fizz accepted the bottle of whisky which he kept thrusting at her but held it on her knee where it could continue to exert a subtle influence on Grampa's reasoning. She said, 'Just hear me out, Grampa. I think you'll find it interesting. Honestly.'

'Oh, go on then. It'll pass the time.'

Fizz shuffled her chair closer to his bed and rested her elbows on the coverlet. 'There's a shelt — ' she started to say, and then realised that if she mentioned a sheltered housing complex she'd lose Grampa straight away. 'Buchanan and I are preparing a case for court and we need information on some unidentified person who lives in a place called

92

Greenfield House.'

'What sort of case is this?'

'It's *sub judice*, Grampa. I'm not supposed to talk about it.' That shut him up for the moment but she could tell by his hitched eyebrow that he wasn't entirely fooled. 'Anyway, we don't know which of the residents this person is. Buchanan wants to keep an eye on the place for a few days so we need an excuse to visit Greenfield House. And that's where I thought you could help, if you felt like it.'

Grampa reared his head back. 'Me? What are you talking about?'

'Just an idea I had while I was on my way here tonight.' Fizz glanced up and down the ward to make sure no one was within earshot. The patient in the next bed had only his wife in attendance tonight and they were oblivious to everything but each other. 'I wondered how you would feel about spending a few days there — maybe as much as a week — if Buchanan could wangle you in somehow. It would give us an excuse to — '

'What like a place is this Greenfield House?' Grampa demanded dangerously. 'It's some kind of a nursing home, isn't it?'

Fizz looked shocked. 'Not at all. It's just a block of flats. I believe there's a communal lounge, but you wouldn't have to make use of

93

it if you didn't want to, and there are elevators to all floors and a nice garden to sit in.'

It took Grampa several seconds to decide how to take this suggestion and his face rippled under the influence of various emotions before he said, 'I never heard such a daft idea in my life. How do you expect Tam to wangle me into a place like that? He'd tell you himself it's a daft idea — and just supposing he didn't, have you thought about what it would cost?'

'No problem about the cost, Grampa. Buchanan's firm would foot the bill — recoverable expenses.' Fizz regarded the bottle of whisky meditatively and handled it a little to make the paper rustle.

'What will you come up with next? This is just typical of your daft ideas — '

'But just think how perfect it would be from your point of view. You'd have a comfortable wee flat of your own — you'd be free to eat what you like, have a wee glass of malt when you felt like it, come and go as you please — and, do you know what else, Grampa? Guess what starts a week on Thursday.'

Grampa's face slackened and his eyes took on a faraway look. 'The Royal Highland Show,' he said, like one speaking in a dream.

'I read about it in the *Scotsman*.'

Fizz rested her case. It was thirteen years since Grampa had last been at the Royal Highland Show — an occasion when he had brought home a first for a Blackface ewe with lamb at foot — and his ambition to return, even as a non-exhibitor, was known to everyone in Am Bealach.

He was visibly hamstrung but he wasn't going down without a fight. 'What does Tam think about this plan of yours? You haven't talked it over with him yet, have you?'

Fizz immediately cursed herself for claiming she'd just thought of the idea on the way to the hospital. It was always a mistake to embroider more than one absolutely had to when spinning a yarn. Now she was forced to say, 'No, I haven't discussed it with him but I'm sure he'd go along with it very happily.'

'Well, we'll see what he has to say about it when I see him tomorrow.'

'Um . . . ' Fizz thought fast. She had managed to carry Buchanan along with her thus far only because he was totally convinced that Grampa would not set foot in Greenfield House. She knew he had been humouring her but once he realised there was a chance that Grampa would concede to the idea he'd back down like a flash.

'Tell you what,' she said. 'I'll talk it over

95

with Buchanan tonight and then if he thinks it's a good idea, which I'm sure he will, we'll see the doctor tomorrow and get him to OK it. We could have you out of here tomorrow afternoon, or at least by Monday.'

It was clearly a supreme effort for the old guy to accede to any plan of Fizz's. She could see the titanic struggle going on between, in the red corner, the longing to be out of hospital and the allure of the Royal Highland Show and, in the blue corner, his inherent distrust of any scheme emanating from the brain of his seriously deranged granddaughter.

In the end, all she could get out of him was a promise to think about it when he heard what the omnipotent Tam had to say, but that was enough. It would, after all, be she herself who would be reporting Tam's opinion.

5

Buchanan was seriously unsettled by the discovery that Fizz had moved her Grampa into the home on her own while he was playing golf on Sunday afternoon.

On the face of it, there was no reason why she should not have done so since, as she lost no time in pointing out, he had given the scheme his agreement in principle. That had been a big mistake, of course, but it had all looked like total pie in the sky at that point. It was — then and now — inconceivable that Grampa would allow himself to be persuaded to spend a single night on the complex. He didn't think of himself as what Fizz called a gerrie, indeed he avoided geriatrics like the plague. He was also so bigoted that, as Fizz was always complaining, it would take a pre-frontal lobotomy to change his mind.

Fizz's telephone call informing Buchanan of her *fait accompli* had come as a nasty shock and it had left him with a nagging sense of unease. He never liked it when Fizz did something unnatural, and it was definitely unnatural for Fizz to fork out for a taxi when, by waiting a few hours, she could have had

Buchanan transport her grampa to the complex. No, there was no doubt about it, she was up to something and he intended to find out what it was before things went any further.

There was no one around the foyer when he arrived at Greenfield House and no one to be seen beyond the glass of the reception window. However, he could discern the sound of music coming from the common room so he pushed open the door and looked in.

A group of elderly people were sitting in the bay window at the far end of the lounge listening to a somewhat younger chap in a cardigan who was playing 'Clair de lune' on the piano. As he walked towards them Buchanan recognised Helen's wine-red corona in the audience and she, turning at the sound of his approach, immediately recognised him.

'Hello again,' she said, in a voice that carried effortlessly the length of the long room. 'I hope you've come to enjoy our little concert?'

Buchanan started to whisper that he was in fact looking for the caretaker but Helen waved a hand at him to stop.

'No need to whisper, my dear. Nigel's only playing background music just now. He doesn't give a hoot whether we chat all through it or not. Do come and sit down.'

Buchanan glanced around at the other faces and saw encouragement in them all. Evidently they didn't see a lot of visitors. And if they were willing to talk he was willing to listen, especially if they were all as outspoken as Helen.

'I shouldn't,' he said, accepting the chair thrust forward by another lady, 'but I must just hear the rest of 'Clair de lune'. I haven't heard it played in years.'

'No,' Helen replied in a voice that must have carried clearly to the ears of the pianist. 'Nigel's repertoire is a bit out of date, I suppose, but he's still good, isn't he? He'll be playing his Rodgers and Hammerstein selection later, when everyone has come down. Cheryl here will be singing, Anthony will be doing some conjuring tricks, Paul — wherever he's got to — has a monologue for us I believe, and I,' she patted a leather-bound book on her lap, 'will be giving a short reading from the Bard. Portia.'

The other old lady, Cheryl, leaned forward with a smile that exposed small, expensively capped teeth. 'Helen would have made a superb Shakespearian actress, you know. She always had such . . . ' she hesitated as though lost for a suitable term, ' . . . such stage presence.'

Helen appeared to be less than flattered by this eulogy. She clearly felt that it drew unnecessary attention to the fact that she had not actually played Shakespeare and, possibly, also inferred that her only talent was stage presence. She lifted her head regally and said, 'Alas, I had my children to consider. Victor and I always put the children first and long runs were out of the question. Television is so much less disruptive to one's personal life, you know, Cheryl. Demanding in its own way, of course, especially when one's face becomes well known, but one can at least see one's family in the evenings.'

That, in some fashion comprehensible only to the in-crowd, put Cheryl's nose visibly out of joint but before she could retaliate Helen turned her attention back to Buchanan. 'But what brings you back, my dear? Is your cute little girlfriend still hoping to find a haven for her grandfather?'

'Not my girlfriend,' Buchanan said, underlining the denial with a shake of his head lest there should be any misunderstanding. 'Just a friend. Actually, she did manage to arrange for her grandfather to stay here — just for a few days, till she can make other arrangements.'

'Well, she must be a very persuasive young lady.' Helen looked faintly affronted. 'Does she know someone at the head office?'

'To tell you the truth — '

But Buchanan was precluded from telling the truth — or even the half-truth he was searching for — by the arrival of an elongated scarecrow of a man who burst into the room with an energy that left the swing doors reverberating behind him.

'Sorry, sorry, sorry! Kept you all waiting. Fifty lines, Paul, 'I must not be late!' Abject apologies!' He worked his way down the room like a whirlwind, greeting each of the oldies who had filled up the vacant seats. 'Never mind, Finella, hunger makes the best kitchen. I shall just have to be worth waiting for, eh, Brian? Hello, Joe, what d'you know? Rose, darling, how's the greenfly? All sitting comfortably? Good! Splendid! Tickety-boo!'

He was an inch or two over six feet but can't have weighed any more than ten and a half or eleven stone. Arms and legs jerked out so awkwardly that Buchanan half suspected that his knees bent backwards like a flamingo's. He was bald apart from a long fringe of fluffy beige hair around his occiput, and two pale grey eyes blazed out like headlights in a face as lean and leathery as a greyhound's.

'Here I am, my dears, better late than never! *Mea culpa*, Helen. I don't even have a note from my mummy. Fell asleep watching the news.' He held out a bony wrist to be slapped and Helen obliged. 'Ouch! You ruthless vixen, you! Well, on with the show! But halt — who have we here? Are you audience or performer, laddie?'

Buchanan, who had fallen into a bemused trance, bounced to his feet. 'Just passing through, actually. In fact I should be going.'

'Oh, don't rush off,' Cheryl cried, dragging him back down by the sleeve of his jacket. 'Stay and see a part of our concert at least. It's very informal. People come and go all evening.'

'Dear me, no. Perish the thought, laddie! We can't have you rushing off without experiencing the mind-blowing wonder of our dear Anthony's legerdemain, and the silver voice of the incomparable Cheryl da Pont, far less the majesty of Helen's Portia. No, no, no. Experience of a lifetime if not longer. And free! Canny whack it!'

Anthony reached for the walking stick that was propped against the table beside him and poked Paul in the leg. 'Sit down and behave yourself, Paul, for God's sake. The lad's here to visit someone, not to watch a bunch of old has-beens like us.' He was lying slouched in an armchair, oblivious to the fact that a string of coloured scarves was clearly visible at the cuff of his left sleeve. 'Nobody else is likely to turn up so we might as well get started.'

Buchanan slid to the edge of his seat but Cheryl still had a grip of his sleeve and before he could make his excuses Paul was perched beside him on the arm of his chair and declaiming, 'Off we go then, chummies! Tallest on the right, shortest on the left! All aboard for the Skylark! Who'll be first?'

'Cheryl's opening,' Anthony said, waving an arm irritably in that lady's direction. The gesture drew his attention to the escaping scarves and he surreptitiously tucked them back into place as he muttered, 'We've been discussing the programme all afternoon, for God's sake!'

Helen was sitting close enough to him to give his arm a soothing pat. 'Do you want to start now, Cheryl, or wait and see if the others turn up?'

Cheryl opted to strike while the iron was hot, there being some doubt among those present whether the unspecified 'others' would turn up at all. She sang 'I Don't Know How To Love Him' from *Jesus Christ Superstar* and she sang it so sweetly and with such tenderness that it seemed churlish to notice that her top notes were not all they might have been. She was a pretty little thing with a vast pile of soft white hair and scarcely a wrinkle. Fizz would probably consider her firm jaw line and taut eyelids highly suspect but, be that as it may, Buchanan thought, the overall effect was charming.

The concert now apparently having started, it looked as if there would be little opportunity of doing any more research for some time so he got ready for a quick exit as soon as Cheryl had brought her song to a close.

As the applause died away, however, and just as Buchanan was gathering his legs under him to make a bid for freedom, he heard light steps on the parquet behind him and turned to see a young woman crossing the room towards the group. She was wearing a longish muted purple dress and a loose open tunic that fluttered out behind her like a pair of wings. Dark hair and eyes set off a skin that glowed golden in the light of the setting sun, and the curve of her neck as she bent to kiss the pianist riveted Buchanan's attention.

'Hi, Pops,' she said, and blew a round of pseudo-kisses — 'Mmwuh . . . mmwuh . . . mmwuh' — to the other members of the concert party. 'Sorry I'm late. I haven't missed much, I hope?'

'You missed my little song!' cried Cheryl,

pouting in mock vexation.

'No, I didn't, sweetie. I was listening from the doorway and you were super as usual. I loved it.'

Nobody appeared at all put out by the interruption and the audience in their individual groups simply chatted among themselves while the proceedings were suspended.

'Dash it all, lassie,' Paul leaped to his feet, waving both hands at the purple ensemble, 'you can't come in here dressed like a houri and playing havoc with a man's blood pressure! Devilish dangerous! Poor old Anthony here's ready to be carried off with an apoplexy. Give us a twirl.'

The girl obliged, spinning gracefully on her toes so that the filmy material floated about her and her hair curved round her cheeks. 'Don't ask me what it cost,' she laughed. 'Pops really doesn't want to know, do you, dear?'

Buchanan was only half listening to the conversation, his mind being wholly occupied with the way her skirt clung to the line of her thigh. Since his teens, diaphanous veils had always figured largely in his exotic fantasies, and this was the closest thing he'd seen to a diaphanous veil for some considerable time. His thoughts were therefore a trifle unfocused when Helen suddenly turned to him and said, 'This is Lizzie, Nigel's daughter. I'm afraid I don't know your name.'

Buchanan lurched to his feet. 'Tam Buchanan. Happy to meet you.'

She shook his hand and, tipping her head to one side, regarded him with smiling brown eyes. 'I haven't seen you here before. Are you visiting someone?'

'No . . . I . . . Well, yes, I am . . . or I should be, but in fact I stopped to listen to your father playing 'Clair de lune' and sort of got waylaid.'

She glanced over her shoulder at her father, who was quietly filling in time with something from *The Merry Widow*. 'He doesn't perform in public any more — I'm afraid his wrist joints aren't what they used to be — but he still loves these little singsongs. It makes such a difference to him — to all of them, really — to have an audience. That's what keeps them going.'

'I can see that,' Buchanan said as she took the seat next to his. 'This must be almost an ideal environment for a retired performer.'

She looked at him carefully, letting her gaze wander from his eyes to his mouth and back again in a leisurely manner. 'Yes, I think it probably is. They all find things to complain about, of course: the flats are a little cramped and the soundproofing isn't all it should be. Pops gets quite aerated when other residents play instruments when he's having his afternoon nap, but those are minor drawbacks. They've all been used to a lot of company — all their working lives — and they can become quite depressed when they retire. Who is it you're visiting?'

Buchanan remembered with a tinge of guilt that he was expected elsewhere — had been for some time — but he pushed the thought aside. 'Not someone you'd know,' he said vaguely, operating on the premise that the less he said the less he'd have to prevaricate. 'He has only been here since this afternoon. I've just come to check that he has everything he needs.'

'If there's anything he's short of, I'm sure Pops — or any of the others — will be able to help him out. They're all very neighbourly. What's his name? I'll tell Pops to look out for him.'

'Fitzpatrick. He's a little deaf but everyone I've spoken to up till now enunciates so clearly that I'm sure he'll have very little trouble fitting in.'

An arresting chord from the piano broke into the background chatter and Nigel stood up from his stool. 'And now, ladies and gentlemen, prepare to be mystified once again by our resident magician, Anthony Bell.'

Buchanan decided the time had come to make his getaway. 'I should go now before Anthony gets started,' he whispered to Lizzie. 'Can you tell me where to look for the caretaker?'

'I'll show you.'

Buchanan waved a hasty adieu to the others and followed her out into the foyer.

'Is the person you're visiting . . . Mr Fitzpatrick . . . is he a relation?' she asked as he shut the door behind them.

'No, just a friend,' Buchanan said, and then added, to keep her talking as much as anything else. 'He's the grandfather of one of my employees but I know him quite well. He's a great old guy. Very spry for his years.'

'He'd get along well with Pops, then,' she said, evincing no great hurry to be gone. 'We must see if we can get them together.'

That sounded to Buchanan like the best idea he'd heard in years. 'I think he'd like that,' he said, swiftly convincing himself of the truth of that assumption. Grampa might not be the most social of animals but, if one could overcome his initial reluctance, he probably would enjoy meeting Nigel and hearing him play. 'I'll bring him down to the lounge tomorrow evening.'

'Good,' she said. 'I'll make sure Pops is

there then. About half seven?'

It was quite clear to Buchanan that she was no more interested in bringing Grampa and her father together than he was himself. It also transpired, when she pointed out the bell marked 'service', that the briefest of instructions could have led him to it without the need for her personal assistance. So it was hardly surprising if his face was a trifle aglow by the time he traced Grampa and Fizz to the former's new abode.

'Well, you're looking very bushy-tailed,' Fizz said immediately, and her denim-blue gaze went straight through him like a laser beam. 'I haven't seen you look so smiley since the day your mother sat on a wasp.'

Buchanan wiped the grin from his face and brushed the implied question aside. He was certainly not going to alert Fizz to the fact that there was a potential new relationship on the horizon. He had long harboured the suspicion that Fizz had some sort of evil influence over his love life and, although he had resisted the temptation to believe it was deliberate, the odds were definitely beginning to swing that way. It went without saying that she had no designs on him herself — she never lost an opportunity to make *that* clear — so her motive had to be sheer maliciousness. And that was where the theory fell down

109

because, whatever other sins Fizz was guilty of — and they were legion! — maliciousness was not one of them. No matter. Fizz and Lizzie would form an explosive mixture and prudence dictated that never the twain should meet.

Grampa was hobbling about from room to room with two walking sticks, pointing out what he considered to be shoddy construction details as he went. 'Look at the height of the ceilings, Tam. And this wee kitchen! You couldn't swing a cat in it. It's like living in a cardboard box. A week's about as long as you'd want to be living in a place like this, and how you're expected to cook a three-course meal on a wee cooker like that is a mystery to me.'

'People don't cook three-course meals nowadays,' Fizz yelled, rolling her eyes at Buchanan behind Grampa's back. 'Nobody but Auntie Duff, at any rate. You can make do with cooking one course and opening a tin of soup or pudding. I bought you some yogurts. They're in the fridge with the rest of your shopping.'

'You never mentioned that I'd be cooking all my own meals,' Grampa muttered, stomping back to his high armchair in the lounge and propping his feet on a footstool. 'At least I got *that* done for me in the hospital. Not that the food was what you'd call wonderful but at least I wasn't expected to be peeling tatties.'

'You won't be cooking all your own meals, Grampa. There's half a cooked chicken there that'll do you tonight, and I put a couple of frozen meals in the ice-making compartment of the fridge. There's enough eggs and cheese and vegetables in the fridge to keep you going for a few days and I'll come round and cook you something later in the week. We'll both be in and out regularly.'

'Tell you what,' Buchanan said, seeing an opportunity to get Grampa down to the common room. 'I'll bring round a chinky for us both on my way home tomorrow night.'

Both Fizz and Grampa regarded him with interest. Fortunately Grampa's question forestalled Fizz's.

'A *chinky*, are you saying?' He looked indescribably shocked, as though he expected it might be some sort of sexual perversion. 'What's a chinky?'

'A Chinese meal,' Buchanan yelled, reminding himself that the benefits of modern culinary expertise had not yet breached the bulwarks of Am Bealach. 'Or we could have an Indian takeaway, or a Thai, or even fish and chips, if that's what you fancy, and then perhaps we could go down

111

to the communal lounge and meet some of the other residents.'

'Aye,' said Grampa without hesitation. 'We'll do that anyway. The sooner I get talking to the other folk in the building, the sooner we'll get some evidence together. I'll maybe even take a wee hurl downstairs in that elevator in the morning and see if I can find anyone to talk to.'

Buchanan was somewhat surprised to hear that Grampa was intending to take an active part in the investigation, since Fizz's original plan had been for him merely to provide an excuse for either herself or Buchanan to make frequent visits to the complex. However, if he was willing there was no particular reason for him not to do what he could. One thing he wasn't and that was indiscreet.

'But you'd have to resist asking questions, you know.' Buchanan sat down so that he could fix Grampa with an emphatic look. 'Or even leading people on too obviously. Your role is simply to listen.'

'Absolutely,' Fizz chimed in before Grampa could answer. 'The last thing we want is for anyone to get suspicious. We have to play it cool. It's much more important to have you here as an excuse for us to hang around.'

'Well, I can tell you one thing already.' Grampa's liver-spotted hand jabbed in the direction of the door. 'I don't like the looks of that caretaker chappie . . . Boston, is it? You saw his broken nose? And there's a great long scar on his arm that looks verra like a knife wound to me. That's a character worth keeping an eye on, for a start.'

Buchanan was willing to admit that Boston's looks were against him but looks could be deceptive. The way he had melted under the fiery blast of Fizz's charm was surely a sign that a soft heart beat below his unprepossessing exterior, and certainly Helen had been far from cowed by his sudden appearance. Not that a kind heart necessarily precluded criminal tendencies, but by the same criterion, a broken nose was no proof of their existence.

'He used to own a garage,' Grampa said out of the blue.

'What?' Fizz had been on her way to the bedroom with an armful of clothing but stopped and came back to stare at him. 'Who told you that?'

'Yon mannie with the zimmer that came up in the lift with us. Did you not hear him saying to Boston that his car was making a funny noise?'

'Uh-huh, and Boston said he'd take a look at it, but — '

'A weel, we had a wee bit chat, him and I,

while you and Boston were footering around with keys and whatnot. He says Boston's a good car mechanic. Used to have a garage of his own out at Currie.'

Fizz swung her head round to look at Buchanan. 'Curious. Catriona said that Mathieson had a garage. You think there could be a connection?'

Buchanan was not particularly excited by the implications of this piece of intelligence but he was willing to admit that it should be looked into, if only to eliminate it as potentially meaningful information. 'It's possible. I'd also be interested to know why he would give up a garage of his own to work as a caretaker.'

'Precisely. Even if his business failed, you'd think he'd have found a better paid job by sticking to his trade.'

'I could easy have a wee chat with him tomorrow.' Grampa's face brightened visibly at the prospect. 'He was out in the garden this afternoon, just picking up bits of litter and talking to people. I could see him from the kitchen window. He'll likely be doing the same thing tomorrow and I could get him talking.'

'I think we should leave that till we see what we can find out by other means.' Buchanan kept his face blank and resisted a temptation to clutch his head. Having one loose cannon assisting the investigation was bad enough but now he had her grampa to control as well. 'For a few days at least it would be better if you just kept your ears open and let things take their own course. Get settled in and let people get used to having you around before you start looking too interested in anything.'

Grampa looked considerably dashed and appeared to be about to put forward a counter-suggestion but Fizz was on her feet and making ready to leave.

'I've turned down your bed and there's a glass of water on your bedside table. Don't forget to lock the door after we've gone. I'll pop in tomorrow during my lunch break just to see you're OK.'

Grampa looked glad to be rid of them as he let them out but he seemed to Buchanan to be quite happy where he was for the present, and was certainly better off here, where he had twenty-four-hour support, than sequestered in Am Bealach with only Auntie Duff around. Maybe Fizz had got it right this time after all.

They could hear laughter and applause coming from the common room as they passed through the foyer on their way out. Fizz wanted to see what was happening but was dissuaded by Buchanan's claim that, if they went in, it would be rude not to stay. No doubt Lizzie was still in there and Fizz would need only one glance at her to know what had been making him so chirpy earlier.

To distract her further he said, 'It certainly appears to be a coincidence that both Boston and Mathieson were in the garage business. It could mean nothing but it will have to be checked out.'

'Shouldn't be too difficult. There can't be all that many garages in Currie, and somebody's sure to remember which one Boston owned.'

Buchanan ushered her towards the car as fast as he dared, keeping her out of view from the bay window. 'Right. See what you can find out, Fizz. If you can get me an address I'll go in tomorrow afternoon and check out the situation.'

A burst of distant applause seemed to indicate that the concert was over. He grabbed Fizz's elbow to hurry her up but her feet remained fixed to the tarmac.

'You want to do that yourself, do you?' she said.

'I think that would be wiser, don't you?'

'Wiser? In what sense of the word?' Fizz enquired politely. 'Given that (a) I'm better at it than you, (b) I look less like a plainclothes cop and (c) you have a full in-tray and I don't.'

'Better safe than sorry,' Buchanan said, knowing that he was looking shifty as he always did when trying to wrap her in cotton wool. 'The garage could have been one of Mathieson's enterprises all along and if we go in there now asking questions — '

'You're saying I don't know how to be discreet?'

'No, you know I'm not saying that. I simply — '

'No. That's fine,' Fizz told him, continuing to resist his discreet urging. 'My share of the action is obviously to consist of doing the research work and collating the information. That's what I thought. So much for your promises.'

Beyond her shoulder Buchanan could see movement in the bay window. People were standing up and moving around. Any minute now Lizzie would be coming down the steps from the entrance.

'*Do it, then!*' He swung away, taking off on his own and leaving her standing there. 'Do it yourself if it's so important to you. Dammit, I don't know why I bother to argue with you in the first place.'

He heard her giggle as she tripped along behind him. 'You'll end up a real old grouch,

117

you know that, Buchanan? You get more like Grampa every day.'

Buchanan thought there was probably some truth in that. But then, it was doubtless true of most of Fizz's friends.

6

The garage that used to trade under the name of 'Boston and Bruce' was now 'McMartin Motors'. It occupied a corner site off the main Lanark Road and, judging from appearances, it had probably never been a serious threat to Kwik-Fit's share of the market. Somebody in disgusting overalls had his head under the bonnet of a rusty van in the forecourt and there were three other mechanics drinking tea at the back of the shed. Nobody took any notice of Fizz as she walked into the empty office and pressed the bell for attention.

The minutes passed and nobody came. She wasn't normally a patient customer but for the moment she was happy to have the chance of a good look around. She had to be discreet about it because, the partition wall being half glass, she could be observed by the group at the back of the shed, but she could be as interested in the decor as any other customer would have been.

The wall behind the counter was covered with pictures, many of them showing the pathetic, pouting, half-naked examples of cosmetic surgery so beloved by car mechanics the world over. Among these, however, there were framed photographs of a boxer in various fighting stances. These were black and white studies but they were noticeably yellowed with age and the length of the boxer's trunks seemed to indicate that they were a good twenty years old.

Fizz had to slip her sunglasses down for a moment to be sure it wasn't Boston's ugly mug behind the defensively raised gloves. This guy was even uglier but he had a body that was worth a second look, long-limbed and muscular, with a six-pack that might have been drawn on with an ink marker.

Finally Fizz decided that she had seen all there was to see in the office. She went and stood in the doorway and shouted across to the group of tea drinkers.

'So, who do I have to bribe to get some service around here?'

They didn't much like that. After a minute or two of disgruntled muttering a young lad of about eighteen detached himself from the group and walked over to her. He was covered with a thick coating of oil and his mouth hung open as though his thick lower lip were weighing it down. Personal freshness was another of his problems.

Fizz mentally closed her eyes to this sight,

conjured up a vision of Ewan McGregor, and blinded him with a smile.

'Hi,' she said with just enough girlish shyness to make him feel in control of the situation. 'I wonder if you could help me?'

He was chewing a large mouthful of the roll and sausage which he still held in his hand but he managed to convey that the possibility was not out of the question.

'I don't know . . . ' Fizz said uncertainly, glancing across to the other two mechanics. 'Maybe you haven't been here long enough to know.'

He regarded her stolidly, his jaw working like a cow chewing cud.

She said, 'How long have you worked here?'

'Here in the garage?'

'Uh-huh.'

He swallowed and licked his lips while he thought about it. 'Coupla years. Why?'

'I was wondering if you knew the last owner.'

'Mathieson?'

That put Fizz off her stride for a second but she covered up quickly. 'No. Boston. I've got an old Austin Seven — it's just a wreck, really, but he said that when it fell to bits he'd buy it for spare parts.'

'Oh, him? Naw. Don't know where he is

now.' He looked at the roll in his hand as though considering whether to have another bite, but decided against it. 'I don't think he's in the motor trade any more.'

Fizz looked deeply disappointed. 'What about Mr Mathieson? Think he'd be interested in an Austin Seven?'

'Naw, I don't think so,' he said seriously and then grinned. 'He just died.'

'That's too bad.' Fizz returned his grin as though it were irresistible and he forgot about his roll and sausage. 'I wonder why Mr Boston gave up his garage. He wasn't old enough to retire.'

'Got into debt,' said the youth, and let go a sausage-scented burp that would have brought a charging rhino to its knees. 'That's what I heard. He borrowed money off Mathieson and couldn't keep up the instalments.'

'So that's how — ' Fizz suddenly realised that the two mechanics at the back of the shed had become interested in their conversation. One of them had got to his feet and was setting down his mug preparatory to coming over. She said quickly, 'If you could remember anything that would help me to find Mr Boston I'd be awfully grateful. I don't want to keep you off your work but if you could just have a think about it maybe we could meet for a coffee later. On your way home.'

He couldn't believe his ears. He looked aside — fortunately not in the direction from which his senior colleague was now approaching — and gave a wobbly laugh. 'Sure,' he said, reddening a little. 'I'll see what I can remember.'

'Easy Eats, then. Round the corner on Lanark Road. When do you finish?'

'Half five — '

'What's the problem?' interrupted the other mechanic, reaching hailing distance at that second and throwing his young friend into a fluster.

Fizz got in fast. 'I've got an Austin Seven that I'm trying to sell for scrap. There's not all that much wrong with it but nobody can get the parts to fix it, so I wondered if it had any scrap value.'

'No. Sorry, doll. We don't do that kind of thing here.' He was recognisably the boxer in the photographs and even uglier than he had been in his twenties. His muscle had turned into fat and his six-pack was now a keg, but you'd still think twice about kicking sand in his face.

'I don't suppose you'd know anyone else who might be interested?' Fizz persisted, just for the look of things, but this guy was a different kettle of fish from the young apprentice.

'No, sorry.' Which Fizz had no difficulty in translating as 'Piss off'.

'OK. Thanks anyway.'

She tried to catch the lad's eye as she went out but he was pretending she didn't exist. His mate, however, followed her departure with an expression of deep concentration and, as she headed for a phone box to apprise Buchanan of the latest developments, she could still see him watching her as clearly as though she had a third eye in her bum.

⋆　⋆　⋆

Grampa was intrigued by his first ever Chinese takeaway but quite transparently unimpressed.

'M-hm. This is chicken, you were saying? Well, well now. Would you believe that? What are all these wee black bits? Are you supposed to eat them as well? And what do you call this? Prawn crackers? Not a lot of nourishment in these, I doubt. Not a lot of prawns either. Still, the rice is verra nice. What? The pineapple? I thought that was our pudding.'

He sampled each dish in turn, professed to be full up, and then discovered he was hungry again before Buchanan had finished clearing up.

'Not what you'd call a high-protein diet,' he commented as he made himself a cheese sandwich. 'Not like your meat and two veg, is it? No wonder the Chinese are so wee.'

Buchanan wasn't in a mood to argue with him even if he'd had grounds, which of course he hadn't. A chinky was demonstrably *not* like meat and two veg and it was clearly not the sort of food that one should allow to form a large part of one's weekly intake — which, in Buchanan's case, it did. He ate a decent restaurant meal twice a week, once on Fridays with an out-of-town friend, and once on Sundays after golf. Sometimes, if he snatched time for a round of golf mid-week, he had a snack at the clubhouse but at least four nights out of the seven he took home a chinky. This was not because he had a particular preference for Chinese cuisine but because the Lee On was on his way home and had plenty of parking space. It was also, if he were honest with himself, because he was pathologically lazy. He had promised himself six months ago that he would start cooking at least one good meal a week but his efforts in that direction had extended no further than the purchase of three cookery books and a garlic crusher.

Grampa, by contrast, appeared quite at home in the kitchen. There was something very practised about the way he washed the plates and forks and tidied the work surface while he waited for the kettle to boil for a pot of tea. Of course, Buchanan realised, he'd been a widower for years before he married Auntie Duff and he'd had two kids to look after into the bargain.

'How did you manage to keep the home and the farm going when Fizz and her brother were young?' he asked, keeping out of Grampa's way as he bustled around. 'What age were they when your son and his wife were killed? They weren't even at school, were they?'

'Colin was at the school — just started that September — and Fizz was three.' Grampa spooned tea leaves into the teapot — no tea bags for him! — and reached for the kettle. 'But we managed fine. They both had their wee jobs to do. They could feed the hens and the dogs, and they could set the table and do a bit of dusting and sweeping about the house. Och yes. It's surprising how fast they learned to pull their weight.'

It always twisted something in Buchanan's guts when he thought about Fizz's barren childhood. 'You didn't have any other help around the house?'

'Off and on,' said Grampa lightly, 'but none of them ever lasted. That two-mile walk from the nearest road is a killer in the wintertime you know. I married Auntie Duff when Fizz was about fourteen or fifteen and away at the school in Edinburgh, but up till that point we more or less managed on our own.'

Buchanan carried the tea tray back to the lounge and Grampa hobbled after him on his sticks.

'That caretaker chappie — Boston — was doing a fair bit of work this morning. Tidying up. Taking the rubbish bins round to that gateway at the garages for the bin men to collect. I went and sat on a bench where he would have to pass me every time he went to and fro but I didn't get a word out of him beyond a good morning and was I settled in all right. A great long-leggedy creature like a greyhound came and sat beside me — claimed her name was *Charmaine* — so I never got the chance to get him chatting.'

'Not to worry. There's no need for you to put yourself out any.'

Grampa poured two cups of tea leaves. 'It would help if I knew what it was you were trying to find out.'

'Fizz didn't tell you?' Buchanan said carelessly, wondering if Fizz had been crazy enough to tell her grampa less than the whole truth. 'She should have.'

Grampa's eyebrows bristled suspiciously. 'She said she couldn't discuss the case with me because it was *sub judice*. Was that poppycock? Is she hiding something?'

'No, no. Not that I know of,' Buchanan said hurriedly. He was constantly aware of the danger of making the precarious relationship between Fizz and her grampa worse than it already was. It wasn't ever going to be wonderful, not since Fizz had defected from art school and taken off round the world for eight years, but at least they were on speaking terms at the moment. 'I can see how she would be afraid to say too much without clearing it with me, but I think it would be only right and proper for you to know what you are dealing with here.'

'Aye?' said Grampa, pushing aside the remains of his sandwich and crossing his arms as though preparing himself to be infuriated.

'The case we're preparing for court concerns the murder of a man called Mathieson — '

'I knew it!' Grampa burst out, although he could have known no such thing. 'I told her not to get mixed up with criminals! That lassie will be the death of me! If I've told her once I've told her a hundred times — '

Buchanan raised a finger. 'We didn't have any choice but to get involved. The accused, Freddie McAuslan, is an old client of my father's and almost certainly innocent.'

'So what am I doing here? Is it all a ploy to keep me from going home to Am Bealach?'

'No. Far from it — though I'm sure Fizz feels happier to know you'll be close to medical assistance for a while. But, actually, we have cause to suspect that Mathieson was involved in some sort of business deal with someone from Greenfield House. He certainly phoned someone here on the evening before he died and we think he made arrangements to meet that person on the morning of the day he was murdered.'

'So it's not just Boston you're curious about? It could be any of them?'

'We've no proof other than what I've told you,' Buchanan admitted carefully, 'but perhaps Boston could be assumed to be more likely than any of the residents.'

Grampa digested that in a grim silence, then said, 'She said you'd be taking me to the Royal Highland Show. Was that just another bit of jokery-pokery?'

Buchanan glanced at his hands, surprised to see that they were not, as he had pictured them, curled into claws. 'I'm looking forward to it.'

'Aye, well. I suppose I'm better off here than in the hospital at any rate, and I don't mind doing what I can to help the pair of you. As you said, it will give you an excuse to hang about the place if nothing else.'

That at least was true, and Buchanan had now more reason to hang about the place than either Fizz or Grampa realised. He said, 'In that case, how do you feel about going down to the communal lounge tonight? Just for half an hour or so. I met a few of the residents there last night and they seemed rather a lively bunch. It might be quite productive if we could get them talking.'

Grampa fairly leaped at the idea. If he had been willing to keep an eye on someone he assumed to be a minor offender he was now visibly agog to unmask a murderer. He downed the remainder of his tea in one gulp and reached for his sticks, leaving Buchanan in no doubt from where Fizz had inherited her dominant genes.

Lizzie was already in the lounge when they got there, looking delightful in a beige tailored skirt and a see-through shirt over a lace camisole. There were only a few people in the lounge tonight and she and her father were alone in the bay window apart from Anthony, the conjurer.

Grampa was duly introduced and eased

into a chair beside Nigel. He appeared a fraction disconcerted by Nigel's plummy accent for a few minutes but was soon launched on the continuing saga of his knee trouble. An unforeseen bonus, Buchanan realised, was that all these ex-performers had voices trained to carry and spoke with a clarity that made a huge difference to Grampa's grasp of the conversation.

Once the three old codgers were launched on a recitation of their various health problems Lizzie leaned close to Buchanan and whispered, 'He's quite a character, isn't he? You said he was a relation of one of your employees — you must have a very close relationship with your staff.'

Buchanan wasn't sure how to answer that question without giving the wrong impression. If he claimed not to have a close relationship with Fizz he would be lying, but the exact nature of that relationship would be hard to put across convincingly and he didn't want Lizzie to get the wrong idea. He said, 'Well, it's a fairly easy-going sort of office.'

'What is it you do?'

'I'm a solicitor.' He fished a card out of his wallet and gave it to her with an old-fashioned look. 'You never know when you'll want a solicitor.' It was a crack he'd used before and it frequently got a smile. It did now.

'I'll give you one of mine.' She took a strip of gold stick-on address labels out of her handbag and tore one off. 'You never know when you'll want a PA.'

Anthony, who was now talking about the good old days of the Pavilion Theatre, drew them into the conversation for a few minutes but, as soon as he could, Buchanan resumed the tête-à-tête with Lizzie.

'Do you visit your father every evening?'

'Most evenings. Sometimes I just drop by for a few minutes on my way home from work, but I like to make sure he doesn't feel neglected. My brothers are both down south so I don't have anyone to share the chore with me. Not that it's much of a chore, really, in fact I look forward to seeing all of them. They're such live wires.' She tipped her head towards the chatting oldies. 'Cheryl and Paul, for instance, have a great social life. They belong to a swimming club, they play bridge, they're involved with an amateur drama group and — oh, heaven knows what else they get up to. They also take off every so often on a round of National Trust properties. I don't know where they get their energy.'

'Sounds very chummy.' Buchanan couldn't

imagine anyone putting up with Paul's eccentricity for very long at a stretch but Cheryl looked the type to appreciate having a beau in attendance. 'Do any of the others pair up?'

'No. Just those two. It's rather sweet, don't you think? They must both be well into their seventies.'

Buchanan discerned something significant in her tone. 'You don't mean . . . they're an item?'

'Oh, absolutely. There are comings and goings in the night, according to Helen. Have been for a couple of years at least.'

'Well, well. Life in the old dog yet.' He took a long look at Cheryl and Paul, side by side on a low couch, and had to murmur, 'She's not deaf, is she?'

Lizzie fought a grin. 'Not Cheryl. She's in perfect working order, but if you're referring to Paul's repartee, don't be fooled. He's a sharp cookie. It's Paul who organises everything here, always coming up with new ideas, keeping the others on the go. One week he decides they're all going to learn to line dance, then they're all writing their autobiographies, next thing he has them singing barbershop or doing gentle exercises to music. Greenfield House wouldn't be nearly such a fun place without him.'

'Did he and Cheryl know each other before they came here?'

'I don't think so.' Lizzie had lost interest in the conversation. She took a coral-pink lipstick out of her handbag and applied it to her lips. 'I must go. I haven't eaten yet and I'm ravenous.'

Buchanan thought to say, 'Neither have I' but rephrased his reply to avoid taking liberties with the truth. 'What d'you think?' he suggested. 'Could we leave them to it now and go and have something to eat?'

'I think that's an excellent idea,' she said, a small smile curving her already delightful lips as she closed her bag and stood up.

As they took their leave and walked out to Buchanan's car, his hand cupping her small, delicately rounded elbow, there was a song running through his head like a mantra.

The sun has got his hat on, Hip-Hip-Hip Hooray!
The sun has got his hat on and he's coming out to play!

7

By twenty to six Fizz was beginning to wonder if her celebrated olde worlde charm had lost its potency. She had chosen a seat close to the window of the café so that she could watch for the arrival of the apprentice mechanic but she was developing a crick in her neck before he hove into view, weaving hurriedly through the throng of rush-hour pedestrians.

When he reached the café he passed by the door in order to peep in at the window and was visibly embarrassed to see her sitting there looking out at him, a witness to his diffidence. Fizz quickly assumed an expression of maidenly delight which reassured him enough to propel him through the door and on to the bench opposite her.

'I thought you weren't coming.' Fizz breathed, devouring him with her eyes and trying to hold her breath at the same time. The stench of petrol and diesel oil that emanated from his clothing was enough to cause a hole in the ozone layer.

'The boss gave me an oil change to do at five o'clock and I had to finish it.' His eyes

135

wandered around bashfully, pretending an interest in the wallpaper. 'You don't argue with him even if it's going to keep you working late.'

'Was that your boss who spoke to you when I was there?'

'Uh-huh. Kev. He's a swine.'

'He used to be a boxer, didn't he? I saw his photographs in the office when I was waiting.'

'Yeah. He used to be some sort of amateur champion — East of Scotland light heavy-weight, or something — he's always going on about it.' His slack mouth tightened momen-tarily. 'Still thinks with his fists. He'd take a swing at you as soon as look at you.'

The waitress came over, removed Fizz's empty cup, and took their order for two more coffees. When she'd gone Fizz said, 'What's your name, by the way?'

'Arthur. Arthur Bundell, but they call me Bundy. What's yours?'

'Hope,' said Fizz without hesitation and continued seamlessly, 'But surely your boss wouldn't actually punch you? He couldn't get away with it.'

Bundy didn't look too sure about that. 'I've seen him slap one of the other guys about and he quite often comes into work with his knuckles all cut and bruised. Just laughs and says he was in a bit of a bust-up at the dog racing or something like that.'

'Gosh.' Fizz toyed with the cruet set, trying to look as if she were just making conversation. 'But the guy he slapped about . . . didn't he go to the police?'

'No. One of the older guys told him to forget it.' Bundy accepted delivery of his coffee and seemed to be searching for some other topic of conversation but Fizz got in first.

'Why was that? Why did he tell him to forget it?'

He watched the retreating waitress for a second and then shrugged. ''Cos Kev's a thug, that's why. He could break your legs if you got him rattled.'

Fizz found this absolutely riveting. Taken in conjunction with Mathieson's reputation for violence it seemed to warrant further investigation. The difficulty was in appearing only marginally interested.

'Does the garage belong to Kev now?' she said, assiduously stirring her coffee.

'No, he's just the gaffer. The owner died a couple of weeks ago so I don't know what's happening now. Maybe we'll all be up the Job Centre.'

'Oh, yes. I remember you said that. Somebody called Mathieson. What was he like?'

Bundy poked at a crumb on the melamine tabletop with a finger, leaving an oily smudge. 'I never had anything to do with Mathieson. He just used to swan in on a Friday, pick up his money from Kev and scram. I never once saw him speak to anybody else, but Kev said he was an evil bastard — and if *Kev* thought he was an evil bastard he must have been a nightmare.'

'So Mathieson just put up the money and Kev managed the shop?'

'Uh-huh,' he said, and added quickly, 'So what do you work at?'

It looked to Fizz as though he wasn't particularly uncomfortable with the subject, just bored with it. She said, 'I haven't got a job right now, that's why I need to sell my car. I wish I'd sold it to Mr Boston while I had the chance but it was still running then and it never occurred to me that he'd go bankrupt. Imagine him borrowing money from someone like Mathieson! He must have been daft. Do you think Mathieson cheated him out of the business?'

'Probably.' He looked away from her, turning his head to follow the path of an unexceptional blue Anglia as it passed beyond the window. In profile he wasn't bad-looking. In a few more years, when life had ground the softness of youth from his cheeks and mouth, he could turn out quite tasty. He was beginning to look as though he'd rather be talking about something else but couldn't think how to change the subject. Fizz let the silence lengthen, knowing that it made him uncomfortable and finally, when he couldn't think of anything else to say, he muttered, 'He duffed up Boston's brother too — to make an example of him, Kev says. Mathieson's into making examples of anybody who crosses him. Used to be.'

Fizz had to keep her eyes down to hide her excitement. 'Was he badly hurt?'

'Reckon he must have been. Mathieson doesn't — didn't mess around. He blinded a guy once.'

Now we're getting somewhere, Fizz thought smugly. Plenty of motive there for a revenge killing. Bundy didn't seem to be totally *au fait* with the details but those could doubtless be checked by other means.

'I can imagine Mr Boston finding it quite hard to make a living round about here,' she pressed on relentlessly. 'You can't get much passing trade.'

Bundy had now given up watching the traffic and turned to memorising the wording on Fizz's T-shirt. Without shifting his gaze he said, 'You wouldn't think so if you'd seen the wads of notes Kev used to hand over on a Friday night.'

'Really? Wads?'

'Must have been thousands,' Bundy said, carelessly. 'They must charge ridiculous prices for some jobs. My dad says Mathieson was nothing but a crook.'

Fizz waited till he bethought himself to meet her gaze and then said, 'Why do you stay there?'

'I'm learning a trade. Lucky to get the chance these days.' He moved his shoulders in a half-shrug. 'It's OK as long as you just get on with the job. I don't talk to any of them much — that's why I didn't like to ask about what happened to Boston.'

'No — you'd better not ask any of them directly,' Fizz said, shaking her head to emphasise that she meant what she said. 'I wouldn't want you to get into trouble. But if you overhear anything about him I wish you'd let me know because I'd really like to see if he's still interested in my car. Nobody else seems to be and I could do with the money. I'm in here most nights around this time.'

Bundy watched her unslinging her bag from the back of her chair and stood up to help her on with her jacket. She could see him blushing a bit and thinking furiously, obviously trying to psyche himself up to ask her for a date, so she said quickly, 'I'd better dash and get my bus now. I'm looking after my sister's baby in the evenings this week 'cos her husband's away and she works in a wine bar. But I hope I'll see you around.'

'Yeah.' He looked almost relieved. 'I pass here on my way home. I'll keep an eye open for you.'

Fizz gave him a shy but encouraging smile and wondered how much longer she could get away with this sort of thing, even with susceptible adolescents like Bundy. She was twenty-eight last birthday, for God's sake, and even a girlish giggle and dark glasses wouldn't cut the mustard forever.

★ ★ ★

By about four thirty in the afternoon Buchanan had cleared his in-tray and was beginning to wonder if he could justify packing in early and grabbing a round of golf before the light started to go. He had made no particular plans for the evening beyond possibly giving Lizzie a ring to invite her out at the weekend.

Their meal the night before had been undiluted delight. It was a long time since he had enjoyed a woman's company so much and Lizzie had made it abundantly clear that she enjoyed being with him. He had discovered that there was no man in her life right now — although she had been married, briefly, when very young — and she appeared to have a delightfully easy-going attitude towards relationships that really appealed to him. Her enthusiasm, when he suggested meeting again, was just sufficiently low-key to establish a reasonably casual relationship, one that might develop into something special, but might equally well not. Which was exactly what Buchanan had in mind.

She had given him her daytime phone number with the assurance that she'd love to hear from him 'some time' but his interest was sufficiently whetted to make him push his luck. Friday was his birthday and, although there were other options open to him, it would be nice to have something particularly pleasant to look forward to.

Suddenly concerned that she might already have made other arrangements, he looked up his notebook for the number she'd given him and phoned her at work.

'Tam!' She sounded amused to hear his voice but not unpleased. 'How very odd! I was just thinking about you a minute ago!'

'What were you thinking?'

'You first. What made you call me?'

'I wondered if you were free for Friday

night. It's my birthday and I wanted to do something special. I thought perhaps we could have something to eat at Poseidon's and then see *The Merchant of Venice* at the Festival Theatre.'

She gave a little trill of laughter that made him smile in response. 'This is so weird,' she said. 'My boss has just passed on two tickets to me for *The Merchant of Venice* — they were a present from a client — but unfortunately they're for tonight. I've been phoning round all my girlfriends to find someone to go with me but they're all busy — and that's when I thought of you. Do you want to go?'

'Certainly,' Buchanan said without hesitation. 'As long as it doesn't mean you won't help me celebrate on Friday. I'm sure we could find something else to do.'

'Oh, I'm sure we could, Tam,' she said with another delightful gurgle of laughter.

That sounded quite exhilaratingly ambiguous to Buchanan but he couldn't decide whether the ambiguity was intended or not. He made arrangements for picking her up and rang off, not too disappointed at missing his game of golf.

It was, by that time, twenty to five: too late to start on anything new and too early to go home. He could meet up with Fizz at the

143

Easy Eats place in Leith and sit in on her interview with the young car mechanic or he could nip over to Greenfield House and drop in on Grampa. There was no doubt in his mind which option appealed to him the more, but Fizz would not look kindly on any interference so it looked like Grampa got the vote.

That was clearly the best use of his time and would, furthermore, free Fizz from the necessity of making a duty visit that evening. She had promised to phone in her report on her conversation with the car mechanic so he could put her in the picture then. Way at the back of his mind was the unworthy thought that the less time Fizz spent at the complex the less chance she'd have of hearing about Lizzie, but he was able to keep it submerged by concentrating on the practicality of making the visit himself.

It had been a bright enough afternoon but, as it progressed, a cool little easterly breeze had caused a sudden drop in temperature so he was rather surprised, as he parked the car, to spot Grampa in the garden. He was sitting on a wooden bench in the angle of the high wall, in the company of a delightful little old lady. This was obviously not the 'great, long-leggedy creature like a greyhound' of whom Grampa had spoken yesterday, since she was barely five feet tall and decidedly roly-poly.

She was like a picture of a traditional old-fashioned grannie, sweet-faced and apple-cheeked, with snow-white hair twisted into a bun at the nape of her neck. She wore fine-gold-rimmed spectacles, a longish black skirt and a black woollen twin set with a small triangular brooch at her throat.

Grampa greeted Buchanan's arrival with a resigned air and introduced his companion as Miss Moir. 'We were just talking about the rubbish you get on TV these days. Nothing but gardening programmes and cooking programmes and painting-your-house-daft-colours programmes. Does anybody watch them? I wonder.'

'I certainly don't.' Miss Moir's voice was gentle and low-pitched but Grampa seemed able to follow what she was saying. 'I like a good film, myself, or even a TV drama but even those are usually disappointing.'

'Were you in the theatre yourself, Miss Moir?' Buchanan asked.

'All my life, yes, since I was in my teens. Rep, pantomime, a little musical comedy, and later on, the odd character part on TV.' The hint of bashfulness in her smile looked more genuine than the sham modesty displayed by Helen and the others in their little clique.

'But — don't worry — you wouldn't have heard of me. I never got my name above the title.'

'You didn't have the killer instinct,' Grampa pronounced as though he had known her for years. 'It takes more than talent to make it to the top in that profession, or so they tell me, and it's easy to see you don't have a callous streak.'

'It didn't matter to me whether I became a star or not. As long as I made enough to keep body and soul together I was happy just to be part of a performance. The smell of the greasepaint, the roar of the crowd — it may sound like a cliché but it's always with you, you know.'

A curtain moved at a first-floor window in the nearby wing of the complex and, for a moment, Buchanan glimpsed the bony face of Paul looking out at them. He raised a hand in a salute and Paul waved in reply and turned immediately away.

'I'm surprised you didn't take part in the entertainment in the lounge last night,' Buchanan said to Miss Moir. 'I'd have thought you would have enjoyed that.'

She nodded. 'Yes, I had meant to come down but I felt a little tired last night. Paul and Helen have been coaxing me to prepare something but I'm a little rusty so I've been putting them off. No doubt I'll get around to it in time.'

'You haven't been here very long, then?' Grampa suggested.

'No, not long at all. Just about . . . let me see . . . come Friday it'll be a month. How the time flies!' A cool current of wind curled round the angle of the wall and she pulled her cardigan closed across her bosom. 'I feel as if I've never lived anywhere else but, of course, I've been visiting my friends here for a long time, coming to their concerts and barbecues, so it was all quite familiar to me from the day I moved in.'

'Nothing like having a few weel kenned faces around to help you feel at home,' said Grampa.

'Yes, I'm very lucky. I've known Helen and Cheryl for more than forty years and I've been visiting them ever since I moved to Edinburgh in 1988 so I have a lot of friends in the complex. Lovely people, all of them.' She closed her eyes and lifted her face to the sunlight. 'I can't believe I'm really living here myself now. I think another year in Causeyside Street and I'd have been pushing up the daisies.'

Causeyside Street. Buchanan knew he'd heard that street mentioned within the past few days but it took a second or two to make the connection. Freddie. Freddie's address, prior to his arrest, had been 100 Causeyside Street. Coincidence? Yes. Almost certainly. Why wouldn't it be and, for that matter, what would it mean if it weren't?

Feeling unutterably foolish, he heard himself saying. 'A friend of mine lives in Causeyside Street. Don't ask me the number . . . somewhere in the low hundreds.'

'Really? He must be quite close to my old flat. I was at number 100.' She lifted a hand to wave at Cheryl, who was walking across the grass in their direction. 'What is his name? I didn't know a lot of my neighbours, to tell you the truth. The flats around there change hands so quickly — it's all young families and students nowadays — but still, I might know him.'

'I don't think he stayed there very long,' Buchanan began evasively, taking his time so that Cheryl had reached them before it was necessary to say any more. It could have been interesting to hear what else Miss Moir might have had to say about her old flat but she agreed with Cheryl that it was getting too cold to be sitting around and went off with her, arm in arm.

'I'll get away now myself,' Grampa announced, reaching for his sticks. 'It'll be near enough half-past six before I get my dinner and I'm playing a game of Scrabble with Charmaine at seven.'

'Have you something to eat?' Buchanan asked, his thoughts veering towards the possibility of a chicken biriani.

'Food? Have you seen that refrigerator? You couldn't get another egg in there. I've made myself a pot of leek and potato soup, and a nice bacon and mushroom sauce to have with some pasta, and there's bananas and yoghurt if I've room for a pudding.'

Chastened, Buchanan slunk home to his king prawns.

8

Buchanan had already left the office by the time Fizz phoned, and there was no reply from his home number, which meant he was still in transit. She hung around the phone box for a few minutes, dialling and redialling his number, but soon decided she'd be quicker just dropping by his flat on her way home.

He was not only at home but in the shower when she got there. He seemed always to be in the shower when she arrived unannounced and unfailingly made it out to be her fault, not his.

'I thought you were going to phone,' he growled, his expression that of a man finding a dead mouse in a Superburger.

Fizz sidestepped quickly into the hallway as his idiot moggy whizzed past her shoulder with spread claws. 'I phoned, OK? You weren't at the office and you weren't here. Why, in God's name, don't you get a mobile like everyone else?'

'Oh . . . right.' He tried, with moderate success, to look apologetic and took a tighter grip on the small towel he had wrapped around his middle. 'I dropped in to see your grampa.'

Fizz was taken aback by the enthusiasm with which he appeared to be embracing her current scheme. He had been practically apoplectic when he discovered she'd gone ahead with moving Grampa into Greenfield House yet now the *fait* was *accompli* he seemed inordinately willing to make the most of it. 'Brilliant. That means I don't have to pop over myself. How was he?'

'Firing on all cylinders. Give me a minute to put something on and I'll tell you all about it. But it'll have to be brief, I'm going out.'

'I'll put the kettle on while I'm waiting, shall I? Any biscuits?'

'No biscuits,' he said shortly, precluding any argument by slamming the bathroom door behind him.

'You're so generous, you know that?' Fizz said, just in case he could hear her. 'You should have been a pawnbroker.'

She went into the kitchen, which was a mess as usual, and filled the kettle at a sink littered with tinfoil containers and dirty dishes. Selina watched her optimistically from under the table but knew better than to come slinking around her ankles as she did to Buchanan. She had been a skinny little runt of a cat in the days when she had scrounged a

151

living around every house in Am Bealach and, although Buchanan had indulged her in every possible way ever since the day she had adopted him, she was still tiny.

There had always been cats around the farm when Fizz was growing up: not pets, but purposeful, independent creatures who had their paws full keeping down the rodent population. There were seldom more than half a dozen, population control being taken care of by foxes, hawks, the occasional osprey and the adversities of Highland life. Everything on the farm, including the humans, was there to work or to be sold and, although young animals were undeniably cute and fun to play with, Fizz and her brother were not encouraged to view them as anything but resources. It didn't take many heartaches — kittens dying, pups being sold, bobby calves going off to slaughter — to instil the lesson. The one pet she'd ever been allowed was a day-old chick, but that had perished in a Hoover-related incident before they had established much of a relationship.

She rummaged through the cupboards and found some instant coffee and also — virtually without looking for it — half a packet of gypsy creams. Buchanan made no comment when he saw them on the tray and, since she was in a particularly forgiving mood, neither did she.

'So, what's the latest bulletin on my revered ancestor?' she asked dropping on to the couch. 'He's coping, I take it?'

'That's the understatement of the year. He'll be knitting his own socks and dipping his own candles by the end of the week.'

Fizz was unsurprised. 'Yep, that's my grampa. 'Self-sufficiency' is the motto on his coat of arms. He could give a two-hour lecture on the subject with slides and demonstrations. I'm just amazed that he hasn't already discovered the identity of Mathieson's chum at the complex.'

'Maybe he hasn't quite got that far, but I have to say he's already proving his worth.' Buchanan helped himself to an inordinate amount of sugar. 'He introduced me to a Miss Moir this evening — a lady who has been at Greenfield House only a matter of weeks. While I was talking to her it transpired that her previous home was in Causeyside Street: at number 100, same stair as Freddie McAuslan.'

'Uh?' Fizz's hand was arrested in the act of reaching for a biscuit. She could see that this piece of information fitted somehow into the matrix of the mystery but Buchanan's face gave her no clue as to the sense she was expected to make of it. It was like a piece of jigsaw puzzle that manifestly made up part of the picture but had no corresponding cavity. 'Mathieson owned the flat Freddie stayed in,' she said, feeling her way. 'So this establishes some kind of connection. Does that mean it was possibly Miss Moir that Mathieson was phoning when Catriona overheard?'

'You tell me.' Buchanan's wet hair was standing up in spikes at the front, making him look uncharacteristically cool, and prompting Fizz — just for a second — to speculate whether, were some patient woman to take this man in hand, he could yet be saved. Selina sprang to the back of his chair and leaned across his shoulder to rub her whiskers against his cheek.

The idea of Mathieson co-operating in some way with an old lady in a retirement home was doing Fizz's head in. 'What's she like?' she said.

'Miss Moir?' Buchanan took advice from the ceiling. 'Ask Walt Disney to draw a sweet old grannie and he'd come up with something like Miss Moir.'

'You'd have to thaw him out first.'

'Mmm?'

'He's in a cryogenic capsule.' Buchanan did not deign to acknowledge this pleasantry so Fizz had another biscuit. 'What we have to remember is that all of these old darlings are ex-performers. Even the non-actors are used to projecting a phoney persona so we can't take any of them at face value.'

Buchanan indicated with an eloquent droop of the eyelids that he had not been born yesterday. 'I take it you didn't get anything of comparable interest from your friend Bundy?'

'Well, I did, as it happens,' Fizz assured him with a touch of acerbity. 'In fact, until you said that about Miss Moir I thought I'd made a major breakthrough. Now it's starting to look as though the setup is a lot more complicated than it appeared.'

'Uh-huh? What did you turn up?'

'Just that Boston has a first-rate motive for killing Mathieson. He borrowed money from him and, when he couldn't pay, Mathieson claimed the garage and beat up Boston's brother. Probably very severely. The word is that Mathieson was heavily into making examples.'

'Well, he would be.' Buchanan nodded. 'He needed people to be afraid of him. How else could he operate without the Law at his back?' He sat there, absently stroking Selina and thinking for a minute or two and then said, 'So where does this leave us? It seems unlikely that, given their past history, Boston and Mathieson would be collaborating on some business deal at this stage in the game. So, do we assume that it was Miss Moir whom Mathieson was arranging to meet that Friday morning? And, if so, why? Was she there as some kind of spy? Keeping an eye on Boston, possibly?'

'Tell you who I'd like to talk to,' Fizz decided. 'Freddie McAuslan. I bet he knows the whole Boston saga and he could probably tell us a bit about Miss Moir also, if he felt so inclined.'

'Mmm. I think you're right. I'd better make time to see him tomorrow.'

'I'll come with you.'

'You'll be too busy.' Buchanan started to gather up the coffee things, pointedly indicating that the interview was coming to an end. 'You'll be seeing your own witness: Catriona Mathieson. She phoned the office this afternoon to say she'd like you to drop by her place when you have a minute. Nothing important, she said, but you'd better find out what she wants.'

Fizz was unwilling to relinquish a second meeting with Freddie. She had a feeling that Buchanan was too soft with the guy and she wanted to be able to put in her ten cents worth. She said, 'Why can't both of us see both of them? I'll let you see mine if you'll let me see yours.'

Buchanan put on his sour expression and carried the tray into the kitchen. 'It'll be quicker if we take one each.'

'Well, I think you really ought to meet Catriona. She's a very complex lady.'

'She didn't sound all that complex the way you described her at the weekend. Just the usual rich man's toy.'

Fizz leaned in the kitchen doorway and watched him scooping cat food into a plastic feeding dish. She had been fairly meagre in her description of Catriona — not wishing Buchanan to be distracted from the job in hand — but if she were to wangle her way into his meeting with Freddie she'd need him to taxi her around. Besides, if Catriona were already in a relationship, as it appeared she was, the risk was minimal.

'She's not the usual bimbo,' she persisted. 'I think you ought to take this chance of meeting her and forming your own opinion.'

Buchanan hooked an eyebrow at her suspiciously. 'In other words, you want a lift.'

'OK. I want a lift,' Fizz snapped. He was getting to be a step ahead of her far too bloody often these days and she didn't like it. 'I also want to see Freddie again but quite apart from that I think you should meet Catriona.'

'Yes, I probably should,' he said, all

157

complaisance now that he had made his point. 'OK. We'll try to fit them both in tomorrow afternoon. I dare say Catriona won't keep us long.' He looked at the kitchen clock and then checked it with his watch. 'You'd better go now, Fizz. Time's getting on.'

Fizz was perfectly happy to quit while she was winning. 'Where are you off to this evening, then?' she asked on her way to the door.

'Theatre,' Buchanan said briefly. 'See you in the morning.'

The door clicked to behind her before she could ask any more questions but as she descended the stairs she was aware of the first faint stirrings of uncertainty. Had she just been given the bum's rush?

* * *

Buchanan, the following morning, had to keep reminding himself not to look too chirpy in case he gave anyone — like Fizz, say — cause for conjecture. Not that he was habitually grumpy, exactly, but when he went around the office humming under his breath and exchanging pleasantries with the typists it made Fizz's antennae quiver. That sort of behaviour might be expected from the junior partner, Dennis, who had an exaggerated opinion of his own charisma, not to mention an enduring ambition to get into Fizz's knickers, but Buchanan was normally much more reserved.

Today, however, his thoughts kept drifting to the previous evening, wallowing in the delicious afterglow of Lizzie's allure. Throughout the performance he had been constantly aware of her sitting there beside him, the touch of her shoulder against his, the gentle rise and fall of her bosom, the scent of gardenias that drifted up from her hair when she moved her head.

Afterwards, when they stopped for a drink at Lorca's, he couldn't take his eyes off her as they dissected the performance and then progressed to an analysis of books and music, her twin passions. She was beautiful, entertaining, lucid and informed and she was — quite unmistakably — attracted to him.

'I think it's wonderful of you to visit Mr Fitzpatrick so regularly,' she said during the long taxi ride out to her home in Peebles. 'Dad said he saw you there again this evening.'

'Only for a few minutes,' Buchanan said. 'I had a little chat with him in the garden.'

'And with Miss Moir,' she nodded, smiling a comment on the efficiency of the grapevine.

'Isn't she a darling?'

'She's amazing,' Buchanan had to agree. 'If you saw her in a television drama you'd say she was over the top. Is she really as sweet as she looks?'

'No doubt about it. Sweet and gentle and loving: a dream grannie. Helen says she's an 'earth mother' and I suspect they all regard her somewhat in that light. Everyone else is addressed by their first name, you'll notice, but Miss Moir always gets her title.'

'I could tell that she was really fond of her friends at the complex. I'm sure she'll be very happy now that she has her home there.'

Lizzie's face flickered in the intermittent light from passing streetlamps as she turned her head to look at him. 'Wasn't she happy before?'

'No — I didn't mean that — I'm sure she was. But it'll be nice for her to be with her friends. She mentioned that she'd been a regular visitor to the complex for years, so the transition won't be all that traumatic for her.'

Lizzie leaned forward to peer out of the window and then tapped on the glass to signal the driver. They stopped in front of an imposing Victorian mansion of the type which, in this district, customarily went on the market for offers over three-quarters of a million.

'How do you like my pad?' Lizzie asked and then, with a smile, led the way to a neat little stone extension which had probably been added originally as a grannie flat. At the door she turned and slipped naturally into Buchanan's arms.

'I can't tell you how much I've enjoyed this evening.'

'It was great,' Buchanan confirmed, kissing her brow. 'I can't wait for Friday. Where would you like to go?'

'Surprise me.' She smoothed her fingertips across his cheekbone. 'I wonder what I could give you for your birthday.'

'Don't be silly. You don't have to give — '

'But I want to,' she purred, looking deep into his eyes. 'I want it to be a special birthday. I'm sure I'll think of something.'

Buchanan, momentarily bereft of words, did what came naturally and as she responded to his kiss he was convinced she already *had* thought of something. He just hoped they were both thinking of the same thing.

He thought about it all the way home in the taxi and fell asleep thinking about it and woke up thinking about it and thought about it at regular three-minute intervals all morning. Every time his path crossed Fizz's he snapped on a glower till finally she ended

161

up telling him he would end up alone and loveless, an insufferable old grouch.

He had more or less sobered up by the time they arrived at Catriona's house in the early afternoon. He wasn't overly surprised by the ostentation of the place but found it profoundly distasteful. The house struck him as a prime example of unimaginative modern architecture of the 'never-mind-the-quality-feel-the-width' variety and the furnishings were pretentious, expensive and crass.

Catriona met them at the door and ushered them into the lounge, talking all the time. 'I hope I haven't dragged you both all the way out here for nothing. I did tell the receptionist in your office that it wasn't important and that there was no hurry for you to call but you said that if I found anything strange I was to phone you and — well, this isn't strange exactly, but I thought, well, if there's a chance you might find it interesting I'd better show it to you. It's nothing much, so don't be disappointed. Now where did I put it?'

'It's no trouble for us to call in, Mrs Mathieson,' Buchanan told her, admiring the view from the window while she rummaged in a writing desk. 'We were on our way to another call anyway so please don't feel you're wasting out time.'

'Here . . . ' She straightened up and

unfolded two pieces of paper which she handed to Buchanan. One was a sheet of newspaper. The other was a pale blue typewritten page listing seven names, addresses and phone numbers.

'You know these people, Catriona?' Fizz asked, reading over Buchanan's shoulder.

'No, I've no idea who they are. And the newspaper, it's the *Evening News*. Chick never ever bought an evening newspaper and I can't see a single item on that sheet that would have been of any interest to him.'

Buchanan looked at her enquiringly. 'But you think that they're something to do with the project he was involved in around the time of his death?'

'I thought it was possible.'

Catriona waved a purple-nailed hand at the couch, inviting them to be seated. She was dressed in tight, black velvet jeans with high-heeled pumps and a garish beaded sweater. At a short distance, Buchanan thought, and with an arc light behind her, she might have passed for a real stunner but at close quarters she left much to be desired.

'I found them both, folded together, in the pocket of his trench coat,' she said, sinking into an armchair and crossing her black velvet legs. 'He didn't take a coat with him on the

163

morning of the day he died — it was a lovely day — but it had been raining most of the previous day and I'm pretty sure he must have worn it then.'

Buchanan ran his eye down the list of names and addresses in the hope that some sort of recognition or correlation might spring out at him, but drew a blank. All but one of the addresses were within a twenty-five-mile radius of Edinburgh but the names defied analysis.

Mrs P. Whittock, Prestonfield; Mrs S. Foreman, Juniper Green; Revd J. Keir, Inverleith; Mr R. Cannon, Cramond; Mr R. Bryce-Cowan, Glasgow; Dr J. Robinson, Comely Bank; Mr C. Charles, Dunfermline.

'Have you done anything about this yourself, Mrs Mathieson?' he asked. 'Tried to phone these people or contact them in any way?'

'I wish you'd call me Catriona, like Fizz does.' She stretched out an arm for a pack of cigarettes on the table beside her. 'I thought about it, but then I thought I'd better talk to Fizz first.' She swung her eyes to Fizz. 'Like you said the other night, we don't know what we're dealing with here and there's no point in rushing to the police with stuff that could have nothing to do with Chick's murder.'

'Roger.' Fizz nodded, keeping her head

buried in the newspaper she'd been scanning. Buchanan hoped very much that she had not been advising Catriona Mathieson against taking her evidence to the police but knew it would be a waste of time to ask her since she would only deny it. Sometimes, when dealing with Fizz, it was better to operate on a don't-ask-don't-tell basis.

'What about the addresses?' he suggested. 'Did your husband have business interests in any of these areas? Friends? Associates? Employees?'

'Not as far as I know,' she said, looking, for the first time, pretty worn down by the whole business. 'But as I told Fizz the other evening, Chick had a lot going down that he never spoke about. He used to say that he didn't like to bring the office home with him.'

Buchanan stood up. 'Well, we'll look into it, Mrs . . . ah . . . Catriona, and let you know if it's worth reporting to the CID. I'll get back to you, one way or another, in a day or two. In the meantime, thank you for bringing it to our attention.'

Fizz took her leave of Catriona in a noticeably less formal manner and waited till she was settled in the car before saying, 'What do you think? Are we wasting our time with this? There's really nothing to suggest it has anything to do with

165

Mathieson's last project.'

'Nothing in the newspaper?'

Fizz unfolded the double page. 'Not that I can see. It's dated Friday the twenty-third — a week before Mathieson was killed. Human interest stories about people who are allergic to peanuts or have made spectacular gardens out of rubbish tips. Daydreaming lorry driver banned for six months. Unfair dismissal hearing. Silly twat grounded on a mudbank off Port Edgar marina. Complaints about closure of public toilets in Morningside. Camper van fire in Aberlady. That's all on pages three and four. The other half, pages twenty-five and twenty-six are the sports pages. Nothing of any interest whatsoever.' She lifted the paper to her nose and sniffed. 'Maybe it was wrapped around his fish supper.'

Buchanan frowned at the blue notepaper. 'There's nothing to be gained from the list of names either. Men, women, a doctor, a clergyman, city centre, outlying districts, prestigious addresses, council housing. Nothing, on the surface, that would tie one to another.'

'I suppose we have to pursue it,' Fizz concluded, glancing at him in the hope, no doubt, that he would either disagree or would offer to do the legwork himself, but he had no

166

intention of letting her off the hook. She knew as well as he did that the list would have to be checked out and, when it came to thankless jobs like that, rank had its privileges.

9

They found Freddie looking decidedly more optimistic than he had done on their previous visit. This was largely due, it transpired, to a misplaced assumption that Buchanan had some good news for him. Fizz would have been happy to tell him that their likelihood of making progress would be greatly enhanced with some concrete input from his good self but Buchanan was as bland as ever.

'I'm afraid not, Freddie. No real progress to report, but we have one or two leads to follow and it's possible you may be able to help us with these.'

He started taking papers out of his briefcase, which gave Fizz the chance to put the boot in. 'We're unlikely to be successful in keeping you out of prison unless you co-operate with us fully. You know that, don't you? It's not like telling the police or grassing on your mates. Nobody needs to know that you've told us anything. You've nothing to be afraid of.'

Freddie's eyes showed a lot of white as he swivelled them between her and Buchanan but he nodded in a way that seemed to indicate that he accepted the truth of what she was saying.

Buchanan folded his arms and hung an ankle across the opposite knee. 'How long were you living at Causeyside Street, Freddie?'

'Dunno . . . about a week.'

'How many flats in that stair?'

'Uh . . . three . . . an' the shops on the ground floor, like.'

'Did you have any contacts with the other tenants?'

'Weren't none.'

Buchanan's head poked forward an inch. 'No tenants in the other two flats?'

'A furniture van came and took stuff away from the place through the wall from where I was: furniture an' that. That was the day after I moved in. After that I never saw nobody.'

'You never saw a little old lady around the place?' Fizz persisted, unwilling to abandon this topic without a fight. 'Short and plump, with white hair and specs?'

Freddie's lustrous brown eyes locked on to hers. 'No, miss. I never seen nobody like that. Never seen nobody up that stair but they removal men. Nobody lived in them flats. Chick was going to sell them.'

'Mathieson owned all three flats?'

'That's right, miss.' He didn't look as if he

was lying, which probably meant that he wasn't.

'OK. Next question.' Buchanan slid the list of names across the table towards him. 'Take a look at these names and tell me if any of them ring a bell with you.'

Freddie held the blue paper flat on the table and brought his nose down to some six inches above it. Fizz could see his lips moving as he slid his eyes along each line. When he got to the bottom of the list he went back to the beginning and studied each line again.

'Don't know none of them.'

Buchanan didn't ask him if he was sure and even Fizz felt it would have been a waste of time.

'Right. No problem. Maybe you'll have better luck with this.' Buchanan retrieved the list and substituted the sheet of newspaper. 'Chick Mathieson was carrying this around in his pocket and we'd like to know why. I'd like to see if you recognise any of the names mentioned in the news items or if any of the stories strikes you as something Chick might have been interested in.'

Freddie appeared quite stressed out by the magnitude of this request but drew the paper towards him and perused it conscientiously front and back. Speed reading not being his forte, this took about ten minutes, after which he admitted defeat.

'OK. Just one more question, Freddie, and then we'll leave you in peace.'

Freddie clenched his fists on the table top and watched Buchanan's lips.

'Does the name Boston mean anything to you?'

'Aye,' Freddie responded, looking surprised at being able to come up with a helpful answer. 'Jack and Len Boston. They used to have a garage out at Currie.'

'Customers of Chick's?'

Freddie thought about that for a minute, gnawing his top lip and scrutinising the interior of the cubicle for inspiration. Finally, speaking almost incoherently as though that ensured it didn't count as lese-majesty, he said, 'They was on the collection list.'

'This was before you went into prison?' Buchanan prompted.

'Uh-huh. Me and Kennedy collected from them a coupla times. Then they got in bad with Chick.' He glanced down the glass-walled corridor to where the duty warden was currently pacing away from them. 'They couldn't keep up the payments and Chick had to sort them out.'

'How thoroughly did he sort them out?' Fizz butted in, impatient with Buchanan's laid-back approach.

171

Freddie's long lashes batted for an instant, like a starlet's, and he looked at Buchanan as though hoping for assurance that he didn't need to answer. When he received only a raised eyebrow in reply he swallowed audibly and muttered, 'See, if Chick's *other* customers thought they could get away with not paying — '

'That's not what I asked you, Freddie,' Fizz snapped. 'I want to know what happened to the Boston brothers and I don't want any of your crap, do you understand?'

Buchanan made a cool-it signal to her under the level of the table but Freddie, after rolling his eyes for a minute, said finally, 'Len was hurt pretty bad. He was in hospital for a long time and doesn't get around too well these days. I seen his wife pushing him in a wheelchair once. Jack . . . I dunno . . . I think he came through it OK. Never seen him around after that.'

'Can you think of any reason why Chick Mathieson might have been co-operating with Jack Boston in some project just before he was murdered?'

Freddie stared at Buchanan as though he suspected this might be a trick question. 'Boston? Chick was working with Jack *Boston*?'

'I didn't say they *were* working together,

I'm just wondering if it's possible. Is it?'

'See, I've been away for five years, but . . . no, not Jack Boston. Jack wouldn't have . . . Jack was . . . like . . . '

'Straight?' Fizz suggested.

Freddie pressed his lips together and nodded. 'That's right, miss. Five years ago he was, last time I seen him. Also, him and Chick didn't get on.'

'Not surprisingly,' said Buchanan. 'And I can't see five years making a lot of difference to that situation.'

He started to fold up the newspaper and make preparations for leaving but Fizz had a gut feeling that, having started to leak information detrimental to his ex-mentor, Freddie might be cozened into parting with another drip or two. Give him a couple of days to think about it and he'd regret being so forthcoming and clam up again.

'Mathieson had a lot of irons in the fire, Freddie,' she said gently. 'He must have had plenty of people working for him. Didn't you meet any of his other associates?'

'No, miss. Just Kennedy. Chick didn't like his left hand to know what his right hand was doing. That's what Kennedy said.' He turned his hands palm up, one after the other, as he recited the relevant phrase, as though that was how Kennedy had demonstrated it to

173

him. 'I seen him with people sometimes but they was just his mates. I never knew who they were.'

'Where was that?'

'At a restaurant once, and at the Tudor casino. I had to drive his car home 'cause he was pi — because he was drunk, miss.'

'Did he go to the casino regularly?'

Freddie denied all knowledge of his boss's social life but judging from what Fizz had already divined of Mathieson's psychological profile, she suspected that gambling would give him the sort of adrenaline hit he appeared to enjoy.

She tried Freddie out with a few more questions, while Buchanan waited for her with an expression of saintlike patience on his face, but she had no further success. Freddie looked willing enough to be helpful but neither his memory nor his intellect was equal to the task.

'He's coming around,' Buchanan said when they got outside. 'He's finally realising that he has to trust us but, frankly, I suspect he has already told us everything he knows. It's quite apparent that Mathieson ran his outfit like the French Resistance, with no osmosis between cells, so either Boston or Miss Moir could fit in to another sector of his empire. We may have to start looking at some of his

174

so-called legitimate businesses. Not the garage. Your young friend knows nothing about what's going on there and I don't fancy the sound of the other mechanics. However, the second-hand shop could well repay a visit. What do you think?'

'It's a possible,' Fizz admitted, not too reluctantly. She'd always had a bit of a fascination for second-hand shops, jumble sales, car boot sales, auction sales and charity shops. In fact she never shopped anywhere else, except for food. 'Another possible is the casino. I'll give you seven to four that Mathieson was a regular gambler and that's the sort of place where people will talk to us.'

'What makes you think that?'

'I don't think it, I know it. I worked there as a croupier the last year I was at art school. Believe me, there wasn't much we didn't know about the regulars. They treated the place as their local and once they'd had a few drinks they forgot to watch their tongues in front of the dealers. At least one of my old chums is still working there.'

She knew it made Buchanan uneasy when she mentioned any of the more colourful means by which she had kept body and soul together in leaner times. He never asked any questions — not that Fizz would have

175

indulged him if he had — and he invariably changed the subject as soon as he could. It was as if he lived in fear of hearing something too bizarre for the human mind to contemplate. He got in the car and didn't speak again till they were out of the car park but he evidently had not stopped thinking about her suggestion.

'Yes, well, time enough to consider that possibility when we have no other leads to pursue,' he said briskly. 'The list has to come first. The sooner you get started on that the better.'

Fizz was ninety-five per cent certain that the list would yield nothing. Mathieson could have had it in his pocket for months and besides, she liked to think she had a nose for these things and her nose told her that checking out every name on that list would be a complete waste of time. It simply did not speak to her.

'How about if I just phoned them?'

She knew Buchanan wouldn't wear that. She wouldn't consider it herself normally, because you never warned a sucker that you were on to him, but in this case it hardly seemed to matter. Buchanan answered only with a sideways look.

'You realise it could take me days to get round this lot by public transport,' she

176

grumbled. 'It would be much more man-power efficient if you were to do it.'

'No chance. My time is more valuable than yours.'

'Well, I'm not starting this evening. I have to see Grampa today since I didn't visit him yesterday.'

Buchanan stopped for a traffic light and sat staring blindly at the car in front for a few seconds. 'We should drop in on Grampa on our way back,' he said. 'I want to see him myself and I have things to do this evening. If we go just now it means we're both clear for the rest of the day.'

Fizz avoided looking at him. She knew that his face would show no hint of the motivation behind his willingness to spend time with Grampa but she was damn sure, all the same, that he was hiding something from her. Had there been nurses around Greenfield House she would have been on to him — probably even ahead of him — but there was nothing fanciable at the complex unless one were on a sexual progression towards necrophilia.

'What did you want to see Grampa about?'

'Nothing in particular. I just want to make sure he's well and happy. I still feel bad about shunting him into that place — OK, it was you who did the shunting but I should have stopped you and now I have to live with it.'

That was, of course, the truth. Not only because Buchanan was insanely superstitious about manipulating people, but because it was in his nature to feel responsible for everyone and everything. It didn't matter a jot that Grampa was as happy as a pig in shit, Buchanan would not sleep easy till the old boy was back in Am Bealach, safe and sound.

'There's no need for you to see him every day, Buchanan. I can give you a daily report if that's all that's worrying you.'

'I'd be happier seeing him for myself.'

'OK, mein Führer, let's do it. I rather fancy meeting the rest of the cast anyway. Are they all like Helen?'

Buchanan appeared to give this question more careful consideration than it deserved. After a while he said, 'By and large, yes. They're all very outgoing and articulate, as you'd expect. But when I say 'all' I don't mean all twenty-odd of them. I've only met Helen's little clique, so I can't speak for the others. Maybe today would be a good time to catch them.'

'Why today rather than any other day?'

'Uh . . . ' Buchanan studied the road ahead. 'Uh . . . because they'll be sitting around the garden at this time in the afternoon. Best time to get them talking.'

'Roger,' Fizz said, deciding that she was

simply a nasty suspicious person and was doing him an injustice.

She would have been hard put to it to explain why she hated to see Buchanan with a chick on his arm. There was, of course, the fact that the said chicks were uniformly unsuitable for him and likely to cause him indescribable angst when the time came for him to give them the elbow. Besides, it wasn't easy to picture Buchanan steeling himself to break anybody's heart so, had Fizz not been willing to look out for him, he would probably have married the gold-digging harpy he had been virtually engaged to when Fizz first finagled her way into his employ, not to mention the half-dozen or so she had saved him from since. Buchanan was the marrying kind and Buchanan with a wife in the background, no matter how far in the background, would not be the Buchanan he was today.

OK, the Buchanan he was today was not anything to write home about. He was pedantic and conservative and a lot more chauvinistic than he thought he was, but he wasn't half as much all these things as he had been two years ago. These days it wasn't unusual for a week or more to pass without Fizz feeling the urge to dissolve him in corrosive sublimate so, in theory, there could come a time — far, far away in the future — when he evolved into something a girl could stand having around. Not permanently, but at least for a time. And if that time ever came it would be a bit of a bummer if, after all her work, he was married to someone else.

He was right about the residents being in the garden at this time of day. There were half a dozen of them sitting, alone or in pairs, on wooden loungers and another four, including Boston, doing ta'i chi under the direction of a tall skinny man who looked like two small boys, one on the other's shoulders.

'That's Paul,' Buchanan said as they walked across the grass. 'He was an actor, probably a character actor. He's quite eccentric, or appears that way. Maybe it's just his sense of humour. And the lady with the pile of hair is Cheryl da Pont: chanteuse. Still pretty good at it too. Rumour has it they're an item.'

Cheryl looked, to Fizz, much younger than those about her but that could be put down to distance. Her figure was still trim and she performed the ta'i chi sequence with supple movements that made the others look stiff. Helen and the rest of her coterie, including Grampa, were loosely grouped in a bay of the shrubbery that screened off the row of garages. Everyone except Grampa looked pleased to see Fizz and Buchanan approaching, and if the old sourpuss had ever looked pleased about anything Fizz would have been really worried.

'Well, well, Archie, my precious,' Helen told Grampa in her usual fortissimo delivery, 'you can't complain that your friends don't visit you.'

Grampa, who had doubtless never in his life been so addressed, not even by Auntie Duff, didn't turn a whisker. 'Aye. This is my granddaughter, Fizz. She can be verra attentive when she wants. I wonder what she wants this time.'

He introduced the three other members of the group: Nigel Hayes, a Michael Parkinson lookalike; Anthony Canning, a red-faced old buffer with a corporation; and the unmistakable Miss Moir who was actually *knitting*, for God's sake!

Anthony and Nigel squeezed along their bench to make room for Fizz to park one hip on a corner and Buchanan perched on the low retaining wall of the shrubbery. Everyone was very cheery and welcoming, and even Grampa looked marginally less like a schnauzer with piles than was his wont.

'I don't know when I last saw my granddaughter,' Anthony remarked in a growly voice that indicated many years as a heavy smoker. 'If she shows up at Christmas or on my birthday I count myself lucky.'

'Ella is holding down a responsible job, dear,' Miss Moir said, her soft voice resonant with affection; the sort of voice an orphan child might associate with a vision of her half-remembered mother. 'And she has a home to run as well as having to devote quality time to her husband and children. We can't expect the young ones to keep on dancing attendance on us year in, year out, can we? Besides, I don't know about you, but I can't find much to say to my grandchildren any more. They have their own interests and we have ours and, thank God, we're lucky enough to have plenty of company our own age.'

'Ah well, there's some truth in that,' Anthony admitted. 'She was never the most entertaining of company, our Ella. Damn boring, to tell you the truth. We can't all be as lucky as Nigel.'

'You don't feel the urge to take part in the ta'i chi lessons?' said Buchanan abruptly, addressing Grampa, who reacted with spirit.

'I'm thinking I'll mebbe give it a wee try tomorrow. Paul says it's verra gentle exercise and would likely do my balance a lot of good. I wouldn't have to do the kicks, he says, or the bits where you have to stand on one leg.'

Helen laughed her loud throaty laugh. 'Don't do it, Archie! The man's a monster. He insisted that I should do the arm movements and kept me at it for an hour. I was so stiff the next day I could hardly lift a fork to my mouth.'

Her resonant tones carried across the lawn to the ta'i chi students, who were resting between sequences. They turned and stared for a moment and then returned their attention to Paul, who appeared to be the choreographer.

'I don't know where Paul gets his energy,' Miss Moir said, smiling across at the group. 'He's an inspiration to us all and such a sweet, generous man.'

Nigel cleared his throat and turned to Buchanan, raising a hand to shield his eyes from the sun. 'And you are a solicitor, I hear, Tam. Would I know the firm?'

'Buchanan and Stewart. Charlotte Square.'

'Is that a general practice or do you specialise?'

'Just the usual run-of-the mill stuff, mostly. Wills, house purchase, a little company work, minor disputes.'

Nigel twinkled his eyes and pretended faint disappointment. 'You don't do anything as exciting as court work?'

'My partner, Alan Stewart, usually deals

with that,' Buchanan said, restricting his reply to the precise truth but managing, to Fizz's eye at least, to look as guilty as hell at the same time. 'Not that even *that's* very exciting, for the most part. Mainly divorces and bad debts.'

'What a pity I didn't know you when I moved to Greenfield House.' Miss Moir cabled deftly and stuck the cabling needle into her bun for safekeeping. 'You could have handled the sale for me. Not,' she added earnestly, 'that I had any complaints about the solicitor that Paul recommended, quite the reverse, but still — '

'At ease, men! Smoke 'em if you've got 'em,' interrupted a new voice from behind Fizz's shoulder, and Paul gangled into her line of vision followed closely by Boston. 'All those who missed ta'i chi practice are on fatigues tomorrow morning. I'll have no slackers in my crew, dammit! Tam, my dear chap, my favourite solicitor, how are you? If I'm ever arrested for fouling the pavement I shall call you immediately. I see you have brought yet another ray of sunshine into our darkness. A cherub straight out of a Botticelli, if I may say so, my dear young lady. Allow me to introduce myself. Paul Ossian Amadeus Bramley, resident of this parish; born of Portuguese/Russian parentage in Oodnadata,

Central Australia; educated at a Jesuit monastery near Dar es Salaam; explored Mozambique on foot with a troupe of travelling acrobats; personal masseur to Marilyn Monroe; bombardier on the Lancaster that sunk the *Scharnhorst*; more recently a colonic irrigation consultant, head sommelier at Burger King, a thespian, a kept man and a known psychopath. At your charming service.'

Fizz gave him her hand, which he kissed with an elaborate flourish before folding his limbs like a joiner's ruler and sinking to the grass. Boston joined him, leaning back on his hands and turning his battered face up to the sun.

Now that she knew how he'd come by that battered face Fizz saw Boston quite differently. She had suspected, even at their first meeting, that he wasn't as tough as he looked but now, seeing the way the residents reacted to him, hearing his banter and their unabashed retorts, it was very obvious that there was a genuine closeness there. He evidently took his job seriously and spent a lot of time just interacting with the old people and developing a relationship.

Gradually he was slipping down the list of Fizz's suspects. He may have had a motive for killing Mathieson — and a good one — but there was no way he and Mathieson would have worked together. If any of the bunch looked suspicious it was Miss Moir. She was simply too sweet to be wholesome. Nobody was that nice. Nobody could really merit the tender regard so legible on the faces of her companions. It just wasn't natural. Fizz watched her counting the stitches on her needles and shuddered.

When the time came to go Grampa hauled himself out of his chair and said he'd walk them to the car. 'I've been sitting here long enough. The doctor says I've to keep on the move as much as possible.'

'Scrabble parade at nineteen hundred hours,' Paul reminded him, springing to his feet to give Fizz another kiss on the hand. 'If we play again like we did last night, Archie my boy, Helen and Cheryl will be as the dust beneath our chariot wheels.'

'Blimey,' Fizz remarked as soon as they were at a safe distance, 'does he ever let up?'

'Not for any length of time,' Grampa grunted, 'but you get used to him. Once you get him talking he's a verra interesting man. Verra sharp. Never got much work as an actor, Helen tells me, but he made a lot of money on the stock exchange.'

'I'm amazed at how well they all seem to

get along,' Buchanan said. 'Or is that just on the surface?'

'No, they're all pretty pally. Helen and Cheryl get at each other sometimes but not seriously.' Grampa waved his stick at the scattered figures around the lawn. 'The rest of the residents don't socialise as much. Nice enough to speak to if you meet them in the lift — and Charmaine's pally enough — but you don't see them around as much as Paul's bunch. They keep themselves to themselves. I think Paul tries his best to interest all of them in his concerts or join in his Scrabble tournaments but it's always that same half-dozen that form the nucleus of everything that goes on.'

'Have you had any private conversation with Miss Moir since yesterday?' Fizz asked.

'We had a wee chat in the garden before the others joined up but all we talked about was sheep. She seemed quite interested in hearing about how I train my dogs.'

Buchanan stopped as they reached the car and glanced around carefully to make sure they were not overheard. 'We spoke to Freddie McAuslan this afternoon and he told us that Boston and his brother were beaten up by Mathieson some years back for nonpayment of a debt. Boston's brother was crippled in the attack.'

'Dear me. Is that not appalling?' Grampa's eyes needled into Buchanan's face. 'So, now we have the motive, eh?'

'So it would seem,' Buchanan nodded. 'But what we have to remember is that even if Boston *is* the guilty party, he didn't act alone. It would take two strong men to heave Mathieson over that parapet. Two at least.'

Two strong men, Fizz thought glumly. How many geriatrics would that equal?

10

It turned out a lovely evening, much too nice to be trailing around Edinburgh checking out Catriona's list, so Fizz headed for the Pentland Hills and walked from Bonaly to Fairmilehead without meeting another soul. OK, it wasn't the Cuillin but it was glorious in the sunset and for three hours she could have imagined herself in the Highlands.

Normally she did her best thinking when she was alone in the hills; even when she wasn't particularly concentrating on a problem she often found that the solution came floating into her mind, unbidden. But as she followed the track across the summits of Allermuir and Caerketton she made not one iota of headway on the case in hand. In fact, she had a horrible feeling she was drifting further from a conclusion every day.

The idea of a simple revenge killing, perpetrated by Boston, no longer struck her as convincing. He might well be capable of committing a murder — who could ever tell? — and he certainly had the motive, but it was hard to imagine him having the implacable malice to use such a grotesquely public method.

And what about Miss Moir? Could she have done it? Oddly enough, Fizz was less sure of Miss Moir than of Boston. That warm, gentle, unquestioning love that informed her every word and gesture was way over the top. It had to be a mask. And why wear a mask if what was *behind* the mask wasn't too scary to reveal? But even if Miss Moir were perfectly capable, psychologically, of writing off Chick Mathieson, she certainly didn't possess the physique to have done the deed alone. That meant that she'd have to have had at least one accomplice, more likely two or even three and the idea of those accomplices coming from the selection available at Greenfield House simply boggled the mind. The sudden ludicrous vision of half a dozen frail old things attempting to manhandle someone of Mathieson's temperament and bulk made Fizz laugh out loud. Even if he'd been unconscious at that point, it still reminded her of something out of *Gulliver's Travels*.

Which left the fragrant Catriona; and for the life of her, Fizz could not imagine Catriona being that decisive. She'd made the best of her life with Chick Mathieson for eight years and she patently wasn't the type to strangle the golden goose, certainly not for the love of another man. There was not the slightest doubt that Mathieson's death had left her considerably worse off than before so she'd had no motive for hiring a hit man. Besides, she was doing her best to be helpful.

However, it was early days yet and there were at least some leads to follow, primarily the list of names. Boring it might be but she was going nowhere and doing nothing until the damn thing was out of the way.

Accordingly, she made an early start in the morning by catching a bus to Prestonfield, where lived Mrs P. Whittock, who was not only number one on the list but the closest to home. Twenty-seven Kirkhill Crescent, which was given as her address, was a big traditional bungalow on a raised site looking out over Prestonfield golf course and Arthur's Seat, both virtually at the end of the garden. Given that it was barely a twenty-minute walk from Princes Street it had to be a very desirable property but Mrs P. Whittock had evidently found something even better because she was moving out. The solicitor's 'For Sale' sign in the front garden already had a white 'Under Offer' strip angled across it.

It was a bit of a bind that the deal had progressed so far, because there was nothing easier to get into for a good old snoop than a house that was up for sale, but Fizz decided to try her luck anyway. Easy enough to pretend she wanted to state her interest in case the deal fell through. The bell sounded hollowly through the lobby as she pressed it and she knew right away that the place was empty. She rang again, just to be sure, and as she waited she leaned sideways from the top of the steps and managed to see into a corner of the sitting room. Parquet flooring, no pictures on the wall, cheesy old curtains like you'd leave behind for the look of things. Mrs P. Whittock had gone.

On the face of it this was a bit of a bummer but it also had a sort of sinister feeling about it. Had Mrs P. Whittock sold up in a hurry? Maybe immediately after Mathieson's murder? Or was the piece of blue paper in her hand a hit list?

She tried knocking on the doors of the houses on either side but the inhabitants had already gone off to work or were taking the dog for a walk on the golf course. Lesson for the day: always call in the evening. Also: never put off till tomorrow, strike when the iron's hot, gather ye rosebuds, etc., etc.

On her fourth try she raised a scone-faced middle-aged woman with a curly perm and a yappy Jack Russell pup clamped to her bosom.

'Sorry to intrude on you at this hour,' Fizz shouted above the yapping, 'but I'm looking for Mrs Whittock, across the road, and I wondered if you could tell me where she moved to and when.'

'Oh, do be quiet, Toby, there's a good boy. Who? Whittock? At what number?'

'Twenty-seven. The one that's for sale.'

'Oh . . . Whittock . . . right.' She nodded briskly. 'You're not a relative or a close friend, I take it?'

'No. I work for a solicitor,' Fizz said, producing a business card.

'That's all right then. I just wanted to be sure the news wouldn't come as a shock. Mr Whittock passed on, you see.'

'Really?' Fizz said, betraying more interest than Buchanan would have thought wise. She looked down at the list for a moment and waited for the dog to stop for breath. 'Was it sudden?'

'I believe so. I wasn't on chatting terms with the family — kept very much to themselves, they did — but I don't think he was ill. Quiet, Toby! Not for any length of time, anyway.'

Toby continued barking like a machine gun, his beady brown eyes fixed on Fizz with an expression of hatred which Fizz returned with interest. She longed to hold the little rat's muzzle closed a few times while roaring 'Shurrup!' in its ear. That would have put the message across to the pooch quite adequately as well as making its owner a lot more popular with the neighbours.

'So, how long ago did Mr Whittock die?'

'Ah . . . now . . . let me see . . . Oh, Toby, for heaven's sake! A person can't hear herself think. The funeral was on a Friday, that I can tell you, because my daughter was here, but when that was exactly I can't be sure. Not long ago, anyway, because the house has only been on the market two or three weeks. They go very fast around here, you know.'

'And I don't suppose you heard where the rest of the family moved to?'

'I did hear. Dear me, where was it now?' She repositioned the wriggling pup under one arm and shushed it optimistically. 'Somewhere down south, to be close to their married son. Cornwall . . . or Dorset, maybe. You could ask Betty Henderson at number twenty-nine. That's who told me.'

But Fizz had had enough. If Buchanan wanted any more information he could phone up the solicitor who was marketing the house. He'd find out all he wanted, including the forwarding address, without all this hassle.

The next name on the list, geographically speaking, was that of the Revd J. Keir whose manse was a scant twenty minutes away in Inverleith. It was easy to locate because it was adjacent to the church, both buildings being grimy early nineteenth-century edifices surrounded by gravestones and gloomy cypresses. The church door was open so Fizz paused on her way to the manse to take a look inside.

It was the usual dark wood and grey stone interior but there were two very nice stained-glass windows above the altar, one depicting the crucifixion of St Andrew and the other the Annunciation. There was no one to be seen. However, as she was turning to leave, she heard the sound of a voice coming from the vestry. It was very faint but as she got closer to it she heard, ' . . . said to him, 'Well if you really think so but I've sung the solo the last four times and there may be those who feel that they could do it just as well, as I'm sure they could,' but he just turned to me and, do you know what he said? He — '

Fizz wished she had waited just a moment longer before tapping on the door but it was too late now. She would never know what he'd said.

'So sorry to intrude,' she said to the two ladies who were preparing flowers at a sink. 'I'm looking for Mr Keir.'

'Mr Keir?' said the younger of the two, a pleasant-faced woman in her thirties. 'I don't think I know a Mr Keir, do you, Angela?'

'I do not,' Angela replied, drawing in her double chin and rearing her head back to regard her companion with earnest speculation. 'What's Andy the gardener's second name?'

'He's not a gardener, he's a minister,' Fizz explained. 'The Reverend J. Keir.'

'Not here.' Angela shook her head.

'You must have the wrong church,' said her friend. 'Is it the United Free you're looking for?'

'No, it's this church. I have the address here.' Fizz checked the list nevertheless.

'Well, our minister is Mr Frank and the evening service is taken by young Mr Cooper. We haven't had a visiting minister for years.' Angela scratched her wrist with the point of her secateurs. 'You couldn't have got the name wrong?'

Fizz looked again at the list, more for inspiration than anything else. She'd had a feeling this job was going to be a swine and it was beginning to look like she'd just about got it right. 'Maybe he was staying with your minister in the manse for a while. Could that be possible?'

They looked at each other, both of them

frowning a little and shaking their heads. Then the younger one said, 'We'd have known about it, wouldn't we, Angela? There's absolutely no way we wouldn't have known about it. You must have been given the wrong information.'

Fizz smiled and nodded and admitted that, yes, that was probably what had happened, then she went on up to the manse and asked to speak to the minister. Mr Frank was friendly and patient and willing to be as helpful as he could possibly be, but he was no more help than the flower arrangers. The name Keir was simply not known around these parts and nor were the names Mathieson, Boston or Kennedy. Fizz knew she was taking a risk in putting the second part of the question to Mr Frank but in the case of a minister of the kirk it was one she was willing to take.

Two down, five to go, score nil. Bloody great!

Back on the bus again and off to Cramond in the hope of better luck with Mr R. Cannon. According to the list, his house was at number eleven Ferry Road, and so was situated virtually on the bank of the Forth so Fizz should have been able to picture it. She often walked the beach at Cramond, which had a nice open outlook across the Forth estuary and also boasted some interesting Roman remains, but she was unable to recall a private residence at that exact location. Only when she arrived at the spot and had walked fruitlessly up and down for several minutes did the answer to this enigma become apparent. There was no such house.

There had, at one time, been a building of some description on the correct site, that much was deducible by the foundations which were still in situ, but it was long gone. There was a café at number ten and a Tourist Information Office at number twelve and nothing but the Forth across the road.

Somebody was playing silly buggers.

★ ★ ★

Buchanan, meanwhile, was beginning to think he'd have had a more productive morning if he had elected to suss out the list instead of wasting his time stuck behind his desk. He'd had his father on the phone for thirty-five minutes, thirsting for an update on Freddie McAuslan's defence, after which his mother had come on the line with the news that she was arranging a little family get-together tomorrow to celebrate his birthday.

'But, I have something arranged, Mum!'

He knew damn well that the get-together would turn out to be just him and his parents anyway, plus the two uncles who could be relied upon to turn up for anything where there was likely to be booze. Steve and Honour would agree to come and then cancel at the last minute, as was their invariable practice at every family gathering, on the excuse that their twins were peaky.

'Oh no! Really, Tam, you should have told me. I've just wasted almost the entire morning on the phone, not to mention the baking I did yesterday. The twins will be *so* disappointed — I promised them indoor fireworks. Now I'll have to phone everyone again and cancel.'

Buchanan had never won an argument with his mother in his life but he was goaded into saying placidly, 'A pity you didn't check with me first because — '

'Well, it wouldn't have been much of a surprise for you if you'd been the first to know, would it, Tam? Besides, every time I try to contact you at the office Beatrice tells me you're out and you never seem to spend a single evening at home. I don't know why you don't get a mobile phone like everyone else.'

As far as Buchanan was concerned she was answering her own question there. He looked out of the window wishing he could knock off early for a game of golf. 'Yes, well, I'm really sorry, Mum. But there it is.'

'What is it you've arranged to do?'

'Nothing special, just the theatre. Maybe a bite to eat afterwards.'

'Who with? Your golfing friends? Darling, how dull! I suppose it's too much to hope that you've got yourself a new girlfriend?'

Buchanan squeezed his eyes shut. 'Let's not go through all this again, Mum.'

'Well, you know, dear, none of us is getting any younger,' said his mother's voice, sounding as placating as she was able to fake. 'I was just saying to Daddy at breakfast time that thirty-two is just about the right age to settle down. Much later than that and you get set in your ways. I don't know why you don't contact Janine. I was always very fond of her, you know — '

That was a blatant lie. She had made Janine's life a living hell from the first time she'd clapped eyes on her.

'No, that's definitely not on, Mum,' Buchanan interrupted, considerably louder than he had intended. 'I've told you before, Janine is long gone and I don't want her back. It gives me nightmares to think how close I came to marrying her. Tell you what,' he added fervidly, 'why not just postpone the party till Sunday? A couple of days won't make a lot of difference.'

That mollified her a little and Buchanan was shortly able to prise his clenched fingers off the receiver and get back to his paperwork. Ten minutes later it was Fizz exploding into his office like the Third World War, huge with portent, her curly-wurly hair writhing with energy, and her eyes sparkling like Schweppes tonic.

'Well, guess what next?' she demanded, slamming Catriona's list of names down in front of him and giving it a slap with the flat of her palm for good measure. 'This thing's a load of crap!'

Buchanan looked at it curiously. 'In what sense of the word?'

'Crap,' said Fizz, 'as in utter balderdash. Everybody on that list is pure fiction. Either there's no such address or there's no such person at that address. The whole thing is total invention.'

She cast herself into the clients' chair with the force that had already buggered the couch back at his flat as well as half the chairs in the office.

Buchanan could not begin to get his head round this development. 'You've been round them all?'

'I called on the first three before I twigged that something funny was going on. The first address is empty and for sale; nobody at the church has ever heard of a Reverend J. Keir, and number eleven Ferry Road was pulled down after a fire in the late eighties. After that I decided to phone Dr J. Robinson and ask for an appointment. The address and number given on the list refer to a medical practice with six partners but — guess what — none of the receptionists knew of a Dr Robinson.'

She'd obviously been thinking about it all the way back in the bus but Buchanan could see that she was just as much at sea as he was. All he could find to say was, 'Not a lot to be gained by trawling round the others, I don't suppose.'

'I tried their phone numbers — all 'not recognised' — and I checked the names and addresses with Directory Enquiries. All three were 'not listed'. So, no, there doesn't look to be much point in a personal visit.'

Buchanan propped his chin on one hand, drew the paper towards him, and stared at it for inspiration but Fizz soon tired of the silence.

'I had a feeling about that bloody list! I said all along that we'd get nothing out of it — didn't I?'

'Not to me you didn't.'

'Well, I said it anyway — you don't have to be so bloody factual! — and I was right.'

Buchanan found her endlessly entertaining when she was angry. Her face was simply not constructed in a way that could effectively convey bad temper. Her frowns were little more than a fractional lowering of the eyebrows and her grimaces indistinguishable from a pout. Had she been a three-year-old poppet she would have been utterly adorable and even at twenty-eight she could make Buchanan forget — momentarily — what a pain in the arse she was.

'You can't say we got nothing out of it,' he told her. 'The fact that Mathieson was carrying this fake list around with him has to mean something. We just have to figure out what.'

Fizz snorted rudely. 'OK, Einstein, what can you divine from it so far?'

Buchanan was tempted to suggest that he'd make better progress if she'd just shut up and let him think about it but he knew he'd be wasting his breath. 'Well, we have to examine the feasibility of its being connected in some way to the activity that was making him so happy before he died. Maybe he was using it to lead someone up the garden path. He'd find that amusing.'

'A confidence trick, maybe?' Fizz suggested, brightening at the possibility. 'You think he might have been sending someone on a wild-goose chase?'

Buchanan shrugged. 'Could be. Then again, it could have something to do with the newspaper. We should check to see if the names or addresses appear in any of the stories.'

He got the page out of his briefcase and they went over it together, head to head, her rapacious hair tickling the hell out of his ear and her intrinsic green-apple aroma playing havoc with his concentration.

'Zilch,' she said, completing the task while he was still half a page behind her. 'I don't see anything that could possibly refer to any of these names and I don't see anything that could possibly be used as a scam. No Eiffel Towers for sale, no big share announcements, nothing but local news — and none of *that's* wildly exciting.'

Buchanan had to agree. But the fact that the pages of newsprint had been folded up with the list evidently implied some sort of connection and he was loath to abandon the search. 'I'll go over it again when I have a minute,' he said, and put both bits of paper into a plastic cover. 'There has to be something there.'

'It's possible,' Fizz admitted, slipping down in her chair and swinging her Doc Martens on to a corner of the desk, 'but that's not to say it's something you or I would recognise. We don't know half the enterprises Chick Mathieson was engaged in so how can we tell which of these stories would be of interest to him?'

Buchanan could only hope it would come to him in a blinding flash of intuition. 'I suppose,' he said after a minute or two, 'all we can do is to try and find out more about Mathieson's interests.'

'And how are we going to do that?'

'By taking a closer look at the ones we know about.'

Fizz returned her feet to the floor with a thud. 'The casino?'

'Possibly,' Buchanan agreed grudgingly. Going to a casino with Fizz would be asking for trouble. As the old saying went, the only way you'd come out with a small fortune would be to go in with a big one. 'We may have to check out the casino later but, for the moment, let's start with the shop. I expect the executors will be keeping it trading till they've run down the stock. I'll take a look-see on my way home.'

'Right,' said Fizz, bouncing to her feet with renewed enthusiasm. 'I'll come with you.'

'I thought you would.'

'And on the way back we can stop for five minutes to see Grampa.'

Buchanan did a rapid calculation in his head. If they left the office before quarter to five they could spend up to twenty minutes at the shop and he'd still have time to get Fizz in and out of Greenfield House before six.

'Fair enough.' He put on a dour face but inside the sun was shining. The omens said that, this time, things on the romantic front were going to go right for him for once.

11

Buchanan insisted that they walk up and down on the far side of the road for five minutes so that they could take a good look at the shop before they went in. This, to Fizz's mind, was going seriously over the top because it was a place of business, after all, and even if it were manned exclusively by serial killers, they couldn't possibly be suspicious of everyone who went in.

There was little to see in any case, other than a welter of ill-assorted junk piled higgledy-piggledy on every flat surface, hanging from the walls and migrating out towards the street on either side of the doorway. The figures behind the counter were too shadowed to see properly through the cluttered window and were largely hidden by a 'Closing Down Sale' sign, but there appeared to be two of them, both men and both fairly young.

'I'll go in first,' Buchanan said, 'and you can follow me in a couple of minutes.'

He had changed into his old golfing jacket, which he kept in the office against the unscheduled possibility of a quick nine holes, but to Fizz's eye he was still instantly recognisable as a 'suit'. It was the haircut probably, and of course the well-tailored trousers and the shiny shoes, but there was something else . . . maybe the way he carried his shoulders or the speed he walked. She couldn't put her finger on it but she could see how he stood out among the other customers.

She crossed the road half a block away and walked back to the shop at a saunter, pausing to look in the window as if something had caught her eye. Inside she could see Buchanan pretending an interest in a car radio but the two guys at the counter were both attending to customers and paying him no interest. There was a middle-aged woman too, she now noticed, who was dressed in a pink nylon overall and seemed to be pricing a pile of old 78s.

Gradually, as though drawn obliviously by successive items of interest, she drifted past the boxes of books and more 78s in the entrance, into the gloomy interior. There were quite a few customers inside, not surprisingly, because the sale prices were rock bottom. Even Fizz, who was emphatically not a consumer, could feel the first stirrings of a feeding frenzy.

There were things here she *needed*, for God's sake! Sets of pots and anglepoise lamps, and umbrellas and typewriters, none of which would be a luxury. She had lived for two years in her tiny flat with no more than the few sticks of furniture left behind by the last tenant, plus the minimum of utensils. But now she had a little money in the bank, thanks to her job at Buchanan and Stewart and, besides, these prices would never be repeated. She actually picked up two nice china mugs — 50p the pair! — but before her turn came at the counter the madness had passed.

Buchanan had worked his way closer to the counter where he was studying a pile of horrendous watercolours as though he was hopeful of discovering an original Conrad Schlegel but he was also in a position to overhear anything said by the two salesmen.

This seemed like a bit of a waste of time to Fizz, who was already regretting her promise to leave any brain-picking for another visit. It would be easy enough to get the woman chatting, and if she happened to say something relevant to the case, Buchanan could hardly blame Fizz for that, could he?

She wove casually over to the box of 78s next to the ones the woman was pricing and started to flip through them. 'Are these all the same price?' she asked.

'That lot's a pound and the ones at the

back there are fifty p. All the classical music's in the box at the door. Was there anything special you were looking for?'

'Classical,' Fizz replied without hesitation, seeing an opportunity to get her further away from the counter. 'Is there any ballet music? I had a look on my way in but I didn't see any.'

'Ballet music?' The woman's pouchy eyes opened in outrage, as though this was a personal insult. 'There's plenty of ballet music.'

Fizz gave her a wan smile. 'I may have missed them. My eyesight's not too good.'

The woman's expression softened a trifle and she elbowed a passage through the tangle of customers to the entrance. Fizz followed in her wake, pretending she didn't notice the stony glower with which Buchanan was watching her exit.

She let her helper start raking through the covers before she said, 'I shouldn't really be buying records this week but it's such a great sale. Everything's really cheap.'

'Aye. We've to get rid of everything by the end of next week. The shop's getting sold. See, here's *Swan Lake*. That's a ballet, int'it?'

'I've got that one, actually,' Fizz lied apologetically. Her associate drew her breath in through her front teeth and returned to the fray.

Inside the shop Buchanan had appeared at the back of the window, fiddling with a toaster and glaring furiously at her through the glass. Turning her back to him Fizz said, 'You'll never clear all this stock by the end of next week.'

'We're getting through it. You should see what we had to start with. *Nabucco*. That's a ballet.'

'No, that's an opera.'

'Are you sure?'

She looked on the point of packing in so Fizz said, 'Yes, but I thought I saw one with dancers on it just past the place where your hand is now.'

'Here?'

'Just past that.' Fizz waved a hand vaguely and, when the search was again underway, murmured, 'When did the sale start?'

'This is the fourth week, hen. You've missed all the best stuff. You should have seen the bargains — there, that's got dancers on it.'

'Yes, but it's not ballet. It's Latin American music.' That just about did it as far as her helper was concerned so she added quickly, 'It's so kind of you to give me your time. I can't tell you how much I appreciate it. It takes me forever to read the titles.'

The woman had already waved a hand at

the box of discs preparatory to delivering the standard, 'if it's not there we don't have it' type of brush-off but she hesitated and then resumed her raking. 'I know we've got plenty. The classical stuff never sells.'

'I'll miss this place when you close,' Fizz said. 'There are so few shops like this in Edinburgh. I don't suppose you have any other branches, do you?'

'No, dear. Just this place.' She whipped a scruffy cardboard sleeve from the box and presented it to her customer with a flourish that was not to be gainsaid. '*The Nutcracker.* I mind my mummy taking me to see that in the King's when I was a wee lassie.'

'Great,' Fizz had no option but to say, and parted with fifty pence.

Buchanan caught up with her a block down the road, and he was spitting tacks.

'I thought we weren't going to pick any brains,' he snapped. 'I thought we agreed that it would be smarter to check out what we were up against in case we made anybody windy by chatting to the wrong person. I thought — correct me if I'm wrong about this — but I thought I had your promise that you wouldn't make any unilateral decisions this time. I actually thought you had grasped the concept that you'd be playing with fire.'

'Have you finished?' Fizz asked politely,

turning her head to look at him. 'Because if you have, I'd like to point out that I didn't ask a single question that could be described as pertaining to the case.'

'You drew attention to yourself,' Buchanan returned heatedly, but not loud enough to divert any passers-by. 'Both of the guys behind the counter were looking at you.'

'This may come as a surprise to you, muchacho, but lots of guys look at me. It doesn't mean they're going to take out a contract on me.' She handed him the record. 'See, I bought you a present.'

'How kind.' He tucked it under his arm without looking at it. 'Just what I always wanted.'

'And you owe me fifty p. Expenses.'

He hauled out a handful of change and reimbursed her and then walked on in silence, staring into the middle distance and shaking his head at some thought of his own.

'Well, don't you want to know what return I got for the money?'

He lifted his eyebrows. 'You learned something of interest?'

'Not much,' she admitted, 'but I reckon it was worth fifty p. First of all, the sale has been going for four weeks, which means that it started before Mathieson's death. Secondly, they're practically giving the stuff away

213

— most of it would be a bargain at twice the price — so they must be in a big hurry to get rid of the stuff.'

Buchanan didn't look wildly interested. 'No doubt the executors will want to get Mathieson's affairs settled as soon as possible. The sooner the stock's gone the sooner they can sell the premises.'

'Yes, but according to my informant, the sale prices were ridiculously low right from the start of the sale, so it was Mathieson who was desperate to get rid of the stuff.'

'There's a lot of very iffy stuff in there — car radios, video recorders — stuff that's easy to loot and easy to resell. Maybe Mathieson suspected he was about to be busted.'

'Exactly what I thought. How could we find out if that's true?'

Buchanan didn't answer. They had arrived back at the car and he pretended that unlocking the doors was taking all his concentration but Fizz was not to be thwarted.

'Why don't you give one of your pals in the CID a ring? Ian Fleming would know.'

'DCI Fleming does not love me any more. Nor you either. Not after what happened last Christmas. We were both skating on very thin ice that time. And — before you ask — I'm not on comparable terms with anyone else and if I were I probably wouldn't want to ask them.' Buchanan let in the clutch and roared away, just beating the lights. 'The principle of swapping favours depends on neither of the parties pushing their luck, which I've been doing quite a bit these last few months. I'll have to build up my credit balance before I hit on any of my contacts again.'

Fizz could see the sense in that. She, too, had been taking care not to cross DCI Fleming's path for the last six months just in case he'd thought of a few questions he'd forgotten to ask her regarding her last interference with the due processes of the law. It was a pity that diplomatic relations had broken down, because Buchanan was quite often able to save a lot of time by tapping in to the grapevine. However, it was probably wiser in this instance to slog it out for themselves. Some people were so touchy.

'Can't stand the man anyway,' she confided. 'He's got absolutely no control over his temper. The bastard called me a liar!'

Buchanan looked bemused. 'You *are* a liar, Fizz.'

'That's not the point. He had no right to say so in front of a crowd of people.'

'It's nothing to what you called him.'

Somewhat mollified by that recollection, she let the matter drop.

★ ★ ★

Buchanan had worked himself into a poisonous mood by the time they reached Greenfield House. He was really rattled at Fizz because he had managed to convince himself that she was growing noticeably more stable and now she had shown herself to be as headstrong as ever.

What was really alarming was the way he could wipe all memory of her past iniquities from his mind. He could jog along with her quite amicably for weeks, his judgement dulled by her unfailing cheerfulness and her willing diligence around the office and — yes — her cuteness. And then, just as he was about to relax and start enjoying her company — *wham!* — she'd turn round and do something downright dangerous like she'd done today. Bad enough that she'd quizzed the lad from the garage but at least she hadn't done it under the eye of his bosses.

There didn't seem to be any way of dampening her super-confidence. Eight years of blagging her way around the less savoury parts of the globe without being raped, robbed or murdered had made her feel invulnerable and — hell mend the woman! — she now thought she was the female equivalent of Bruce Willis. Somehow or other he was going to have to find a way of getting her off this case.

A chill mist having drifted in off the Forth in the past hour, they weren't surprised to find the garden deserted. A quick scan of the lounge, however, revealed the in-crowd in their accustomed venue beside the bay window. The only other occupants of the room were two bald men playing cards and a tiny lady who was fast asleep (Buchanan sincerely hoped) with her mouth open.

'Oh wondrous dawn! Oh glorious dream fulfilled!' Paul sprang to his feet and galloped the length of the room to meet them, moving like a cross between a giraffe and an arthritic stork. 'Welcome to Greenfield social and athletic club. You find us at the crescendo of our afternoon revels — like a scene from Hogarth's *Gin Lane*, I fear — deep in all manner of licentiousness of which Cluedo is but the tip of the iceberg. So different from the home life of our own dear queen! The blame, I fear, lies at Miss Moir's door — for though I tried to woo her away from such excesses with the promise of a brisk tussle on the Snakes and Ladders board she would not have it and I was afraid to press the matter lest she turn ugly. It'll all end in tears, mark my words. Ah! She tries to hide her shame but observe the downcast eye, the encrimsoned cheek!'

'Paul, for heaven's sake,' Helen cried as they approached the group. 'Won't you give us a little peace and quiet?'

' 'A Little Peace and Quiet',' Paul repeated, cocking his skeletal head on one side. 'I don't usually do requests but if you care to sing it, I'll strum along.'

'Paul,' said Cheryl, and sent him a look that should have welded him to the wall.

'Just making conversation, my heart's darling. Just laying the foundations for a free and frank exchange of ideas. Communication is the cornerstone of every ordinary peace-loving family. Show me a man who — '

'Come and sit down, dear,' said Miss Moir, placidly patting the place beside her on the couch which Paul had just vacated. 'Let's finish the game first and give Archie a chance to enjoy his guests. It's he they came to see, after all.'

'Visitors for some and not for others? Gad! If this gets out it'll be civil war!' Paul rolled his eyes alarmingly and then subsided abruptly and sat down on the couch.

A hushed peace invaded the room, a peace that no one was in a hurry to break. Even

Grampa, whose deafness must have shielded him from much of Paul's inane prattle, took a moment to recover and it was only when the Cluedo players had resumed their game that he grabbed his sticks and levered himself to his feet.

'We'll take a wee bit stroll in the garden. I haven't had my walk this afternoon.'

Anthony snatched a heavy cardigan off the back off his chair and held it out. 'Chilly outside. Better take this. Save you going upstairs for something warm.'

'Verra kind. I'll not be long with it.' Grampa slung the woolly around his shoulders and, when they met the breeze outside, seemed glad of it. He was walking a lot better today, Buchanan noticed, and appeared to be making less use of his sticks. He was also looking younger and more cheerful than he'd looked for the past year.

'You seem to have settled in very well with that bunch,' Fizz said. 'Have you spoken to any of the other residents yet?'

'Oh, aye. I've managed to have a word with all of them now, but the majority of them have nothing of interest to say, or they say it so damn quiet that I can't make out a word. All they do is watch television or play a wee hand of gin rummy once in a while. No life about them at all.' He waved a stick at the

219

row of garages. 'We were out for a run in Anthony's car this morning. He took me and Cheryl and Paul up to the library and then we had a cup of tea and a buttered scone at a nice wee café overlooking the Meadows. A lot of new buildings around there since I was last in Edinburgh.'

'That would break the monotony a bit,' Buchanan murmured, half his mind working on the question of whether to bother informing Grampa of the developments regarding Mathieson's shop.

'Oh, aye, it was verra nice. I could have gone with some of them to the pictures the night before, mind. Some new American 'we-won-the-war' story. Nigel's daughter took them in her car. But, och, they're all the same, these war stories. I just stayed in and watched *University Challenge* with Helen and Anthony.'

Buchanan found himself holding his breath. He was fairly sure that nothing of his shock and alarm showed in his face but the moments he spent waiting for Fizz to ask about Nigel's daughter stretched out like hours. He didn't dare turn his head to look at her but he could see her in the periphery of his vision and she appeared to be bending forward to look at the path verge just ahead of her.

'Look,' she said, pointing to the glint of gold in the grass. 'Somebody's dropped their specs.'

The likelihood of such a thing happening, at the precise millisecond when he needed her to be deaf to what Grampa was saying, stunned Buchanan into silence. He watched Fizz pick up the specs, discuss their ownership with Grampa and decide to give them to Boston, but took no part in the conversation. It was uncanny, the way things were going so smoothly. It was almost as if this relationship between himself and Lizzie were *meant*, somehow, and the gods were on his side.

By the time they reached the bench at the far end of the garden Grampa was ready for a rest. 'Just five minutes and then I'll need to be getting back. Helen has invited me for dinner tonight and it takes me a while to get ready.' He leaned his sticks against the arm of the bench and drew Anthony's cardigan closed across his chest. 'There's one small thing I thought I would just mention to you. Something I noticed two or three days ago but I thought I was mebbe imagining things.'

'What's that?' Fizz asked, but her grampa was not to be hurried.

'No point in going off half-cocked and then looking a fool when it turned out I was

221

wrong. However, I just bided my time and ran a few trials and I think I'm right.'

Fizz and Buchanan indicated that they were hanging on his lips.

'I think they don't like to see me talking to Miss Moir.'

'Who don't?' Fizz asked.

'All that clique. Helen and Paul and Anthony at least, and I'm pretty sure the others don't like it either. Aye, and Boston's at it too now.' Grampa's eyes blazed suddenly in the shadow of his bushy brows. 'I can't sit down beside her for two minutes but one or the other of them appears out of nowhere and either joins us or takes her away to do something else. I thought at first it was just Paul that was doing it but now I think they're all at it.'

Buchanan looked at Fizz but she didn't seem any more able than himself to deduce anything from this information so he said to Grampa, 'What do you think they're nervous about? They can't be worried that you might say something to upset her . . . or tell her something they might be trying to hide from her.'

'Away and don't be daft! What do *I* know that would be of any interest to any of them? More likely they're afraid of what *she'll* say to *me*. She must know something that they

222

don't want her to let slip.'

That, at first glance, seemed much the more likely answer but the picture of Miss Moir being mixed up in anything shady wasn't an easy one to assimilate.

'Even if this is true — and I'm sure it is — it doesn't necessarily mean that it has anything to do with Mathieson's murder,' Buchanan pointed out. 'There's no telling what that bunch could get up to. They could have an illicit still in somebody's garage, they could be smoking pot, they could be into cock fighting or shooting crap or ram raiding. With a pied piper like Paul at their head, they could get up to anything and Miss Moir is not quite as . . . as worldly as the others. Maybe they recognise her as the weak link.'

'Aye, that's a point,' Grampa nodded.

'Still, it's something we should keep in mind, Grampa,' Fizz put in. 'It would be interesting to note if there were any special subjects they didn't like you to discuss with Miss Moir, anything they shy away from. That might give us a pointer or two.'

'Right, I'll keep my ears open.' He got his sticks under him and struggled to his feet. 'Time I was getting back. Helen has a duck in orange sauce for us and I don't want to keep her waiting.'

If there was a gene for independence, Buchanan thought, and another for attracting the support of others, the Fitzpatrick family had probably been bred for both of them for generations.

12

Fizz spent the morning in the office catching up with her backlog, making telephone calls, and, thanks to Buchanan's being otherwise engaged when he called, bringing Mr Buchanan senior up to date with developments.

Buchanan's daddy was transparently disappointed at the lack of progress. 'You seem to be going backwards instead of forwards, Fizz. Why are you wasting your time on these elderly people when it's patently obvious they could have nothing to do with the case? Chick Mathieson could have blown them away with a . . . a sneeze. You should be concentrating on the wife and her boyfriend. She may claim that she and Mathieson had an open relationship but even if they did, she'd not be too happy if she thought some other woman was likely to get the bulk of his money.'

'We don't know that there *was* another woman. That's pure speculation.'

'Well then, that's what you should be looking into.'

'How?'

He hesitated and then chuckled in the way that made Fizz ready to forgive him anything. 'I just come up with the ideas, Fizz. It's up to you to figure out how to make them work.'

'Roger. I'll put my mind to it.'

He was right, of course, up to a point. It would be nice to know if Mathieson did have another woman and if she had come out of the relationship with a fortune, but Fizz doubted if it would be worth the time and effort. Mathieson's killing was obviously not a *crime passionnel*. Crimes of passion were seldom so brutal: they were either spur-of-the-moment or well covered up. Whoever had topped Mr Big had done it the way he himself would have done it in the past — with ruthlessness, brutality and the maximum of publicity. The killer wanted it known that he'd had his revenge. No doubt the entire criminal community of Edinburgh knew who had topped him and why.

For the rest of the morning, as she worked, the thought of a revenge killing was never far from Fizz's mind. It would surprise nobody if Mathieson turned out to have several deaths to his credit. Morgan, for whose killing Freddie had served five years, had been a loner and a down-and-out; so it was difficult to imagine some friend or relative emerging from the mists of time to settle his account but, of course, one could never dismiss the possibility. Much more feasible, however, was the likelihood that Mathieson had been murdered in retribution for a more recent death, and possibly one committed by precisely the same means. What better way for the murderer to put his signature on the crime?

She shared these thoughts with Buchanan just before lunchtime, when she had more or less cleared her desk for the weekend, and he managed to look fairly interested.

'There's a sense of aptness about that theory that I like,' he said, looking out at the sun-filled square with an almost blissful expression on his face. 'Justice must not only be done but must be seen to be done. The killer was also, when you think about it, proclaiming that the Big Bad Wolf was dead.'

He went on staring out the window and thinking for so long that Fizz had to clear her throat to wake him up. 'So?' she said.

'So — what?'

'So what are we going to do about it?'

'What do you want to do about it?'

Fizz assailed him with a terrible frown which had no effect. 'I want you to get on the blower to your CID contacts — not necessarily Fleming, there must be others — and find out if there have been any recent killings similar to Mathieson's.'

He shook his head, still not losing his good humour. 'You know I can't do that, Fizz. The minute I tell anyone at St Leonards that we're investigating Chick Mathieson's murder we'll have Ian Fleming making life difficult for us. And you know whose fault that is,' he added with a sad but gentle smile worthy of Miss Moir at her best. 'If it hadn't been for that trick you pulled — '

'He didn't know about that.'

'He couldn't prove it, Fizz, but that doesn't mean he's not out to get you next time you put a foot wrong.'

Fizz inflated her cheeks and let the air out with an explosive puff. 'OK. Well, in that case I'll have to see if there's anything in the papers. It'll take hours.'

'How far back are you going to look?'

'I don't know. Maybe a couple of months to start with. I'll see how I get on.'

'Mm-hmm.' He fiddled with his pen, clicking the retractable point in and out. 'If it runs on into the evening don't worry about Grampa. I'll call in on him on my way home.'

Fizz was quite happy to go along with that since Grampa wouldn't care if he never saw her from one week to the next. 'Roger. And if I turn up anything of interest I'll either phone or drop by later in the evening.'

'No, don't bother with that,' Buchanan said, returning his gaze to the window. 'I'll be out all evening and it could be midnight before I get back. It's unlikely you'll discover anything that won't keep till the morning.' He suddenly whipped his head round to glare at her. 'But don't come round too early. In fact, don't come round at all tomorrow. And Fizz, please don't phone till lunchtime at the earliest — and *then* only if it's urgent.'

'OK, OK. I know Saturday is your Sabbath — just you and Selina in silent communion. I won't intrude.' Fizz hesitated and then decided to strike while Buchanan was in a receptive mood. 'There is the question of the casino, however. I think we should make an early visit a priority, don't you?'

She could tell by his face that he was no more enamoured of the idea than he'd been the last time they discussed it, but he couldn't procrastinate for ever. They were now a week into the case and they still didn't have a single clear lead so they could do nothing but explore the leads they had.

'I suppose you're right. We'll have to do it sooner or later — but not tomorrow, Fizz, I may have something on. I'm not sure, but I think we'll have to leave it till Sunday.'

'I'll phone you tomorrow afternoon and you can tell me then.'

He seemed more than usually relieved to see her take her leave and when she glanced back he was staring out of the window again in another daydream. It was quite obvious that his mind was on other things today, probably the frolic he had planned for this evening. Unfortunately, she was out in the street before she realised that she should have asked him what that was.

She grabbed a sandwich on the way up George IV Bridge to the library and ate it on the hoof because you weren't supposed to eat in the Edinburgh Room and the clerks had eyes like hawks. She wasn't hopeful of reaching her objective before closing time, which was eight o'clock, so a little sustenance at this point was necessary to stave off severe malnutrition.

The Edinburgh Room was seldom busy during the summer months when all the colleges were on holiday, and today there were only a half-dozen serious-looking researchers plus a couple of old gents perusing the map section. Fizz ordered the relevant editions of the *Scotsman* and the *Edinburgh Evening News* at the counter, carried the microfilms over to the reader, and fed in the first spool, starting with the *Scotsman* of the day after Mathieson had died.

She didn't expect to find anything at that

date but one had to come at the problem in a logical manner and that weekend's was the first edition on that section of the reel. She made reasonably good progress for the first two or three editions but the task quickly became boring and, increasingly, she found herself reading an entire story through to the end even though her first glance had told her it was not what she was looking for.

It took her till seven fifteen to establish that the *Scotsman* had reported no deaths similar to Mathieson's for the two months prior to his demise. She was tempted to call it a day at that but, since she had the *Evening News* microfiche to hand she reckoned she might as well go for the burn.

She had already read some of the stories in the *Scotsman* so she was able to zap along quite nicely and was a couple of pages into the Saturday edition when the word *Dunbar* caught her eye. It headed a mere snippet tucked away in a half-column of similar short Stop Press items.

Dunbar Killing. The body of a man found in his home early this morning has been identified as that of Simon Harvey, a local fisherman. He had been shot several times in the head and chest. It is thought that the killing may be drug-related.

Apparently the news had reached the *Scotsman* office too late for the morning editions but before the *Evening News* had been put to bed. What it meant was that the fisherman had died within hours of Chick Mathieson and in the same small village where he had left his car. And Fizz did not believe in coincidences.

She had barely five minutes to skip to the following Monday's edition of the *Scotsman* and locate the full report, and the beat-it bell was ringing before she had the microfilm set up. But it was all there: the neighbours seeing the door of Harvey's cottage lying open, the brutality of the shooting, the fact that he was a fairly recent incomer to the village, with a boat that was bigger and better equipped than the norm, and the strong implication, between the lines, that he had been under suspicion for importing drugs.

Turfed out into the balmy evening, Fizz decided to take a circular route home through the Meadows and down the Pleasance. She had promised herself a couple of hours' studying but she wanted to think about what she had found while her brain was still popping with possibilities.

Her first reaction was to assume that Mathieson had murdered Simon Harvey and then faked his own suicide and tried to disappear. That would mean that Harvey was either one of his own minions or part of a rival gang. Probably the latter, judging by the way Mathieson had been caught and punished. Shooting wasn't Mathieson's *modus operandi*, as far as one could tell, but he could have been in a hurry. That would tie in with the half-cocked way he had left the disposal of his car till the last second.

Then again, she thought, blind to the joggers and dog walkers and cricketers and footballers around her, it was possible that Mathieson had got wind that someone was after both Harvey and himself. He could have dashed down to Dunbar to warn Harvey and, finding him already dead, had realised that he himself had to disappear pdq. Hence his hurried phone call to Freddie and his attempt to fake his suicide.

On the whole, she preferred the second possibility but she was impatient to hear Buchanan's thoughts on the matter. It wasn't what you could term urgent, she supposed, and that was just as well because it would probably be tomorrow afternoon at the earliest before he could give it of his best.

★ ★ ★

Buchanan had tasted nothing of his main course and if he'd been asked what he'd had for his starter he'd have had a hard job remembering. He could, however, have described to the last detail the filmy, low-cut garment that made Lizzie look like an exotic Egyptian dancer, the delicacy of her hands, the entrancing frown that appeared between her brows as she laughed, and the silver filigree choker from which dangled a pendant that swung to and fro in her cleavage like a hypnotist's watch.

She was saying, 'I haven't seen you at Greenfield House these last few evenings.'

'No. The way things have worked out it's been easier for me to fit in my visits on my way home from work. I'm not sure whether Mr Fitzpatrick gives a hoot whether he sees me or not but I feel I have to keep an eye on him.'

She sipped her wine. 'He seems to have settled in really well, from what Pops tells me. They've all taken to him enormously and, of course, they're all enchanted with his little granddaughter — Fizz? Is that her name?'

'That's what she answers to, yes,' Buchanan murmured, casting about for a way to divert the conversation into other channels. 'I — '

'Anthony is full of her praises. A sweet

234

old-fashioned miss, the likes of which he has not seen for sixty years, so he tells me. High praise coming from Anthony. For him, civilisation ended in 1959 and humankind has been hurtling towards perdition ever since. I'm so curious to meet her.'

Buchanan squeezed a smile. 'There's nothing abnormally saintlike about her, I assure you, but she does have a very cherubic expression. I suspect you'd find her . . . possibly a little irritating.'

'Really? What a pity. I thought I'd found something quite unique. A twenty-first-century phenomenon.'

Which, of course, she had, Buchanan reflected, only not in the way she thought. He caught the eye of a hovering waiter and instigated the serious business of choosing their desserts, hoping that this would facilitate a change of subject, but Lizzie returned almost immediately to talking about Greenfield House.

'How much longer is Mr Fitzpatrick planning to stay?'

'Just a few more days, I believe. His doctor at the hospital wants to have a final look at him next Wednesday and I've promised, all being well, to take him to the Royal Agricultural Show, after which he'll be raring to get back into harness.'

'He's really amazing for eighty-two. In fact, I hear there's a little romance coming into bud.' She shook with silent laughter and the pendant went *tick-tock* in its peachy hollow. 'He and Miss Moir are becoming very close.'

Buchanan dragged his thoughts above her collarbone and considered what she'd said. Is that what was worrying Paul and co.? Did they truly believe that Miss Moir might become enamoured of a married man? Well, Love had happened to Paul and Cheryl; presumably it could happen at any age.

'I'm sure he must enjoy Miss Moir's company,' he said, in heavily reassuring tones. 'She's such a charming lady, and Grampa is currently rediscovering the joys of conversation. He's very deaf, you know, and the excellent diction and projection of these trained voices means that he can, for the first time in years, follow what's being said without demanding a recap every few minutes. I can see that everyone takes pains to speak clearly but possibly Miss Moir's voice is better pitched than the others.'

Lizzie nodded but there was still a glint of amusement in her eye that told him she was not entirely convinced that romance was not in the air.

So he added, 'Besides, anything verging on infidelity would be anathema to Grampa.

He'd never dream of being unfaithful to Auntie Duff.'

She paused with a spoonful of syllabub halfway to her mouth. 'Auntie Duff?'

'That's his wife. His second wife. Everyone in Am Bealach calls her Auntie Duff because that was what she'd been called for twenty years before she married Grampa.'

A waiter appeared at her shoulder and topped up their glasses as she said, 'You call him Grampa. Does that mean you're a friend of the family?'

'I suppose you could call me that,' Buchanan nodded. 'I spent a couple of weeks on his farm last year when I was recuperating from an operation and I got to know him quite well. He introduced me to salmon fishing and to a collection of malt whiskies that were new to me, and I had a great time. Not as relaxing as I had planned but . . . well, interesting.'

'And Fizz,' Lizzie said, dabbing her lips with her napkin, 'did she work for you at that point or was that when you met her?'

Buchanan was at a loss to imagine why she should be so interested in Fizz. It wasn't as if she could suppose there was anything between them other than a normal boss/ employee relationship — well, perhaps a slightly more chummy relationship than the average, but not much. She had never come into contact with Fizz, either directly or on the phone, so she couldn't have become contaminated by the mystery hate virus to which so many of his girlfriends had fallen victim. So who had been telling her stuff that had made her suspicious?

He said, 'Fizz was in her first year at law school at that point. She'd been working for me as a volunteer the year before in a legal clinic I was running, and since then she's been working part time in my office to eke out her grant.'

Determined to stop discussing anything even vaguely connected with work he topped up Lizzie's glass and said, before she could start off again, 'Would you like a liqueur? Or a brandy?' He signed to the waiter, gave the order and hurried on, 'They're going to chase us out of here shortly. How do you feel about going on somewhere — like Aurora, for instance?'

She propped her chin on an elegantly curved palm and drooped her eyelids lazily. 'Aurora? I've never been there. Is it a nightclub?'

'I suppose it is, in a manner of speaking, but a very laid-back nightclub. Soft lights, good music, comfortable seating, small dance floor. And it doesn't close till dawn.'

Her eyes, still lazy, smiled into his. Her free hand lay some eighteen inches from his on the white table top. 'It's been such a happy evening,' she murmured, raising her hand and walking it two finger-steps closer to his. 'I don't want it to end but, to be honest, dancing has never really turned me on.'

'That's too bad,' Buchanan whispered. He hadn't meant to whisper but that's what came out. He finger-walked his hand two inches towards hers. 'What does turn you on?'

'That's a difficult question. Let's see. Mmm. Well . . . blue eyes. Black, straight eyelashes. A voice that's low-pitched and gentle and runs down my spine like warm chocolate sauce. Long straight legs . . . ' Her hand crept a hesitant six inches closer.

'You're very particular,' he said stiffly, stealing a sneaky two inches while she wasn't looking. 'You may have difficulty finding what you're looking for.'

She looked thoughtfully at her hand, crept it forward till it was nail to nail with his, and then looked up at him with what could only be termed a brooding look. 'It's possible. But I don't really think so.'

Buchanan took his turn of looking at the two hands, hers so fine-boned and pale, his so strong-looking and brown, separated by less than a millimeter. He could feel, in anticipation, the silkiness of her skin and the warm pulse of her blood beneath. He could sense the sexual tension darting like an electric spark across that tiny gap and knew that she was waiting for him to make the final move.

He moved, but it was to summon the waiter. As someone had recently remarked in his hearing, hunger was the best sauce. Let her simmer.

And simmer she did, all the way home in the taxi, till the driver must have been getting ready to sell tickets. Somewhere along the way Buchanan started to get a little worried. If she was thinking along the lines of a one-night stand he was her man. However, one should perhaps have made an opportunity, earlier in the evening, to plant the understanding that commitment was not included in the package. Not for any appreciable length of time.

He had found it very easy to convince himself, in his anticipation of this evening, that Lizzie was the woman of his dreams but now that it came to the bit he was assailed by doubts. Not only by doubts, but by a faint tingle of guilt which he was able, with Lizzie's assistance, to ignore almost completely. The source of the guilt was certainly not something he wanted to examine at this

240

juncture, just in case the consequences might interfere with his performance. He was already becoming concerned about the onset of a sharp pain in his spine, which had been getting worse all evening, and he could only hope that Lizzie's approach to sex was not overly athletic. However, all that aside, whatever she had in mind he was determined to give it a damn good try.

Arms around each other's waists, they climbed the stairs, and let themselves into the flat.

13

'HAPPY BIRTHDAY TO YOU! HAPPY BIRTHDAY TO YOU! HAPPY BIRTHDAY DEAR TA-AM! HAPPY BIRTHDAY TO YOU!' sang Buchanan's parents, his cousin Mark, two uncles and an aunt, his golfing mates, The Wonderful Beatrice, Grampa, both adjacent neighbours, sundry hangers-on and partners of the above, and Fizz.

Almost all of whom were pretty well stewed to the eyeballs by this time since they had been conscientiously partaking of the lavish refreshments since around ten thirty. Fizz had done nothing other than enjoy herself, since Mummy and Daddy Buchanan had organised everything. They had lost a few guests along the way, those who had made other arrangements since the original party had been cancelled, but The Wonderful Beatrice had found the phone numbers of the golfing coterie, which had proved a much more laddish bunch than Fizz would have expected and some of them rather dishy.

It was largely due to the lads that the wave of noise that greeted Buchanan was so thunderous. Even the 'happy birthday' chorus

242

clearly shocked him to the core, making him lurch backwards so precipitately that he raked his shoe down his companion's shin, thus putting quite a damper on the poor girl's evening. Close on the heels of the choral tribute, however, came a roar of drunken laughter, an explosion of bursting balloons and party poppers, hoots, cowboy yells, ribald remarks and deafening salsa music as someone turned up the volume on the CD player.

You had to hand it to him, nonetheless, the birthday boy handled it pretty well, considering he had been within minutes of getting his end away for the first time — unless Fizz was much mistaken — in many months. His smile might have been slow in surfacing and of very low wattage but, with Lizzie in extreme pain at his shoulder and his mother covering his face with baby kisses in front of everyone, it was as much as could have been expected. For a minute or two he was kept busy with people hugging him and decking him with streamers and paper headgear, et cetera, but when she saw his eyes start to scan the sea of heads in an uncomfortably intent manner Fizz decided it was a good time to be elsewhere. She ducked into the kitchen and washed some glasses under the venomous stare of Selina, who had been shut into her travelling basket for the night.

She was pretty sure there was going to be trouble this time. Even though she had taken great care, when putting the idea into his father's head, that he would believe it had sprung entirely from his own imagination, Buchanan was an entirely different kettle of fish. He no longer believed that Fizz was the embodiment of all innocence — that phase hadn't lasted long — and he was definitely beginning to suspect her of interfering in his sex life. It had taken him nearly two years to start wondering if she was doing it deliberately, but in the past her interventions had consisted merely of nipping things in the bud. This time it was damn near coitus interruptus.

She would deny everything, of course, and his father would back her up, so Buchanan would have no proof, merely a very much stronger suspicion than hitherto. What he would make of it was anybody's guess. He wouldn't be fool enough to infer that she wanted him for herself because he had to be just as aware as she was that she found his fussiness, his untidiness, his constant soul-searching and his rigid code of ethics just as irritating as he found her much more acceptable failings. Being from Mars, he'd never be able to conceptualise the idea that, in spite of all the aforesaid, she just could not bear the thought of him shagging someone else.

It occurred to her after about ten minutes that she might be safer from his fury in full view of his friends and family so she sidled carefully forth and latched on to his father, his uncle Graham and Grampa, who had entrenched themselves in a corner out of the way of the dancers. Grampa was giving a lecture on malt whisky, its history, manufacture and effect on the central nervous system, which appeared to be holding the other two enthralled but which Fizz had heard many times before. No matter. Protection was more important right now than entertainment and as she was not expected to play an active part in the conversation she was able to keep an eye open for a sudden attack.

Buchanan was currently being kept safely occupied by the wounded Lizzie, whose leg now sported a bandage worthy of an amputation, probably applied by cousin Mark, who was a doctor. She wasn't bad-looking, if you liked brown eyes, and her figure was at least a little better than the cotton bud lookalikes that Buchanan was often drawn to, but she was no stoic. The fuss she was making about what was barely a scratch was like a footballer trying to get his opponent sent off for a bad tackle. She had Buchanan patting her hand and Mark propping her leg on a stool and half the golfing fraternity milling around her and plying her with food, drink and sympathy.

During a break in the music Fizz heard her say, 'No, you will *not*, Tam darling. It's your party and I wouldn't dream of letting you drive all the way to Peebles tonight. No, please, I mean it! Put me in a taxi and I'll be just fine.'

There was a general upsurge of indignant voices through which Mark's was heard to say, 'Look, I have to go now anyway, so why don't I run you home?'

The argument seemed to go on a little longer but someone had replaced the CD by that time so Fizz could only guess at what was being said. Then Buchanan lifted his head and looked straight into her eyes across the room. For a second his brows came down and then he turned away, lifted Lizzie to her feet and helped Mark support her to the door amid a clamour of commiseration and farewell.

Fizz knew at once what had finally tipped the balance with Buchanan. He didn't want her getting anywhere near his little playmate, and that meant he was pretty sure what she'd been up to. She worked her way round till she was wedged in between Grampa and Buchanan's father and waited for the wrath to come. It didn't take long. As soon as he came back into the room he made a beeline for her with a face like a cold chisel and a gleam in his eye that might have been the onset of insanity.

'Happy birthday!' she carolled blithely before he could say anything, and planted a kiss on his jawbone, that being as high as she could reach without his co-operation, which was not forthcoming.

'Wonderful party,' said his uncle, bellowing to be heard above the music. 'Brilliant piece of organisation. I think your parents deserve a round of applause for pulling it off so successfully.'

'All it took was a few phone calls,' said Buchanan senior modestly. 'Dorothy had done all the baking already. We were in a bit of a rush at the last minute, right enough, because I didn't think of it till this morning, but it seems to have worked out all right.'

'It was your idea, was it, Dad?' Buchanan asked in a just-checking voice.

'You don't think it was your mother's, do you?' He turned to Grampa, laying a hand on his shoulder and shouting in his ear. 'She's a great one for tradition, my Dorothy. She likes everything to be done the way her mother did it, but I talked her into it. I'm not sure she's convinced it was a good idea even now but she'll come round.'

'I don't know why but I assumed I had Fizz to thank.' Buchanan was smiling but the look he threw her was like a lethal injection.

'Not at all,' she said quickly, not allowing Buchanan senior to be generous about it. 'Your dad did all the organising and your mum did all the catering. I didn't even know it was your birthday till your father told me. But I think it was a great idea, don't you?'

Buchanan said what was expected of him with a convincing warmth that fooled three of them and then turned to the fourth. 'Care to dance, Fizz?'

Like hell she did. 'I'm not much into dancing,' she said.

'Of course you are. You were dancing like St Vitus himself at Christmas time. Come on.'

He extracted her from her sanctuary with a grip on her wrist that verged on GBH and they inserted themselves into a fissure in the throng of dancers. It wasn't a large sitting room so there was no space to do anything but twitch to the music.

'So,' he said politely, 'when did you hear about Lizzie?'

'Uh . . . how do you mean?'

'Did your grampa mention her?'

Fizz narrowed her eyes in a puzzled way. 'Sorry, I'm not with you. Does Grampa know her?'

His smile was not one to gladden the heart. 'She's Nigel's daughter.'

'Really?' Fizz portrayed surprise and then couldn't resist putting the boot in. 'Grampa never mentioned her. Maybe he expected that you would have kept me posted. Particularly if she forms a regular part of the setup at the complex.'

She saw the shaft go home but he said only, 'You didn't know about her?'

'The first time I clapped eyes on her was when she walked through that door.' She knew Buchanan wouldn't be fooled by that half-truth but she rattled on, 'And I have to say, I thought it a bit thoughtless of your folks not to have anticipated that you might have company. It must have been embarrassing for you both.'

'I hadn't mentioned Lizzie to anyone so it's nobody's fault,' he said, watching her face. 'Is it?'

Fizz ignored the question as if she regarded it as purely academic and went for the banal. 'Well, it's not the end of the world, I suppose.'

'No,' he said in a gravelly voice which she could barely pretend not to register, 'and it's not the end of the relationship.'

'Right,' she returned chirpily. 'Which is nice. So you can relax and enjoy your party. Your golfing buddies are a great bunch. You should have seen them earlier dancing their version of the haka. They had everyone in hysterics.'

She kept talking fast, knowing that Buchanan wouldn't interrupt her to resume his interrogation because that would have been descending to open hostility. Besides, what could he say that wouldn't sound like he was accusing her of having the hots for him? All his dealings with people were conducted firmly within the bounds of good manners, which meant she was fairly safe as long as she exhibited no sign of guilt.

Gradually she could see his anger being replaced by a sort of grim acceptance as though he had finally realised that, suspect what he might, he had not the slightest grain of proof that she'd had either the means, the motive or the opportunity to interfere with his romance.

This gave her the confidence to say, 'By the by, I don't want to spoil your party by talking business, but I found some valuable information this evening. I think we should discuss it fairly soon. Maybe tomorrow, if you can spare the time.'

'Something important?'

'Mmm ... not urgent but definitely intriguing.'

'You'd better tell me about it now. Come into the kitchen where I can hear you speak.'

The minute they stepped through the door Selina let loose with a whole catalogue of complaints, scratching at the door of her wicker prison and pretending she'd been subjected to mental torture for hours. While Buchanan made his abject apologies to her and carried her through to the living-room window, which was her usual exit, Fizz restored her strength with a large gin and tonic and several pastries.

She was inclined to hope that, as far as direct retribution was concerned, the matter was closed but it would be bound to take some time to airbrush the incident from Buchanan's memory. His manner, as he returned to the kitchen and sat down across the table from her, only confirmed this assumption. It was strictly me-boss-you-menial-and-a-not-too-likeable-menial-at-that.

'OK. You picked up something from the papers, did you?'

'Uh-huh, but not what I'd hoped to pick up. There haven't been any murders similar to Mathieson's for at least the last two months — not reported in the *Scotsman* anyway — and no trial reports of anything

251

like that. But what I did find was a report of a fisherman called Simon Harvey being found shot in his home in Dunbar.'

Buchanan lifted an apathetic eyebrow. 'That's where Mathieson dumped his car.'

'Right. And Harvey was shot on Friday the thirtieth. The same night Chick Mathieson was murdered.'

Buchanan forgot about being apathetic. 'What would be the connection between Mathieson and a fisherman?'

'No ordinary fisherman,' Fizz told him, topping up her G&T. 'This guy had a state-of-the-art vessel and had only been operating from Dunbar for about a year. The police are treating the murder as drug-related.'

A cacophony of loud laughter and cries of encouragement burst out from the living room where some poor mug was making a fool of himself. It was now after two in the morning but at least Fizz had had the forethought to ensure that the neighbours were among those making the noise.

Buchanan ignored it. 'One of Mathieson's agents, you think?'

'Looks like it, but whether Mathieson bumped him off or not is another thing. It's also possible that Mathieson discovered they were both for the high jump and dashed down to Dunbar to warn him. Then, arriving too late, he faked his own suicide in an attempt to escape.'

Buchanan put an elbow on the table and used the fingers to pinch his eyebrows together above his nose. It didn't seem to concentrate his thoughts any. 'That's one explanation,' he said after a minute, 'but I don't see Mathieson dashing anywhere to warn anybody. He doesn't strike me as the caring type. He'd be more concerned with saving his own skin.'

'Well, maybe it was the stash of drugs he was worried about,' Fizz substituted. 'Harvey may have had millions of pounds worth of Mathieson's drugs in his house. I could see Mathieson galloping to the rescue of that, couldn't you?'

They were both sitting there silently mulling this over when Buchanan's father came in with his hands full of empty glasses and had to be told what they were discussing so intently.

'Well, at least things aren't standing still,' he commented, a slight malfunction of the tip of his tongue signalling mild intoxication. 'Now, Fizz . . . what I wanted to ask you . . . Dorothy and I are ready for our beds and so, I think, is your grampa. We're going to share a taxi home and, if you're ready to call it a day, it would be no trouble to drop you off.'

Fizz hesitated. Then she said, 'I'd really appreciate that. I'll get my coat.'

At any other time Buchanan would have insisted she stay and boogie the night away with the younger contingent but he made not one move to defer her departure. OK, so she was in the doghouse but, hell, she hadn't expected to make an omelette without breaking a few eggs. And, anyway, she was knackered. He could stuff his party.

★ ★ ★

The revelry went on till around four o'clock, none of the remaining guests being in a fit state to notice that their host had keeled over on the couch. They woke him up to say goodbye, and he retained control of his senses long enough to shamble through to the bedroom and fall into the comforting embrace of his duvet.

About two in the afternoon he was awakened by the slam of the front door and his mother's voice singing out, 'It's just me, darling! Where are you?'

He groaned and clawed a pillow over his head muttering, 'Oh God, let it be a nightmare.'

But a minute later she was in the doorway tut-tutting like a woodpecker and declaiming, 'I don't believe it! Still in bed, Tam, at two in the afternoon? The party must have gone on for quite a while after we left. Well, just you stay where you are, darling, and I'll bring you a nice cup of coffee.'

'What are you doing here?' he managed to croak, peering out at her through one slitted eye.

'You didn't think I'd leave you with all that clearing up to do by yourself, did you? As if I would — especially as a lot of it consists of my good glasses and china. Don't worry, I'll have it all cleared away in no time.'

Buchanan was asleep again before the door closed behind her but she was back a minute later with a mug of coffee and went out leaving the door open for Selina to dash in and start demanding nourishment. He withstood her offensives for about ten minutes by wrapping his head in the duvet and trying to ignore the drumming of her paws as she strode furiously up and down his backbone.

He'd never felt less like facing another day. This time yesterday he'd felt like a million dollars; now he wasn't worth ten cents. Life had turned grey overnight. True, his relationship with Lizzie could probably be salvaged

— in fact he'd send her some flowers as soon as he got up — but some of its magic had faded. Yesterday he had been able to tell himself that this could be love at last, but now he had to fight the temptation to admit that, lovely though she was, her main attraction had been, and would continue to be, that she was — as Fizz was fond of phrasing it — hot to trot.

The thought of work was also pretty dismal. Freddie's defence was making no progress — every succeeding piece of information they came up with only confused the issue more — and at the same time his other work was starting to pile up. He'd have to start bringing work home in the evenings, something he'd not had to do since Fizz had started to be a worthwhile paralegal. Either that or call in his father. No, that was *not* an option.

But what was dragging him down more than anything was his suspicion of Fizz. From the moment he had switched on the living-room light last night his mind had been a maelstrom of conflicting emotions: Fizz had done this to him — she couldn't have done it — nobody else would think of it — yes, but Fizz would have known better — it had to have been deliberate — but how could Fizz have known? — and why would she do it anyway? WHY? Why, when she thought of him as a bore and an anachronism? Why, when he had never done anything to hurt her? Beyond sacking her a few times, of course, which had barely impinged on her consciousness. Why when, if all she wanted was a whirlwind romance, all she had to do was whistle? No, maybe that last inference wasn't true. Pretty though Fizz was, sexy as she could often appear, he wouldn't touch her with a bargepole. He wasn't that desperate. All the same, it hurt even to consider the possibility that she might have been the Machiavelli behind last night's fiasco.

He wasn't sure whether he wanted to face her today or not but she had said, on her way out, that she'd pop round in the afternoon and he had concurred in the hope that they could make some progress with the investigation. That meant he'd better get up.

His mother was charging around with Classic FM blaring out so that she could hear it over the racket of the vacuum cleaner, so he dashed into the bathroom and ran a bath. Fortune allowed him a blissful twenty minutes in a state bordering on sensory deprivation before Fizz turned up.

He heard her in the hall saying. 'How's the birthday boy this morning? Is he up?'

'Just. He's in the bath.'

'Not opening his veins, I hope?'

'Oh, Fizz, what a thing to say! Come through to the kitchen and we'll have a coffee and chat.'

Buchanan threw himself out of the bath with an alacrity that caused a minor tidal wave to precede him, sweeping everything in its path and soaking the pile of magazines he kept in the only place he ever had time to read them. Fizz and his mother in conversation was one of his most frequent recurring nightmares. God only knew what could result from a union of those two minds.

He didn't take the time to dress but threw on his bathrobe and caught up with them before Fizz had time to launch into any of her bizarre memoirs. She was wearing a white T-shirt and her old blue jeans but she looked shining clean and pretty and demure, just the sort of girl his mother approved of. They were discussing the party, which was bad enough, but it took only about fifteen minutes for him to shunt his mother back to her hoovering and leave Fizz and himself in possession of the kitchen. He could have seen both of them far enough, this morning, but he was also desperate to get Freddie's case settled and get back to his real work, even if it meant working flat out till they cracked it.

'Right,' he said. 'For God's sake let's try to make some headway over the weekend. We seem to have done nothing but collect information, and none of it is actually getting us any further forward. What is it we're doing wrong? What is it we're missing?'

Fizz leaned her elbows on the table and cupped a hand over each eye. After a minute she said with a sigh, 'God knows. Maybe we're letting ourselves be sidetracked by the situation at Greenfield House. Your father thinks so. He reckons Catriona and her boyfriend are worth watching. *Cherchez la femme*, and all that.'

Buchanan wasn't convinced. 'The boyfriend, maybe, but not Catriona. She's too keen to help.'

'Is she?' Fizz said doubtfully. 'I mean, what has she actually told us that we couldn't have learned from someone else? What has she done, other than give us that list of names? And that turned out to be nothing but a red herring.'

There was no arguing with that, of course, and when you thought about it Catriona could have as good a motive as anybody for killing her husband. But it was inconceivable to Buchanan that a woman would kill like that, even if she'd had the necessary strength. Only a man would possess that savage malevolence, and only an unbalanced man at that. The thought made him wonder what he was about, allowing Fizz to be involved in the investigation. Easy enough to claim that he'd had no chance of talking her out of it, but was that entirely true?

'Fizz,' he said abruptly, 'I want you to keep a really low profile in future. I know I've said it before but I really mean it: this is not the sort of case you've been used to. We're not dealing with enthusiastic amateurs. In future I don't want you to do anything or go anywhere unless I'm with you.'

She looked at him sadly for a long moment. 'You're easing me out, is that it?'

'No — honest to God, Fizz, it's not that. But — '

'We've known from the beginning that Mathieson wasn't topped by the paramilitary wing of the Brownies. What's the difference now?'

'The difference is,' Buchanan said, 'that I'm getting windy. I've got a really bad feeling that we could both be out of our depths on this one. I think we should tread very carefully from now on.' He expected a long argument and was surprised when, after a moment's sombre thought, she caved in without a fight.

'If that's the way you want to play it, Kimosabe, it's OK by me, but if we're working in tandem it's going to take a lot longer than if we each pursued our own line of inquiry.'

'That can't be helped. It's simply too risky to go any deeper into Mathieson's affairs without taking precautions.'

'You think that's the next step?' she said, perking up.

Buchanan poured them both another cup of coffee. The next step, if he'd had any choice in the matter, would have been to leave her bound and gagged and suspended in a sack from the top of the Scott monument till this case was closed. He couldn't think of any other way to be shot of her.

He said, 'I'd hoped we wouldn't have to probe that deeply but it looks like we're not going to make any progress till we do. We should really try to get some more facts out of Freddie — possible hideaways where Kennedy might be holing up, the names of the customers he and Kennedy used to collect money from, any information about who Mathieson talked to in the pub. We should also try to track down any of the other residents who were Miss Moir's neighbours before she moved. If Mathieson owned all three of those flats, as he appeared to, the tenants might have worked for him like Freddie did. But pursuing any leads we get along these lines could take us right into the centre of Mathieson's web and, even if the spider is dead, there could still be some nasty characters in there.'

'And don't forget the casino,' she advised, buttering the last of his mother's home-baked scones. 'I bet the place is buzzing with gossip about him.'

'It must be ten years since you worked there, Fizz. Surely — '

'My pal Louise is still there. The place changed hands a couple of years back and she was kept on as manageress. I met her in the Grassmarket one Sunday morning.' She chewed happily and smiled at a passing thought, probably some recollection of her student days. 'Saturday's much the best night to go. From about ten-thirty onwards the big spenders start to come in and it can get quite exciting. You're not doing anything tonight, are you?'

Buchanan thought that extremely unlikely. Even if Lizzie were not still incapacitated by her gouged leg it was unlikely she'd feel much like delivering his delayed birthday present so he might as well press ahead with the investigation. The casino was at least the sort of scene where they could blend into the background.

'I suppose not,' he admitted, 'but I'm tempted, before we do that, to take a look at Miss Moir's erstwhile abode. Maybe the names on the other doors could tell us something.'

'Roger,' said Fizz. 'Sounds like a good idea. Grampa's going out for a run to St Andrews this afternoon with Cheryl and Paul and won't be back till late, so we won't have to rush.'

'You don't have to come,' said Buchanan wistfully, but she just smiled.

14

Miss Moir's flat at 100 Causeyside Street was accessed through a solidly made door between a cyber café and a bookie's shop. There were three entryphone buttons beside the entrance, labelled McBain, Fry and Moir, but the lock was broken and the door had sunk on its hinges so that it was jammed half open.

Beyond it was a narrow passageway, littered with free newspapers and circulars, smelling of piss, and leading to a flight of stairs. At one time, and not so long ago, it had been a reasonably pleasant entry: the walls were painted primrose above the dado and rust below, and there was a good oak handrail on the banister. Upstairs, the three doors opened off the same landing. Sunshine poured in through a square cupola on to a jungle of dead plants that lined the edge of the stairs and trailed over into the void below.

All three doors were painted high gloss black with the panels outlined in white, and the brass letter boxes, bell pushes and nameplates — noticeably Miss Moir's — showed signs of regular polishing. Fizz, who had polished a large assortment of horse brasses every Saturday from the age of four till the day she went off to senior school, found this collection quite interesting.

'They didn't all leave at once, did they?' she remarked. 'You can tell that all three of them kept their door furniture polished but Miss Moir's is only a little dulled, McBain's is noticeably tarnished, and Fry's is almost as black as its going to get.'

Buchanan checked out this theory and then stared at her with exaggerated awe. 'My God, you're getting to be a regular Miss Marple.'

'Gee, thanks, boss.'

She started peering through each of the letter boxes in turn but there was little to see apart from more junk mail. Miss Moir's hallway was empty of furniture but the carpet and such areas of adjacent rooms as could be seen through open doorways were spick and span. The same could be said for the view from McBain's letter box, but the flat between them was a tip. The hallway was thick with dust and the few sticks of furniture were strewn with rubbish: chocolate wrappers, bits of paper, a baseball cap, open lager and Coke cans, one of which had dribbled a wide brown stain on the carpet. Chez Freddie, without a doubt. Even the bits of Sellotape that had attached his temporary nameplate were still in situ.

'Shall we go?' Buchanan suggested, and when Fizz hesitated he added, 'You weren't wondering about the possibility of breaking in, I hope?'

'Who, me?' Fizz frowned as though the idea had never crossed her mind. In fact she had rejected it immediately because, even if the lock had not been Tower of London surplus, the chances were that the police had already taken away anything that might have been worth breaking in for.

They retraced their steps to the street and had a brief recce through the window of the cyber café next door. There was only one cyber-customer, a youth of about fourteen who was skittering his fingers over the keyboard like he was playing 'The Flight of the Bumblebee'. The girl behind the counter was in her late twenties, tall, heavy, and wearing a disgusting pair of damn near flesh-coloured leggings. They looked positively indecent and left little to the imagination: the roll of flesh where her thighs sagged over her knees, the indentation where the legs of her panties cut into her fleshy hips, even the intimate details of her pudenda screamed for involuntary attention as she moved around wiping tables.

Fizz was moved to utter a very rude

comment but managed to stop herself in time. The only way to get Buchanan in there would be to let him pretend he didn't notice. They sat at a table as far away from the nerd as they could get and ordered two coffees and a salad roll for Fizz.

When the girl came back with their order Fizz got her talking about the Internet facilities for a couple of minutes and then said, 'Actually, we came to visit someone who used to live upstairs. The name's Fry. I don't suppose you'd know where they've moved to?'

'I don't. Sorry,' she said, but her eyes showed a quickening of interest. She brushed a crumb off the tabletop and threw a lightning glance at Buchanan who, his eyes being on a level with her crotch, was making an in-depth study of the menu.

'That's a pity,' Fizz told her pathetically, 'because their son's critically ill and the post office is closed so I can't find their forwarding address.'

That concentrated her mind a little. She folded an arm across her middle, propped the elbow of her other arm on it and used the fingers to twiddle her earring. This effectively shielded her mouth from the computer nerd who was neither interested nor within earshot. 'You do know they had a bit of trouble upstairs? Not just your friends, all three of the owners. With the guy who owns the rest of the corner here.'

'Dear me. What sort of trouble?'

She glanced again at Buchanan, who had now lowered the menu and was looking right back at her. This seemed to unnerve her somewhat and she went a bit pink and stuttery. 'Oh . . . I'm not sure. I didn't hear the whole story but somebody said the landlord — our landlord, that is, not theirs — wanted to buy them out and was making things nasty for them because they wouldn't sell at the price he was offering.'

'He owns the whole place now?' Fizz asked.

'Yeah. Our lease is up in August and Harry in the betting shop has to clear out then too, so the whole corner will be empty.'

Buchanan helped himself to milk. 'Are there any rumours about what's happening to the premises? Are they being relet?'

'Harry next door says he heard we're to get a new supermarket. Tesco. See, there's the whole bit in at the back that used to be the brewery till they knocked it down.' She observed Fizz getting happily outside her salad roll and said to Buchanan in doting tones, 'Would you not like a nice wee doughnut? Or a fruit slice? They're aw'fly nice.'

Buchanan succumbed to a fruit slice, probably because he couldn't bear to disappoint her, and she rushed it back to him with cosy murmurings. 'There now. You'll like that, and if you want another just you give me a wee wave.'

Buchanan's grateful smile dropped off his face as soon as she turned her back and his residual expression did not encourage Fizz to be witty. 'Well, we've learned something at any rate,' he said quietly. 'Mathieson stood to make a lot of money if he could buy up this whole corner.'

'Megabucks,' said Fizz briefly, not wishing to interrupt his train of thought, but he had apparently no more to offer. After a while she said, 'Not very nice for Miss Moir but hardly sufficient motive to hang him off a bridge.'

Buchanan looked at his fruit slice and made a visible attempt to convince himself that he wanted it. Failing, he pushed the plate aside and said, 'Who knows what she and her friends at the complex might consider sufficient motive?'

'But they're physically incapable, even all six of them together.'

'They could have hired somebody,' Buchanan said stubbornly. 'It wouldn't surprise me in the least if Boston had some heavies among his associates. The bunch of them are all very friendly with Boston — and they're all very keen that Grampa shouldn't have private conversation with Miss Moir. Looks to me like they're scared she'll talk too much.'

'About what? Mathieson's murder? For God's sake, Buchanan, get a grip!' Fizz swallowed her last bite of roll and eyed Buchanan's fruit slice. 'If you're not going to eat that flies' cemetery I think I could manage it.'

Buchanan slid the plate across as though he had never doubted it.

'I'm not saying I don't agree that the gerries are hiding something,' she went on. 'And I'm not saying that some of them — i.e., Paul — might be capable of seriously erratic behaviour and — yes, OK — he could probably carry the others along with him. But taking out a contract on Chick Mathieson? Come on, muchacho! Besides, that wasn't a contract killing, you know that yourself. Contract killers are in and out fast, no frills, no risk. Mathieson's murder was *personal*.'

Buchanan conceded that with a nod. 'It was a message. A message to other oppressors or to other victims: nobody is safe from vengeance.'

That sent Fizz off on her own train of thought: why had no one hit back at Mathieson before? Was Kennedy his only minder and, if so, where was Kennedy when he needed him? And were Mathieson's other heavies now hunting down the killer? And if they found him before she and Buchanan did, would that make the police think twice about Freddie's case? Probably not. So they had to find him first.

She finished her coffee in a single gulp. 'Right, Buchanan. Let's get this show on the road.'

⋆   ⋆   ⋆

Buchanan was not a gambler. He had played the tables once before, on holiday, but only because the friends he was with wanted to have a flutter. He'd had only the vaguest idea what he was doing and still wasn't interested in learning more so he didn't listen too intently while Fizz showed off her insider knowledge.

It was only half-past ten so the casino was not by any means busy. Two of the six roulette wheels were still unmanned, as were a couple of baccarat tables, and there were vacant seats at the one operational stud poker table. White dinner jackets and backless evening gowns were not *de rigueur* although, according to Fizz, neither were they unknown later in the proceedings when the big spenders were liable to arrive.

The current clientele were just your ordinary Edinburgh punter, a considerable sprinkling of them from the Chinese community. There was very little conversation: in fact, if it hadn't been for the low background music it would have been like the reading room of the British Museum, and nobody looked in the least like they were enjoying themselves. Now and then a burst of laughter would greet a long-awaited win or a humorous remark but for the most part the faces around the tables showed only an impassivity that verged on apathy.

Fizz could not immediately see her friend Louise, so she and Buchanan sat at one of the tables that ringed the room and ordered soft drinks, that being all that was on offer in the gaming room. It was fairly apparent to Buchanan that Fizz was more in tune with the atmosphere than he was and maybe he should have expected that, but he hadn't.

'You go for this sort of thing,' he said, making it an observation rather than a question, and she broke into a smile.

'Bet your sweet ass I do. Even at this time in the evening, when there's nothing much happening, there's a tension — like a coiled spring — like there's something cataclysmic about to happen. But some nights the atmosphere is so electric you could run a trolleybus on it. When a party of big spenders come in, late on, and start piling on the money like it was going out of fashion, and the croupiers start getting nervous and the tables have a gallery of spectators around them, and the pit bosses are scared to blink — that's when you see what it's all about.'

Buchanan looked at the young croupiers, the girls in black velvet evening dresses, the men in white ruffled shirts and black bow ties, and tried to imagine an eighteen-year-old Fizz stacking chips and calculating odds at the speed of light. It can't have been easy for her to work till four in the morning, put in at least seven hours a day at art school and still find the time to produce a portfolio of work for her exams. Perhaps that's why she'd packed it in without qualifying. One day he'd ask her.

It didn't sound like the Fizz he knew now, who was tenacious to the point of bloody-mindedness, but ten precarious years would make anybody tough. He'd been tempted to ask her about it more than once but he was aware that it was one of her many no-go areas and she would only put his nose in a sling. He was sure it was connected somehow with the mystery of why, since her father had been an

273

established solicitor in Stirling and presumably not a pauper, she had been so short of cash that she'd had to burn the candle at both ends. At college and ever since.

There were possibly ways he could find out but some respect for Fizz's privacy prevented him from trying. One of those days she might tell him off her own bat, otherwise he could live without knowing.

She was too interested in what was going on at the tables to make conversation, and was taken by surprise when a tanned girl in a black trouser suit hove into view and came for her with a crow of delight.

'Fizz! You made it at last. I was beginning to think you'd changed your mind or that someone had lost the pass I left for you at the door! How're you doing? You're looking great!'

They went through the so-are-you-you've-lost-weight-you're-positively-anorexic routine that appeared to be obligatory on such occasions and then Fizz said, 'This is Tam Buchanan. He's my boss.'

'Oh, hi.' Louise had a wide red mouth and a nice smile.

She accepted Buchanan's seat while he stole another from the next table and she and Fizz launched immediately into an orgy of reminiscences and a review of where various people were now. Buchanan let them run and was rewarded with the odd crumb of information regarding Fizz's past: nothing he could sell to Reuters but interesting, if only because of their rarity value. Eventually, and purely by accident it seemed to Buchanan, the discussion turned to Mathieson.

'Everybody knew Chick Mathieson.' Louise said, her eyes dancing from table to table as she watched the play. 'Half the stories you'd hear about him weren't true.'

'But he was a bit of a gangster, surely?'

'Oh, I'm quite sure he was. I think he was a major drug dealer and probably worse. He used to sashay in here every Friday night with that thug Kennedy, and make out that he was such a big pal of Mr Hunter, the new owner. In fact, I suspect Hunter was scared stiff of him. Used to give him all the credit he wanted, right up till last month.'

'And what happened last month?' Fizz asked softly.

Louise's gaze withdrew itself from the baccarat table and lit on Fizz with faint consternation. 'I shouldn't be talking about things like that. We're not supposed to discuss big wins or losses.'

Fizz grinned. 'Like I'm going to quote you all over town? For God's sake, Louise, the man's dead. What's he going to do, haunt you?'

'No, sorry, Fizz. I really can't discuss casino business. It's more than my job's worth.'

Fizz wouldn't leave it at that and Louise was just as determined to remain shtoom so, after a minute or two, Buchanan took himself off to the loo in the hope that his absence might grease the wheels of negotiation. He took his time and when he returned to the gaming room Louise was nowhere to be seen and Fizz was watching the play at one of the roulette tables.

'Any success?' he asked, coming up behind her just as the croupier spun the wheel.

She whirled round so fast her hair lashed against his face. 'Quick, Buchanan, gimme a fiver!'

Buchanan would have argued — in fact he had come prepared for this eventuality with a firm refusal in mind — but the blaze in her eyes carried such conviction that he responded with knee-jerk speed.

She snatched the fiver from his fingers while half of it was still in his wallet, threw it on the table with a pound of her own and said, 'Tier.'

In an instant the banknotes were raked into a hole in the green tabletop. Buchanan hadn't a single clue what was happening and Fizz refused either to explain or to move her eyes from the spinning wheel. All the fire had gone out of her now and her expression was just as apathetic as all the others. Except that it wasn't apathy, Buchanan realised that now, it was acquiescence; an acceptance that one was now in the hands of Fate.

The wheel seemed to spin forever, giving him plenty of time to realise that Fizz had suckered him again. Had she asked him in her normal manner to put on a bet for her he'd have told her to get lost. Not that he'd have minded a small speculation of his own but there was no way he was going to finance her gambling. But she had foxed him by catching him on the hop with her now-or-never act. He'd never learn.

He watched the spinning ball come to rest on number twenty-three and sighed. Whatever it was that Fizz had called to the croupier, that wasn't it. Someone at the other side of the table had made a reasonable profit but his face remained blank as the chips were raked across to him. The same could not be said of Buchanan's when a similar pile of chips ended up in front of Fizz.

'How — ' he said, when he had regained control of his lower jaw, but she silenced him with a dig in the solar plexus.

'I'll cash these in and then you can buy me a drink.'

Their winnings came to seventeen pounds. Fizz deftly divided the notes and tried to hand him half of them.

'Don't be silly, Fizz.' He turned and made his way to the door that led downstairs to the bar, Fizz tripping along in his wake.

'Fifty-fifty, Buchanan. Plus your fiver. That's fair enough.'

'No it isn't. Give me my fiver back if it makes you happy, but you earned the rest.'

She desisted while they descended the stairs, there being a lot of people around, but once they'd found a table she laid the bundle of notes in front of him and held them there when he tried to shove them back.

'You might as well take them now because I'll find some way of slipping them to you, one by one if need be.'

'My God, you're the most aggravating woman, Fizz! I don't want the bloody money!'

She smiled at him as though he were a fractious child. 'But this isn't about what *you* want, Buchanan, it's about what *I* want.'

There was no point in arguing further. He had long ago given up trying to plumb the dark intricacies of Fizz's mind. She would happily screw the last five pence of expenses out of him if she felt it was her right but she'd dig her heels in about a thing like this — even though she was saving up for a new pair of Docs. Well, dammit, she'd get the bloody money one way or another.

'And don't think I won't be watching for it cropping up in my wages over the next few months,' she murmured as he tucked it into his wallet. 'I'm not daft, you know.'

Buchanan sunk his double tonic water in a one-er and waved for another. 'How did you do it?' he asked, wondering if he really wanted to know.

'It's just a matter of watching the play.' She smoothed back the tendrils of hair that were supposed to be woven into the tight knot behind her head but were, in fact, all over the place. 'There was only one other bet on that side of the board.'

Buchanan regarded her closely. 'What are you saying? That the wheel's loaded?'

'God, no!' She glanced around quickly to see if anyone had overheard the question and whispered, 'You can't get away with that these days, but it's surprising how often, when the bets are one-sided like that, the result is in the bank's favour.'

'And why should that be, do you think?' Buchanan enquired, in two minds whether to take her seriously or not. 'Because God loves bankers?'

'Because a good croupier can put a spin on the ball. It doesn't always work but it works often enough to make it worth a wager. I've seen real money paid out on a call bet. *Mucho, mucho pesetas.*'

Buchanan consulted his conscience and decided their win was legitimate. 'It's a good job Louise wasn't watching you,' he said. 'She might have felt it wasn't quite cricket.'

'Actually, I'm not supposed to play the tables, either here or in any other casino,' Fizz said without visible qualms. 'At least, I signed an agreement not to but that was ten years ago. I'm not sure that it was a lifelong ban. Anyway, do you want to know what Louise told me?'

'She came across?'

'Eventually. I had to squeeze her pretty damn hard, I don't mind telling you, but I knew she'd cough in the end.' She finished her gin and tonic and looked sadly at the empty glass. 'You don't get much of a helping in pubs, do you? It's hardly worth dirtying the glass.'

Buchanan ordered her a double and she said, 'It seems Mathieson was quite a compulsive gambler. He often lost all the cash he had with him and the boss, Mr Hunter, would give him credit. Obviously, he was a good risk and there was never any trouble. He'd pay his account the following Friday and it might be weeks before he asked for credit again. However, a few — '

She broke off as her drink arrived and filled in the hiatus by fiddling with the strap of her dress which had slipped off her shoulder. It was the same navy-blue thing she wore over a T-shirt at work, four pounds fifty from Oxfam and probably her only dress, but tonight it looked amazingly sexy.

'However,' she said when they were once again in camera, 'a few weeks back — Louise claims she can't remember exactly when it started — Mathieson began to forget to settle his debts and things started to get distinctly hairy. Hunter was too scared of him to refuse him credit but the total was mounting up and Mathieson kept just brushing the matter aside as though it was of no consequence.'

'How much are we talking about?'

Fizz made a exasperated face. 'That's where Louise dug her heels in. She claimed she didn't know, and maybe she didn't, but she knew it was a lot. A *whole* lot.'

'And it was never paid?'

'Not as far as she knew.'

Buchanan shook his head in confusion. He could think of no reason why a guy like

Mathieson, who had to have been seriously well-heeled, should have reneged on his gambling bills. Why, in the first place, had he run up debts that he had clearly no intention of honouring? And did this mean that it was Hunter, the owner of the casino, who was behind his killing?

Fizz was unable to answer any of these questions and, since she was preparing to indicate her readiness for another drink, Buchanan suggested that it was time to hit the road. The bar, in any case, was fast filling up and conversation was becoming difficult.

Just as they were getting into the car he remembered he hadn't sent Lizzie flowers.

15

Buchanan senior turned up at the office just as Fizz was about to stop for her tea break and requested her presence in his son's office for a detailed account of their investigation thus far. It was a complete waste of time, Buchanan junior being laconically polite and his father interested only in driving home his conviction that Catriona was at the bottom of everything.

Fizz took pains to acquaint him with Mathieson's zero credit rating at the casino but he refused to admit that it had to be noteworthy, on the grounds that people with that amount of money tended to be careless about paying bills. Finally, more to get rid of him than anything else, Fizz agreed to subject Catriona to another grilling A.S.A.P. and that seemed to cheer him up.

Neither she nor Buchanan expected to glean any useful information from the visit but she was going to have to see Catriona anyway. Somebody had to ask her what she thought of the list of names being a fake, in case its fraudulence prompted her to view it in a different light. It was just one of the myriad loose ends and red herrings that would have to be tidied away in the hope that, thereafter, they'd be able to tell the wheat from the chaff.

'I'll come with you,' Buchanan said after his father had gone. 'I've made arrangements to see Freddie at four thirty so we can see Catriona first, spend ten minutes with Grampa, and then I can drop you off at your place on my way to the prison.'

'I'll come with you to see Freddie.'

'No point,' he said, gathering up the papers he'd been reading when his father arrived and walking with them, somewhat pointedly, to the door. 'I'm really only going for the sake of keeping up his morale but . . . ' he paused with his hand on the door handle, 'to be honest Fizz, I'm also wondering if he'd talk more freely if you weren't there. Sometimes a quiet chat reveals more than a third degree. If you want to do anything practical this evening you can sit quietly and use your brain. We've been running around so much this past week we haven't had time to think.'

Fizz was much inclined to agree with him on that at least. Her brain was so bunged up with unconnected information that it felt like the mental equivalent of a bad head cold. A brisk walk in the fresh air, perhaps along

Cramond beach, would blow away the cobwebs.

She phoned Catriona and made an appointment for three o'clock, so she was expecting them and dressed accordingly when they arrived. She led the way through the house and out, by way of patio doors in the dining room, to the landscaped back garden. A manicured beech hedge surrounded the lawn on three sides but the ground sloped away so sharply at the end of the garden that they could see over it to the panorama beyond.

She arranged herself on the sun lounger, where she had obviously been whiling away the afternoon with a pile of magazines and a copious supply of G&T, and waved her guests to chairs beneath the beach umbrella.

'Can I offer you a drink?'

'No, thanks,' said Buchanan like a flash before Fizz could get past 'Y — '. He looked at his watch. 'We don't have a lot of time, I'm afraid.'

'Has something happened?' Catriona said hopefully, screwing up her eyes against the sun as she reached for her sunglasses. 'Have you found out anything?'

Fizz started to say they'd found out too damn much but Buchanan spoke virtually in tandem, cutting her off.

'We're making progress,' he said noncommittally, and started to open his briefcase just as Catriona said, 'What about the list of names and addresses? Did you . . . ?' She paused as Buchanan produced the blue sheet of paper and handed it across to her. 'Yes? You spoke to them?'

'No,' Fizz told her flatly, accompanying the words with a hard look just in case Catriona had known all along that the list was a fake. 'There are no such people.'

Catriona slid down her sunglasses and looked at the list as though she'd never seen it before. 'You're sure? None of them?'

'Not a one.'

She lifted her eyes to Buchanan's face, swivelled them to Fizz and back again. 'What does it mean?'

Buchanan raised an eyebrow. 'We were rather hoping that you could throw some light on that, Catriona.'

She laid two fingertips to her breastbone as though she were about to say, *'Moi?'* but instead she returned speechlessly to the bit of blue paper and gave it another going over. At last she said, 'I don't know . . . maybe he was trying to trick someone . . . somehow . . . ' She shook her head. 'Honestly . . . I haven't a clue.'

Fizz was much inclined to endorse that

claim. The chances were that she and Buchanan could probably make as good a guess at the significance of the list as Catriona could. At least she'd tried, which was reassuring.

Buchanan zipped the paper back into his briefcase but as Fizz was gathering her feet under her to rise he said, 'Do you happen to have a recent photograph of your husband, Catriona? I think it could help us in the next stage of our inquiries.'

'Yes, I'm sure I have,' she said earnestly, hauling herself up from her lounger in the manner of one eager to prove her good will. 'Several. Just give me a minute.'

'What do you want a photograph for?' Fizz asked when she was out of earshot.

He looked a bit shifty. 'I just thought that, if we don't get a break soon, we might be reduced to revisiting the areas on the list — the doctors' surgery, the church, et cetera — in the hope of finding someone who recognised Mathieson.'

'That was a royal 'we' you used there, I hope?' Fizz enquired respectfully.

Buchanan was saved having to answer by the reappearance of Catriona carrying two photographs.

'I brought both of these,' she started saying when she was still a hundred yards away. 'The big one is clearer but this one here is actually a lot more like him.'

She handed them to Buchanan, who let Fizz commandeer them and take a quick look. Buchanan was always going on about evil not showing in people's faces but Chick Mathieson didn't just throw doubt on that theory, he demolished it. He was probably the most evil-looking bastard she'd ever seen in real life. In the smaller of the two pictures he was smiling but the smile didn't reach his eyes — it didn't even reach his cheeks! — and the very sight of it gave Fizz a cold feeling in the pit of her stomach. Any judge would have taken one look at it and given him twenty years on the spot. He was a big guy and totally bald, so the chances were that anyone who'd seen him, even a couple of weeks back, would remember him.

Catriona resumed her seat. 'I knew I could put my hand on them in a minute because I'd only just put them in the writing desk. I spent all day yesterday going through Chick's papers with a fine-tooth comb, looking for anything unusual, but there was nothing at all . . . ' She lifted her head from the back of the lounger and listened to the sound of an approaching car ' . . . that would be of the slightest help to you.'

The rattle of car wheels on gravel grew

louder and an oldish Vauxhall Astra appeared round the corner of the house and slid to a halt beside Catriona's shiny blue Toyota.

'It's Sam!' Catriona's face lit up as she bounced out of her lounger and rushed across the lawn to welcome the new arrival.

Fizz turned to Buchanan and muttered, 'Sam! That's the boyfriend.'

'No it's not,' he returned, looking over her shoulder. 'Not unless he's a master of disguise.'

It was, in fact, a woman getting out of the car. Not a Samuel, Fizz realised, but a Samantha. A laughing, brown-haired Samantha in a pair of beat-up jeans and a last year's Festival T-shirt. Which was the final straw for the *crime passionnel* scenario. Catriona could be bi, of course, but the two of them — even hugging and cheek-kissing like they were at the moment — didn't give the impression that they were more than close friends. They were gabbling like a passing flight of geese while Sam reached into the car for her shoulder bag and a gift-wrapped package which she presented to Catriona.

'We ought to go,' said Buchanan uncomfortably. He fastened his briefcase and got to his feet, at which Fizz was forced to do likewise. However, Catriona brought her friend back to them and introduced her, showing no impatience for them to be gone.

'This is my friend, Sam Phillips. Sam, this is Fizz Fitzpatrick and . . . and this is Tam Buchanan, who is a solicitor acting for Freddie McAuslan — you know, I told you about him in my letter.'

Sam shook hands, her clasp limp and a little damp. She wasn't unattractive, in a dull sort of way. She was wearing the wrong shade of foundation — too pale for her recent tan — but her bright grey eyes made her otherwise ordinary face rather interesting.

'You're trying to prove Freddie McAuslan's innocence?' she asked, clearly overcoming a certain shyness in order to fill the silence while Catriona opened her present.

Buchanan inclined his head. 'We're acting for his defence, yes.'

'And do you think he's innocent?'

'Fortunately, I'm not required to have an opinion about that,' he said, smiling down at her, 'just to present the facts. But, yes, the facts would lead one to suppose that the police may have got the wrong man.'

Sam remained standing, pretending not to watch Catriona's face. 'Oh dear, that's too bad.' Then, realising what she'd said she rushed on, 'Oh . . . I didn't mean . . . Of course it would be dreadful if — as you say — the wrong person was punished but, oh dear, how long will all this unpleasantness go on for? I know Catriona is just living for the day when it will all be over and she can start to pick up the pieces of her life. It's traumatic enough for her to lose Chick, but all the rest of it . . . it's agony for her.'

Catriona, having divested her present of its glittery paper, its ribbons and rosettes, its pretty box and its layers of pink tissue paper, revealed a jazzy necklace and earrings which she greeted with delight. The trinkets were rather pretty, delicate concoctions of crystal beads and feathers, but compared to the redeemable assets Catriona was already sporting, they were mere baubles. Fizz suspected she would never actually wear them — she was much more into ostentation — but it was evident that she appreciated the thought.

'Not from Tiffany's, my darling,' Sam said, ducking her chin almost humbly. 'But I thought they were unusual. I hope you like them.'

'Love them!' Catriona held the necklace around her neck and, at her coy look, Buchanan fastened it for her, complimented her politely, and immediately added that they really had to rush.

'Oh, must you? What a pity.' She was concentrating on fixing on her earrings and her absorbed eyes showed that she didn't give a damn whether they stayed or left. 'Well . . . I'm sorry I couldn't help you with the list of names but I'll keep it in mind. Something may occur to me.'

They saw themselves out while, behind them, they could hear a torrent of girl talk bursting out as if they hadn't seen each other for months.

'Well, that's one loose end snipped off,' Fizz admitted when they were back on the road. 'I don't suppose your dad will be too happy about it.'

'You know what he'll say, of course.' Buchanan turned left towards the distant speck of white at the base of Blackford Hill which Fizz had identified as Greenfield House. 'He'll say that just because Sam turned out to be female it doesn't mean that Catriona doesn't have a boyfriend as well.'

Fizz could only groan. She knew that Buchanan was absolutely right, and spent the next ten minutes planning how to be out of the office all tomorrow morning.

There was no sign of Grampa, nor indeed of any of his clique, either in the garden or the lounge. They checked out the TV lounge but found three cardiganed granddads in sole possession and only then considered the possibility that he could be in his room.

'Well, I'm not sorry to see you, and that's a fact,' Grampa admitted straight out, as he let them in. 'I haven't had an intelligent conversation all day. I'm telling you, some of these old souls are nothing short of doolally and the rest of them have nothing to talk about but their grandchildren, their aches and pains, and the time they were on the same bill as Mike and Bernie Winters. Dearie, dearie me, is that not sad? Eh? What a thing to boast of as your life's achievement!'

'Where's your gang?' Fizz asked. 'There's not one of them to be seen downstairs.'

'They're all away out to different places.' Grampa stomped back to his seat by the window. He had dispensed with one of his sticks altogether and looked like he wouldn't be long in discarding the other. 'Nigel is driving Helen to the opticians for an eye test and they're going to the museum afterwards. Miss Moir went with them, and the others, Cheryl and Paul and Anthony, took a picnic lunch up Blackford Hill and aren't back yet.'

'Didn't anyone invite you along?' Fizz said, immediately suspecting that he had rubbed up some or all of them the wrong way, as he was apt to do.

'Och, yes, they invited me but my legs are not just back to what they were yet and I was afraid I'd hold them back. I'll not be up to climbing hills for a while and as for museums, I can only take them in small doses. I don't mind walking,' he said to Buchanan, by way of explanation, 'and I don't mind sitting, but don't ask me to stand around.'

Buchanan was lounging beside him with his hands in his pockets, looking out the window. 'Did you enjoy your run to St Andrews yesterday?'

'Aye, I enjoyed it fine. There was a bit of a snell wind blowing when we stopped at Crail to stretch our legs but I had my thick cardigan with me that Auntie Duff knitted me last winter so it was quite pleasant.'

'I just wondered . . . ' Buchanan started to say and then stopped.

'What was that you said, Tam?'

'I just . . . ' He paused again and then said, 'You don't think that maybe the trip yesterday and the various activities today could all be part of a ploy to keep you away from Miss Moir — and possibly some of the others?'

Grampa glowered at him from under his bushy eyebrows.

'I mean, it has done, effectively, hasn't it? You haven't had a chance to talk to her for two days. The only ones you've spoken to — tell me if I'm right about this — are Paul and Cheryl, and I'll bet they're the two hardest nuts to crack. Cheryl could possibly let something slip but not while Paul's there to keep an eye on her.'

'Aye, you might just have put your finger on it there, Tam.' Grampa's glower deepened as he thought about it. 'D'you think they've tumbled to it that I'm a spy? Have I — what is it they say? — blown my cover?'

Buchanan's smile as he sat down in an adjacent chair held a trace of affection, although how anyone other than a blood relation could feel affection for the old nark was a mystery to Fizz.

'No, I'm sure they don't suspect anything concrete,' Buchanan said. 'They're just being careful. I'm pretty sure they have something to hide, something that has to do with Miss Moir and, possibly, with her previous flat in Causeyside Street. But it doesn't look to me as if it could be anything to do with Mathieson's death so I reckon they're just making sure that one of the less acute conspirators — and in particular Miss Moir — doesn't blurt something out. You're almost certainly under no more suspicion than anyone else, though the fact that you're in close contact with a solicitor may be making them wary.'

Grampa was willing to accept that view of the matter. 'So what's this about Miss Moir's flat?'

Fizz left Buchanan to explain about that while she went into the kitchen and checked on Grampa's food supplies. There was freshly made Cullen skink in the freezer, a smoked haddock soup that they rarely had at the farm because it was regarded as a luxury. Not too much of a luxury for Grampa, however. There was also a pork chop marinading in something spicy, a pot of potatoes cut into chips, enough fresh vegetables for another week, and the ingredients for at least three other main dishes.

Fizz was putting on the kettle for a cup of tea when Buchanan stuck his head round the door.

'We have to go now, Fizz. It's nearly four.'

'I'll stay and keep Grampa company for a while,' Fizz decided. 'I can get a forty-one to the High Street from just outside.'

Buchanan took a couple of steps into the room. 'Let's just stick to what we arranged, huh? I'd feel a lot happier — '

'No, really, Buchanan,' Fizz interrupted before he went into his mother-hen routine. 'Get a grip. None of the gerries from hell is even around the place. What's going to happen to me, for God's sake? You can't expect me to live in purdah till Freddie's cleared.'

'No, I suppose not.' Buchanan chewed the inside of his lip for a minute. 'OK, but promise me you'll leave as soon as you feel able to, and go straight home. And don't do anything silly.'

'OK. Yeah. Sure. Now beat it.'

He went, visibly beset by doubts, but that was typical of Buchanan. He spent half his life worrying about things that would never happen and blaming himself for everything that did. The man was a walking jungle of neuroses.

Fizz hung around till quarter past six, by which time it had become obvious that Grampa was not going to offer her a share of his Cullen skink and would be just as happy on his own, watching the news on STV. She had considered waiting to see if Lizzie turned up to visit her father but that could mean another hour or more, and Grampa was obviously not going to eat till she'd gone.

The hillwalkers had arrived home just after Buchanan's departure and about an hour later Grampa had spotted Nigel and Miss Moir escorting Helen down the path from the garages. None of them was in the lounge as Fizz passed by, but just as she got outside she spotted Nigel hurrying back to the garages on his own.

Partly out of curiosity and partly because she wanted to know if Lizzie were due soon, Fizz took a short cut across the grass to close with him. Disappointingly, he was up to nothing nefarious. He unlocked a garage, revealing a flashy maroon camper van, opened the back and retrieved Helen's tartan lap rug. He did look startled when he turned back and saw Fizz walking towards him, but that couldn't really be termed suspicious.

'Hi,' Fizz said, giving him a medium-sized smile. 'How was your day at the museum?'

'Oh . . . wonderful. Absolutely.' He locked up the garage and they started to walk back across the grass while he rabbited on about this and that exhibit, what they'd had for lunch, where they were going next, etc. He might have been monopolising the conversation to prevent Fizz asking questions but, on the other hand, it was just as likely that she was becoming as paranoic as Buchanan.

She had to block his escape at the entrance to say, 'I met your daughter last week — or rather, I ran across her, but we didn't get a chance to speak. Will she be visiting you this evening?'

'No. Dear me, what a pity.' He looked no more than politely distressed. 'She normally comes every evening, at least for a little while, but I told her not to bother tonight in case we were late back. I had thought the ladies might want to have dinner somewhere before we came home — in fact Helen was too tired — and, in any case, Lizzie is going out somewhere later on. She lives quite a bit out of town — in Peebles — and sometimes it can take her almost an hour to drive into town, so she prefers to fit in her visits on her way home from work. But I'm sure you'll meet her soon. In fact, it's surprising you two haven't met properly already.'

It wasn't at all surprising to Fizz but she was gladdened to know that she could have a lazy evening without feeling that she was wasting an opportunity. It wasn't until she was waiting for the bus that she started to wonder what, exactly, Lizzie was doing this evening. And with whom.

Buchanan had shown no sign today that he was hopeful of getting his leg over: no uncharacteristic smileyness, no bursts of unconscious whistling, no nipping out for a haircut. However, he was now becoming suspicious — if not convinced — that his recent lack of success with the ladies was not due to bad breath, so he could well be playing it cool. The bastard.

The High Street, at that hour of the

evening, was as quiet as it ever got during the day. The rush hour was over and the tourists were still in their hotel rooms shaving and showering and putting on lipstick and getting into their new holiday outfits in preparation for strutting out to dinner.

Fizz's head, as she turned into the unlit entry to the staircase of her flat, was full of depressing thoughts, and she was taken completely by surprise by the hooded figure that came at her out of the shadows. Before she knew what was happening, she was caught by the shoulders, spun around and slammed, with appalling force, against the wall. A bomb exploded inside her skull — pain too excruciating to register as such — and her face seemed to blaze with sudden fire.

She was whipped back round as easily as if she were a child, her attacker holding her upright with one hand. She saw him only in what seemed to be a series of split-second images, as though someone was flicking the light on and off or as though she were fighting off unconsciousness. Dimly, she saw one fist drawn back to punch her in the face.

Instantly, operating entirely on autopilot, she went totally limp, throwing her whole weight on to his one supporting hand and forcing the bastard to use both hands to pull her upright. As he did so, he had to spread his legs to regain his balance.

Fizz knew she wouldn't get another chance so she put every adrenaline-packed ounce of her strength behind the knee that took him square in the *cojones*. He didn't yell, in fact the only noise he made was a horrible high-pitched whistle. He didn't even grab his balls, he just fell to his knees which made it convenient for Fizz to Doc him hard in the face before legging it for the stairs.

There was a locked door at the foot of the staircase and it took years for her shaking fingers to get the key in the lock but, even after she'd slammed it behind her, she didn't feel safe. He could still kick his way through it and catch her before she could stagger up the hundred steps to her eyrie so, in desperation, she punched every doorbell on her way up.

She was home and dry before the sound of indignant voices floated up from the half-dozen neighbours down below, grumbling and complaining and bonding happily in a common belief that the High Street wasn't what it used to be.

16

Lizzie was wearing trousers to cover her bandaged leg. They were black and sort of drapey, and they tapered down to a pair of spike-heeled black pumps that showed a lot of toe cleavage and gladdened her escort's heart exceedingly.

'I like your cousin, Mark,' she said, undressing her after-dinner mint in a fascinating way. 'He has a wonderful bedside manner — or in my case, a couchside manner. I'm sure he's a first-rate doctor.'

'He is. He can be a bit dizzy in other ways and — as you saw — he has the dress sense of an unmade bed — but I'd trust him with my life. He got married last Easter and his wife's now in the early stages of pregnancy and throwing up all the time. That's why she wasn't at the party.'

'Was it a good party?' she said, biting off a tiny corner of her mint. 'There seemed to be a lot of fun people there. I was sorry I didn't get to meet them.'

'I can't say it was the best party I've ever been to.' Buchanan sketched a wan smile and she giggled in understanding. 'The guests seemed to be enjoying themselves but by the time I got over the shock they were all starting to go home. Frankly, I've never understood the thinking behind surprise parties. Who are they for? The guests or the recipient?'

Lizzie's brows twitched together as she laughed. 'Yes, they do go horribly wrong sometimes but it's nice to think that someone cares about you. Whose idea was it? Your parents'?'

'My father's claiming responsibility,' Buchanan said, keeping his suspicions to himself.

As though reading his mind, Lizzie said, 'And I was sorry to have missed the chance of getting to know Fizz. She's a sweet little thing, isn't she? What age is she?'

Buchanan nodded to the waiter to indicate that he was ready for the bill. With any luck he'd bring it over before he had to answer Lizzie's last question. No point in raising any further doubts in Lizzie's mind.

'What age do you think she is?'

'Oh, I don't know. Seventeenish, maybe. I couldn't see her face clearly with all that wonderful golden hair floating about.'

Buchanan watched the waiter's approach and took his time looking at the bill. As he laid his credit card on the plate he turned back to Lizzie and, as though he'd forgotten what they were talking about, said, 'Back to my place? I'll guarantee a total absence of merry revellers tonight.'

She shook her head, putting on a devastated expression. 'Not tonight, I'm afraid, Tam. It's a bad time for me.'

Buchanan tried to mask the fact that he was reeling from the blow by hiding behind a nonchalant expression. After all, sex was not supposed to be the main point of this rendezvous. 'We could play some CDs. I could show you my etchings.'

'I don't think so, Tam. I'm feeling a bit washed out, to be honest, and I have a heavy day ahead of me tomorrow.' She tipped her head on one side and regarded him soberly. 'You're looking a little drawn yourself tonight. You've been working too hard. I don't suppose your job takes you out and about much.'

'Sometimes it does. I was out most of the afternoon, as it happens.'

'Round about town?'

'Uh-huh. Just around the suburbs and then over to Saughton to talk to a remand prisoner.'

'I thought you didn't do court work,' she said as Buchanan signed the chit and reclaimed his card. 'Is it an interesting case?'

304

'It's not my usual line of operation,' Buchanan said evasively. People were always curious about court work but the fact was that ninety per cent of it was agonisingly boring. 'Normally my partner would attend to it but this is a favour I'm doing for my father. You didn't meet Dad properly, did you?'

Lizzie said, no, she hadn't, which led to other topics, and she went with the flow of the conversation apparently without noticing she'd been sidetracked. He dropped her off at her grannie flat, promising to phone her later in the week, and drove disconsolately home to Selina.

She was comfortingly glad to see him and was still riding around ecstatically on his shoulder when the bell rang.

'Bloody hell!' he said to her but she had already deserted him and was racing up the hessian wallpaper to her vantage point.

It was Fizz, of course. Buchanan didn't even have to think about it. Nobody else would have the gall to turn up at eleven forty-five at night. No doubt she thought to interrupt yet another cosy assignation with Lizzie but this time she'd made a big mistake. This time he'd have it out with her once and for all.

He marched into the hallway and pressed

the release button on the downstairs lock. As he did so he caught sight of his furious face in the hall mirror and took a moment to compose himself before opening the door.

In the split second he turned the handle, however, the door flew open in his face and he was confronted by a man in a Balaclava who was already lunging for him with what looked like a heavy spanner. Buchanan leaped backwards fast, crashing into his golf bag and bringing down the mirror with a crash, but the man dived forwards just as nimbly and was swinging his arm down when Selina, misjudging her jump in all the excitement, landed on his head.

The guy screamed, either in shock or because Selina was clinging on with all eighteen claws. She had also pulled his mask askew so that he was unable to see what was happening to him. The eyepiece had slipped down to his nose and this gave Buchanan all the time he needed to grab a driver and let the intruder have it round the head.

It wasn't really a wholehearted blow; even when it came to the crunch he couldn't put his heart into it, and for a long time afterwards that occasioned Buchanan the most caustic regret imaginable, but it was enough to unnerve his assailant. Grabbing at his mask, he fell face up in the doorway, scuttled backwards like a crab and threw himself down the staircase. His footsteps could be heard retreating at speed and by the time Buchanan collected his wits and got to the downstairs door there was no sign of him.

There didn't seem to be a lot of point in charging after the guy. The eighteenth-century mews where Buchanan lived was ill lit and full of doorways and alcoves: not the sort of territory through which to search for a madman with a monkey wrench. He locked the door securely, went back upstairs, and watched from the window for ten minutes without seeing any movement below.

Selina was sitting on the floor in front of the couch, washing herself with brisk application as though she wished to eliminate all trace of a distressing experience from within her aura. She looked so tiny and helpless sitting there it was incredible to think that she had just — quite possibly — saved his life or, at the very least, delivered him from a very severe beating.

Buchanan was about to go into the kitchen to see if he still had a tin of cod roe, to which she was very partial, when he realised how much she reminded him of Fizz. She had the same apparent frailty, the same indomitable will, the —

Something like a monkey wrench hit him

just below the diaphragm, taking his breath away. *Fizz! Jesus God! FIZZ!* Had there been a visitor at *her* door tonight?

He was down the stairs and into the car in under a minute, his heart pounding and the sweat running down the back of his neck. It was a scant ten-minute drive between his place and Fizz's at this time of night, and he did it in six, groaning, swearing and talking to himself all the way. This wasn't the first time he had galloped to Fizz's rescue and none of the other times, as she was fond of pointing out, had he turned out to be instrumental in her survival. But the nitty had to turn gritty eventually and he could only pray that it wouldn't be this time.

Double parking at the gated entry, he skidded through the passageway and jammed his thumb on the bell of her entryphone. As he waited for her to answer he realised he was panting like he had run all the way. He rested his forehead against the reinforced glass of the door muttering. 'Come on, Fizz . . . Come on, baby . . . just answer . . . ' over and over like a mantra and telling himself, at the same time, that she was fine, she was sleeping, she was just taking a long time to wake up.

When it looked as though she wasn't going to answer his mind started to throw up alternative suggestions, like ringing someone else's doorbell and getting them to open the downstairs door and then breaking down Fizz's door somehow and —

There was a sudden click and a voice that was barely recognisable as Fizz's croaked, 'Fuck off.'

'Fizz? Is that you? It's Buchanan. Are you OK?'

Silence. Then, after a minute the door lock whined and he pushed his way in and took the stairs in a mad rush. *Had* that been Fizz or was there someone in there with her? Dammit, he should have thought to pick up some sort of weapon.

The door at the top of the stairs was jammed ajar with one of her boots but there was no sign of Fizz. The whole scene was decidedly spooky and Buchanan's muscles were tensed as he slid quietly round the door. It was dark inside but he could see a faint line of light under the bedroom door. He edged towards it but almost immediately fell over what was probably the other boot and decided, thereafter, that caution was probably a waste of time. Whoever was in there knew he was coming.

'Fizz?' he said, tapping on the door, and heard a noise from inside that sounded alarmingly like a groan.

She was in bed, lying on her back and lit only by a little lamp on the table beside her.

For the first couple of seconds Buchanan's mind refused to accept that it was her and then realisation hit him like a bus and he burst out, 'Oh my God, no! Oh, Fizz!'

He dropped to his knees beside her and stretched out a hand involuntarily towards her virtually unrecognisable face. He wanted to touch her but there was no place he could rest his fingertips that wasn't bloody or bruised or swollen grotesquely out of shape. He wanted to ask her what had happened but his throat had closed up and speech was beyond him.

Her face! Her baby face! He couldn't handle the thought of a fist — or a monkey wrench? — smashing into her face. What kind of an animal had done this to her?

She turned her head. 'Not looking my prettiest, I take it?' she said, barely moving her lips which were crusted with blood and swollen to twice their normal thickness. 'You should see the other guy.'

'I think I did,' Buchanan said unsteadily. 'He paid me a visit about fifteen minutes ago. I wish I'd killed him!'

'I doubt it was the same guy,' she said, wincing. 'The guy I'm talking about won't be visiting anybody for a day or two; he'll be too busy putting ice packs on his balls.'

'You could do with an ice pack yourself. I'll get you one.'

He went through to the bathroom and ran a handtowel under the cold tap. For a moment he held it to his eyes. It helped the stinging a little but it didn't do a damn thing for the horrors. In the fridge in the kitchen/living room he found an ice tray containing six cubes which he wrapped in the wet towel and took back to her. Afraid to hurt her, he let her apply it herself, which she did with gingerly little dabs.

'I'm going to phone a doctor,' he said.

'No.'

'Don't be silly, Fizz. You need a doctor. You could have broken bones.'

'I loathe doctors — and there's nothing broken.'

'You don't know that.' He hated making her argue when he knew it hurt her to speak but she was obviously in need of more medical care than was currently available. Her face alone needed attention and the bedclothes might be hiding ravages he couldn't even bring himself to ask about. 'I'll get Mark. You don't loathe him.'

She raised no objection to that so, taking the set of keys that was hanging beside the door, he charged down to the call box next to the entrance and punched in his cousin's number. As he waited for him to answer he noticed his car, still sitting in the middle of the road, and still unnoticed by the authorities.

'Mark Buchanan.'

'Mark, it's Tam. Fizz has been badly beaten up. Can you come right away?'

'She's at her own flat?' Mark was never one to waste time on unnecessary conversation. 'OK. I'm on my way. Give me ten minutes.'

Buchanan reparked the car and sprinted back to Fizz.

'He'll be here in ten minutes, Fizz. I'm sure he'll be able to make you feel a lot more comfortable.'

She hadn't moved since he'd been away but, with the extra light spilling into the room from the hallway he could now see the full extent of her injuries and the sight sent a shockwave through him like an electric current.

Both her eyes were blackened and swollen, the left one totally closed, and its lid streaked with blood from a deep cut across her eyebrow. Below the same eye her cheek bone stuck out like an open drawer and livid crimson and purple bruises covered her nose and the side of her mouth. Buchanan had seen similar injuries often enough before, in

312

his rugby days, but never all on the same face, and never on a face so sweet and delicate and soft-skinned. Never on Fizz.

He tried to think what he should be doing for her. Keep her warm? Well, she'd done that for herself. Hot sweet tea? Or nil by mouth till seen by a doctor? Hot water? That was it. He hadn't a clue what it was for but the first thing the doctor always called for in such cases was hot water. He put the kettle on and spent the next ten minutes between it and Fizz, keeping one simmering and stroking the other's hair in helpless anguish.

Mark arrived full of calm assurance, strolling in as though he'd just happened to be passing and felt like a chat. Only a faint shortness of breath betrayed the fact that he'd run up the stairs.

'OK, Tam,' he said, when Buchanan started to babble out the whole story in the hallway. 'I'll just take a look at Fizz first and then we can sit down with a cup of tea and you can give me the background.'

'Right,' Buchanan said, starting to relax a little now that somebody else was in charge. 'I have a kettle of hot water on the boil if you need it.'

'Fine.' Mark nodded approvingly. 'No milk, one sugar.'

He closed the bedroom door behind him,

leaving Buchanan to wander aimlessly around the living room like an expectant father, and it was fifteen minutes before he emerged.

'How is she? Is her nose broken?'

'She's fine,' Mark sighed, lowering himself into the only armchair and taking in the Spartan surroundings at a glance. 'I don't think anything is broken but we'll have her into casualty when the swelling's gone down a bit and do an X-ray. I had to stitch her eyebrow — that'll show, I fear, but not too obviously. We'll see.'

'Can I take her a cup of tea?'

'No, leave her just now, Tam. I think she'll sleep.'

Buchanan made the tea and spent a fruitless few minutes looking for white sugar. Finally he discovered two café packets of demerara sugar in a coffee jar and they made do with that.

'You want to tell me what happened?' Mark suggested, eyeing him with a hint of professional concern, as though he and not Fizz were the patient.

Buchanan did want to tell him, wanted to share the horror with somebody, but halfway through the recital he knew it had been a bad idea. Describing the viciousness of his own attacker and imagining Fizz's experience at the hands of a similar thug suddenly brought the whole thing into perspective and he was swept up in a tidal wave of rage.

He had loathed the very thought of physical violence all his adult life, despised it as a solution to anything, and abhorred the mentality that would stoop to it. But for a long time after Mark had left, as he sat sleepless in the armchair beside Fizz's bed, his soul burned with a consuming desire to have an hour alone with the man who had done this to her.

★   ★   ★

Fizz woke up somewhere around 7 a.m. feeling pretty rough but not as bad as she'd felt on many a January first. Buchanan was stretched out in her armchair with his legs sprawled half across the room and his face arranged in the expression of saintliness that he always wore when unconscious.

She sat up, moving very carefully, and hooked up her T-shirt from the floor on the other side of the bed. It was barely long enough to cover her nakedness but it sufficed to get her as far as the loo and, thereafter, to the airing cupboard where there were clean panties and shorts.

The face she saw in the bathroom mirror was like something out of a horror movie but the sight of it left her virtually untraumatised because she couldn't really think of it as hers. On the contrary, she was rather proud of it. OK, it hurt a bit but getting a mouthful of Doc Marten had to hurt a lot more, particularly when your balls were somewhere under your ribcage.

She was making herself a herb tea when a blue-chinned, shadowy-eyed Buchanan stumbled into the room in a way that reminded her of Lurch in the Addams Family.

'What are you doing up?' he demanded.

'I didn't want to wet the bed.'

'But Mark said you were to stay in bed today till he saw you. You might have concussion.'

'What rubbish,' she said, inserting a sliver of dry bread between her sore lips.

'Please, Fizz. Will you just go back to bed and I'll make you a nice breakfast?' He looked in the fridge. 'Scrambled eggs? You could manage that, couldn't you?'

Fizz didn't usually eat a cooked breakfast and she doubted, moreover, whether Buchanan had the first idea of how to go about cooking one, but she discovered that she was very hungry. She'd missed her dinner last night, which meant she'd eaten nothing since yesterday lunchtime and suddenly the thought of scrambled eggs, even scrambled by Buchanan, sounded almost tempting.

'OK. But I'm getting up later. I've things to do.'

He let that go without an argument, doubtless hoping that Mark would talk her out of it, and started bustling around the stove in a businesslike way that fooled nobody. It took him a good half-hour to produce two tablespoons of watery scrambled eggs on sodden toast, served with the cooling herb tea she'd made herself, and it was difficult for her to regard the offering with the degree of enthusiasm he clearly felt it merited. However, she was inclined to be generous this morning, in return for his unexpected sweetness the night before.

Her expectations of male sympathy were not high, her previous experience of such being largely of the 'would a shag cheer you up?' variety. Buchanan, however, had surprised her with his genuine empathy and, although she had been doing just fine on her own, she had to admit that he'd been a real comfort.

He sat in the armchair and watched her efforts to get food into her mouth without opening her lips more than a quarter of an inch and it didn't help much to have him sitting there wincing and making unconscious mewing noises all the time. She got him started on a summary of his own attack, but that wasn't a good idea because she laughed so much at the thought of Selina wrapped round the attacker's head that she started her lips bleeding again.

'Well, it sure as hell wasn't the same guy,' she told him with absolute certainty. 'And it sure as hell wasn't any of the gerries. Nor was it Boston — not my little playmate anyway, he was half a head taller than Boston.'

'Mmm . . . I think the same could be said of my chappie. He was a lot bigger than Boston all over. Which means, basically, that we're back to the drawing board.'

'Looks like it,' Fizz had to admit, and was immediately depressed by the thought that Buchanan would try his damnedest to keep her wrapped in cotton wool for as long as it took — and that could be weeks. 'Of course, it's possible they were hired thugs,' she added wishfully.

Buchanan considered that but not for long. 'It struck me — if you'll forgive the pun — that the intention was not to kill us but merely to indicate that we should mind our own business. If they'd wanted to kill us they'd have used a gun, not a monkey wrench. Which makes one wonder . . . '

'If it's Mathieson's replacement who's

worried about what we could uncover?' That seemed, to Fizz, to be eminently possible. The attacks were, in fact, just a continuation of Mathieson's actions-speak-louder-than-words technique.

'So,' Buchanan said, scratching his unshaven cheek, 'that would indicate that we're up against the A-team and the smart thing would be to take a long holiday in Samoa and forget the whole business.'

'I couldn't agree more,' Fizz mumbled. 'Except that you're not going to do that. You wouldn't drop Freddie in the shit and neither would I. So where do we go from here?'

'You don't go anywhere, Fizz, not for a few days at least — and, before you start, that's not even open to discussion. I'm going to get a joiner to put a better lock on your door and I'm going to arrange someone to stay with you till — '

'Forget it.' Fizz hauled herself upright. 'I don't share my space with anybody, Buchanan. Not ever. I've had that scene and I didn't like it and I'll never do it again, so forget it!'

He took that badly, if his face was anything to go by, and it usually was. Fizz couldn't see why it was such a big deal because she couldn't imagine who he could induce to move into a flat in the expectation of its being invaded by a toothless thug with a high-pitched voice and poor social skills.

'You can't expect me to leave you here alone, Fizz.'

'I don't expect you to leave me here — full stop! Whither thou goest I will go, and if you want to sleep behind my door with a pair of horse pistols in your hands you're welcome to do so. But, get this clear: as soon as Mark has been and gone I'm out of this bed.'

Buchanan looked at her expressionlessly. He was very pale this morning and there were brownish smudges under his eyes as if he hadn't slept. Fizz saw his hands shaking as he gripped them together on his thighs and suddenly realised that he was fighting with a towering anger.

Without saying anything he got up and left the room, shutting the door very quietly behind him.

17

Buchanan was still in a murderous mood when Mark arrived later in the morning. He couldn't look at Fizz's face without a fireball of rage exploding in his chest and his mind blanking out in a red haze. The anger filled his whole being and leached out in pointless bursts of irritation against inanimate objects, politicians on the radio, dogs barking in the street. Every minor inconvenience weighed on his spirits like a death threat, and Fizz's idiotic recalcitrance — in the face of unarguable common sense — was about as much as he could take.

Mark gave him a hard look as he went into Fizz's bedroom and when he came out again he took hold of Buchanan, who happened to be just outside the door, and drew him into the other room.

'What's up?' Buchanan gasped, his bowels dissolving with alarm. 'She's not — '

'She's fine,' Mark said, combing his fingers distractedly through his untidy hair and making it worse than before. 'There's not a thing wrong with her that won't be cleared up in a week or so. It's you I want to talk about.

321

You're not doing Fizz any good by making such a big production of this. What's got into you, Tam? This is so unlike you. Is there something you haven't told me?'

Buchanan affected a puzzled frown, unwilling to accept that his inner turmoil could be visible, even to Mark. 'What are you on about?'

'Are you scared that something like this will happen again? Is the guy likely to come back?'

'It's possible, but I don't think it likely. I'm pretty sure that all he wanted was to scare her off.'

'So why are you overreacting like this?' Mark propped a hip against the table and waited patiently for the answer Buchanan couldn't give. And went on waiting.

Finally the silence forced him to say. 'Her face . . . if it hadn't been her face . . . '

Mark said nothing, just let the silence go on and on while Buchanan tried to find a palatable excuse for his reactions — palatable not only to Mark but to himself. There didn't seem to be any way he could explain his feelings for Fizz. He could say it wasn't love, but that wasn't true. He did love Fizz, when he wasn't hating her, but in a purely platonic, nonsexual way. Only that wasn't true either. Quite often he fancied her like nobody's business — but God, he fancied anything these days, and it was obvious that the complications arising from that sort of relationship could be quite horrendous for both of them. There was no way to explain what he himself couldn't understand, but Mark was still waiting for an answer and he felt, for some reason, that he had to supply one.

'I knew all along that I should have kept Fizz out of this,' he said. 'She was determined not to stay on the sidelines but, all the same, it's my fault this happened to her.'

Mark surprised him by bursting out laughing. 'You'll never change, will you? Everything's been your fault since your mother's morning sickness.' He stood up, slapping Buchanan on the shoulder. 'But Fizz — don't get me wrong, Tam, I've got a lot of time for Fizz — but she'll do what she damn well chooses to do and neither you nor me nor anybody else will stop her. It's nobody's fault but her own that she got a doing-over last night. She had it coming to her; it was only a matter of time. Maybe this'll teach her a lesson.'

Buchanan knew in his heart that Mark was talking sense, as he usually did, but he also knew that Mark's arguments applied equally to himself. He too had had it coming to him for a long time. Poking one's nose into criminals' business was no part of a solicitor's remit. It was, however, fun. That was his problem and, no doubt, Fizz felt the same way, so had he any right to oppose her?

'I can see how you'd want to safeguard her, when possible,' Mark said on his way out, 'but she has as much right as you have to decide where to draw the line.'

'She won't stay in bed, you know,' Buchanan said, seeing how he liked it.

'I didn't even bother telling her to. She hates being indoors. Take her out in the car this afternoon. She'll be fine.'

As Buchanan was locking the door behind him, Fizz appeared in the bedroom doorway, dressed in T-shirt and shorts. 'I heard that,' she said brightly. 'What do you say we trundle round some of the people on Catriona's little list. We can show them Mathieson's photo, like you said.'

'Fine. Whatever you say.'

She blinked at him in an alarmed manner and headed for the bathroom whence, presently, came the noise of the shower running.

There was something quite liberating in letting her have her own way, Buchanan discovered, but he was also smitten by the suspicion that he had been treating her in a manner closely akin to chauvinism for the last couple of years. She was a responsible adult — well, maybe not responsible, exactly, but she knew what she was doing — but he had been disgracefully autocratic. He felt bad about that; then he felt good about at least having the decency to feel bad about it; then he felt bad about feeling good; then he warmed up a can of tomato soup for lunch.

Fizz was already getting on top of the eating problem and claimed that she was so good at talking without moving her lips that all she needed was a glove puppet. She still had to be in pain but she wasn't going to admit it and she certainly wasn't going to let it keep her indoors. Buchanan was conscious of a few shocked stares as he helped her into the car but Fizz had always enjoyed shocking people and wasn't embarrassed in the least.

Driving at a sedate pace, they went first to the doctors' surgery and then to the church but, at neither location could Buchanan find anyone who recognised Chick Mathieson's photograph.

'OK,' Buchanan said, 'you want to take a run out to Cramond?'

'No, I don't think that's worthwhile,' Fizz demurred. 'There weren't a lot of close neighbours around that one. Let's check out the ones I didn't visit — the out-of-town ones.'

Buchanan consulted the list. There were three out-of-town names: one in Glasgow, one in Dunfermline and one in Juniper Green. Glasgow was out: too far for Fizz to travel today. Dunfermline was about fifteen or twenty miles away, and Juniper Green probably less than five. Working on the premise that Fizz was safer here beside him in the car than she would be at home, Buchanan chose Dunfermline and headed for the Forth Road Bridge.

The address in Dunfermline was, allegedly, that of a Mr C. Charles and turned out to be an impressive stone villa, circa 1900, standing in an avenue of similar houses on the edge of the town. It was fronted by a massive area of lawn, and a long driveway edged with overgrown shrubs and trees curved down one side to a pair of iron gates.

'You'd better stay in the car,' Buchanan said, driving straight up to the front door. 'We don't want to give her nightmares.'

'No point in both of us wasting our energy,' Fizz agreed willingly enough. 'Mr Charles won't even be there.'

And, of course, he wasn't. The name on the door was Wallace.

'Charles? No. No one of that name around

here,' said the stout middle-aged man who answered his ring. 'Sorry I can't help you.'

'Just one other thing,' Buchanan said as he started to retreat. 'Could I ask you to take a look at these photographs and see if you've seen the face before.'

'What is it, George?' said a woman's voice from the depths of the hallway.

George was looking at the photographs and didn't answer but a moment later she appeared at his shoulder, a fat lady with dyed chestnut hair. 'What is it?'

'Chap wants to know if we recognise this man. No.' He raised apologetic eyes to Buchanan. 'I don't think he lives in this street.'

'You've never seen him around?' Buchanan asked as the lady took the photograph from her husband's hand.

'Sorry. I think I'd have remembered him. A face like that — '

'But, George,' interrupted his wife, 'this is one of the men I was telling you about. Remember? The day you were at Bruce's funeral.'

Buchanan took a second to register what she'd said. 'You've seen him before?'

'Yes, I have. I'm sure of it.' She turned impatiently to her husband. 'Don't you remember, George? The men who were selling a camper van out there in the street. I told you about it when you came home. Oh, honestly George, you never listen to a word I say!'

George slid a weary glance at Buchanan, silently enlisting his support in what was evidently an ongoing battle, but Buchanan was wholly on the side of his better half.

'Would you mind telling me what you saw, madam?' He produced a second business card, George having pocketed the first, and handed it to her. 'I'm not at liberty to tell you what it's about but your recollections could be rather important.'

'Certainly,' she said, giving her husband a so-there look. 'There were three of them: this one; a short, stocky one with a broken nose; and a very strange-looking man — very tall and thin with an odd, jerky way of walking.'

Buchanan could scarcely hide his incredulity. 'You got a good look at them?'

'Oh, absolutely. They were just down there outside our gate — well, you can't see the place from here because of the trees, but I was at the end of the garden cutting some greenery for a flower arrangement and I could hear every word they said.'

'Can you remember any of it?'

'Not word for word, no, I don't think so — it was two or three weeks ago, you know.

But they were selling the camper van, I can tell you that. The skinny man was. The other two seemed to be together but it was the big man — this one in the photograph — who was interested in buying it.' She paused, thinking, her fingers to her lips. 'There was something — I can't tell you what, exactly, but they were signing papers — possibly receipts. I think I came back in the house at that point, but I watched them from the window for a while, till they drove off.'

'Did they all leave together?'

'The big man drove away in the van and the smaller man was in a big white car, I'm afraid I didn't note the make — dash! I should have taken the number down, shouldn't I? I didn't notice where the thin man went to — I was back and forward all the time making the tea, you see. I can remember telling you, George, and asking you whether I should have phoned the police.' She looked Buchanan in the eye. 'It was a stolen vehicle, wasn't it?'

'I'm really sorry,' Buchanan repeated, 'I'm not at liberty to talk about the case but what you've told me has been very helpful. Could you, I wonder, give me a description of the camper van?'

'Oh, dear me, I'm not the best person to ask about anything like that.' She thought for a moment. 'It was a nice one, but a good few years old, I would say. Turquoise coloured — quite pale turquoise — duck-egg blue, I suppose you'd call it, and with one of those little jutting out bits with tiny windows above the driver's cabin.'

'A Luton,' said George, and she rolled up her eyes a fraction as though to say, nobody loves a smartass.

'I *knew* they were criminals, I just knew it,' she assured Buchanan. 'That's why I took careful note of their descriptions.'

'Great. You've been enormously helpful.'

'If I can be of any further help . . . ' said George's wife, ducking to peer into the car as Buchanan made his retreat. She could have seen very little, since Fizz had the sun visor down, but she kept trying till he had turned the car and disappeared down the drive.

'You hit pay dirt?' Fizz demanded before he could open his mouth.

'I hit a corner of something worth digging a little deeper for, that's for sure.'

He pulled out on to the quiet road, parked just out of view of the house, and gave her a one-sentence résumé of what he'd learned. It was difficult to tell behind the bruises whether Fizz was excited or not and her muffled diction conveyed nothing.

'Boston and Paul, obviously. Had to be.'

She hitched painfully around in her seat to face him. 'The camper van — it wasn't maroon was it?'

'Maroon? No it was pale turquoise. Why do you ask?'

'Because Nigel has a maroon one. I saw him in the garage with it last night after he came back from his day out with Helen and Miss Moir. A real stonker. More of a mobile home, really. Shiny and new. Must have set him back twenty thou. Minimum.'

Buchanan had enough on his plate without adding that factor into the equation. 'So, what was Paul up to, selling a camper van to Chick Mathieson?'

Fizz shook her curly mane. 'And why was he doing it outside the house of a fictitious person?'

Silence invaded the car. After a while Fizz found a strip of chewing gum in the glove compartment and posted it gently between her lips.

'We'll have to see if anybody living near any of the others on the list remembers either Mathieson or a camper van,' she decided. 'It's the only way we have a chance of turning up some more information.'

Buchanan had already come to that decision. It was not yet three o'clock and Fizz still looked reasonably fresh, and anyway, it was as good a way as any of passing the afternoon. They went first, since it was on their route, to pay a repeat call at the address in Cramond — the vacant site facing out across the Forth — but drew a complete blank with the few neighbours, as Fizz had predicted. Ms S. Foreman of Juniper Green was also a waste of time since her address was occupied by an isolated market garden whose delightful owners claimed to be currently too busy to wipe their noses never mind count the number of bloody camper vans that passed by.

That left only the Glasgow address, and it was beginning to look like Buchanan was going to have to check that one out by himself when Fizz suggested they give the doctors' surgery another go.

'It's on our route and we're not in any particular rush,' she pointed out. 'We may as well see if the mention of a camper van jogs someone's memory.'

Buchanan was willing to give it a try and, for once, persistence paid off.

One of the receptionists, an alert-looking older woman who hadn't been around earlier, listened curiously to his description.

'Funny you should ask that,' she mentioned when the other receptionists had pleaded ignorance. 'I haven't noticed a turquoise camper van about the place but I did see a white one, a couple or three weeks ago, that caught my attention.'

Buchanan leaned on the counter. 'What made it catch your attention?'

She gave the facial equivalent of a shrug. 'It was out there in the car park but the people with it weren't patients. I should have gone out and told them the car park was reserved for patients and staff but it was raining and they weren't there all that long. Less than half an hour. Also, it looked to me that there was money changing hands.'

'Did you get a good look at the driver?' Buchanan asked, not daring to hope.

'Not his face, no. There were two or three people around the van for a while. There was a bald man in a trench coat and ... I couldn't swear to it but I think there was another man — yes, there was! A shorter man, quite thickset. And also an elderly woman in a wheelchair.'

A wheelchair? Buchanan's mind reeled. 'Did you see what they were doing?'

'Not really. I got the impression they were giving the woman money. Then the two men drove off, one of them in a white Merc and the other in the camper. The woman — I think she must have left her car round the back where the doctors park. She went round that way anyway. The cheek some people have. It says quite clearly 'Staff Parking Only' but — oh, why should I bother? It's not my responsibility.'

Buchanan was confident that nothing of his inner turmoil showed in his face, since he could see it in the two-way mirrored doors of the dispensing hatch behind her, but it took him a moment to collect his thoughts and formulate a thank you.

'God, what next?' he said to Fizz as he got back in the car. 'It looks like they're all in this up to their eyebrows. One of the receptionists saw Mathieson, Boston, and *Helen*, of all people, with a *white* camper van this time. The two men drove away in the vehicles, as before, and Helen disappeared round the back of the clinic.'

Fizz found this funny. She started to make ha-ha-*ow*! noises which changed to stifled snorts and then sounds that were new to Buchanan and defied description.

'Shit, Buchanan, I wish you wouldn't make me laugh,' she complained at last.

'What's to laugh at?' He began to start the car and then changed his mind. He needed to think. 'This is terrible. It could mean that we end up getting all those old idiots arrested for murder. Is that something to laugh at? Because if it is I'm missing the joke. There's not one of them could survive two weeks in Saughton.'

'You don't honestly believe they had Mathieson killed, do you?' she said, her pupils skittering like two black beetles along the slits in her eyelids and focusing on his face. 'And sent a couple of thugs to put the frighteners on us? What are you *on*, Buchanan?'

Buchanan was a long way from believing it but stranger things had happened. 'It looks like Boston was an ally of Mathieson's. It must have been Boston he phoned the evening before his murder.'

'No, that can't be right.' Fizz held up a finger to indicate that she was thinking and didn't want to be distracted for a minute. Then she said, 'They had to be pretending to Mathieson that they lived — or worked — at those locations. That long, overgrown drive at Dunfermline . . . It would have been easy for Paul to hang around there unseen, maybe with a spade or a pair of secateurs in his hand, till Mathieson arrived, and then show him the van, which was parked out of view of the house. Same for Helen. Who'd know whether she was a doctor at the practice or not?'

'Boston would know.'

'Right. Which means that Boston is on *their* team — not Mathieson's.' She gave Buchanan one of his own sticks of chewing gum and helped herself to another. 'They were adopting fake identities to sell camper vans to Mathieson. It was Mathieson who was being fooled by the fake list of names — not the other way round. Don't ask me why — and don't ask me where the gerries were getting the mobile homes.'

Those were both questions that had been exercising Buchanan's mind, particularly the second one. If Paul and co. had stolen both vehicles they were in big trouble, maybe thirty thousand pounds worth of trouble. If so, they weren't going to get off with a few weeks' community service.

'And what about the other names on the list?' he said. 'Were they also fake mobile home vendors? That would mean that we're talking about seven vehicles altogether — maybe a hundred thousand pounds worth, maybe even more.'

'And the other five vendors would have to be played by people other than Helen or Paul.' Fizz started to snigger again. 'Like you said, compadre, they're all in it. Oh, God, I love it! The idea of those old devils taking on Edinburgh's Mr Big!'

Buchanan refused to believe that the scheme was some sort of crusade against crime. He was convinced that none of them could have guessed that they were dealing with a shark of Mathieson's magnitude. They weren't that foolish.

'It's one of Paul's crazy games,' he said, hoping he was way off the mark but suspecting somehow that he wasn't. 'It has his fingerprints all over it. Whatever it is they've been up to, it's just the sort of mad thing he'd conceive. No wonder they don't want anybody spilling the beans.'

He leaned his arms on the wheel and tipped his neck from side to side to take the kinks out. He was starting to crave the sleep he'd missed last night and his mind was definitely sluggish.

'It wasn't anything criminal,' Fizz stated positively. 'I don't believe for a minute that they were running a stolen van syndicate. I'll bet you anything you like that it was just a bit of playacting. They'd all love that. What bothers me is that they'd need seven fake owners. Even including Miss Moir — the mind boggles! — they're one short.'

'Boston?' Buchanan wondered.

'Boston drove Mathieson's car away from the address in Dunfermline, and one or other of the vehicles from the clinic. That would put him — ostensibly — on Mathieson's team so he could scarcely pose as an owner as well.' She reached backwards over her shoulder for her seat belt. 'Well, come on, then. If we're going to see the Glasgow one we'd better get on the road.'

'I'd planned to give that one a miss,' Buchanan said firmly. 'An hour to Glasgow and an hour back, and probably another hour finding the place and talking to people. That means it'll be seven o'clock before we get back.'

'So? Do you have a date?'

'No, but you do. With your bed. Mark said — '

'Oh, Mark-schmark! What's the difference between taking to my bed and lounging here? I'll tip the seat back if it makes you any happier.'

'We could leave it till tomorrow,' Buchanan suggested, just so he could tell himself he'd tried.

18

They stopped for coffee at the motorway service station so it was after five when they located the last address on the list: a Mr R. Bryce-Cowan, of The Old Mill, Giffnock Toll.

It was probably a couple of hundred years since there had been toll gates at the crossroads and The Old Mill was no longer an old mill but a bar/restaurant. There were a dozen or so sunshaded tables on the paved forecourt and a large car park at the back, currently almost empty.

Fizz was, by that time, totally bored with being fed second-hand information and decided to sit in on Buchanan's chat with whoever he found to talk to. The headache she'd woken up with had now cleared and she felt a lot less woozy, and besides, there might be a G&T in it if she played her cards right.

'I'm looking for a Mr Bryce-Cowan,' Buchanan told the barman when he brought their drinks, and was about to say something further when the chap straightened and surveyed the virtually empty lounge as if expecting to see someone of that name.

'He doesn't seem to be here yet,' he said,

taking a surreptitious glance at Fizz's face as he set her glass neatly on a paper coaster.

Buchanan said, 'Is he a regular customer?'

'No, not at all, sir.'

'Yet you know him by name?'

The barman smiled politely. 'Only because someone asked for him once before, like you did, sir. It's a name that tends to stick in your mind.'

Buchanan fished a business card out of his wallet and handed it to him. 'I'm trying to locate Mr Bryce-Cowan. Could you tell me when it was you last saw him?'

'Gosh . . . it must be . . . ' He swished his cloth across the spotless table top and stole another peep at Fizz as he searched his memory. 'Two weeks ago at least. About this time of day . . . but we were busy.' Recollection dawned on his face. 'I'll tell you when it was. It was the day before the Celtic/Milan match. The place was full of Italians.'

'And do you remember the person who asked for Mr Bryce-Cowan?'

'I remember one of them: a big, heavy-built guy with a face like — ' Whatever he had been about to say, he suddenly realised that he might be talking to the guy's affectionate brother and changed it to, 'Well, I'd remember his face. Also his head — he was

340

bald as a billiard ball. The other guy . . . no, I can't remember him — but he was quite a bit shorter.'

'What did Mr Bryce-Cowan look like?' Fizz mumbled.

'Uh . . . elderly . . . maybe about seventy, and walked with a stick. What you'd call portly.' He narrowed his eyes and studied the light fitting as though he were searching for a hidden mike. 'Nope, can't recall his face. Sorry.'

'So, how did you know who he was?' she persisted.

He withdrew half a step. There was someone waiting for him at the bar but, as his eyes fell on the fiver Buchanan was sliding out of his wallet, he said, 'He told me, miss. He came up to the bar and said, 'My name's Bryce-Cowan. I'm meeting someone here shortly, so if they ask for me I'll be over there.' Funny thing, though — I've just remembered. It was raining that evening but he didn't have a coat. Or even a jacket. Just a cardigan. And another thing: when he went out with his friends he said to me, 'I'll not be more than fifteen minutes.' I thought he meant for me to keep an eye on his drink, but he didn't come back.'

'You didn't see any of them after that?'

'No. His two pals drove off in a white car

and a flashy maroon mobile home but none of them came back in.'

'You've been very helpful. Thank you,' Buchanan said, slipping him the fiver.

Fizz could barely contain herself till he was out of hearing. '*Maroon!*' she whispered. 'That's *got* to be the one in Nigel's garage. Maroon's not all that common a colour for mobile homes. And the vendor sounds like Anthony, don't you think? He's what you'd call portly.'

Buchanan nodded, beginning at last to look a little amused by the audacity of the escapade. 'That's who I thought of. Sitting in here like mine host, wearing indoor clothes, probably circulating in a proprietorial manner, and telling the staff he wouldn't be long. I must say I like his nerve.'

Fizz lifted her G&T in a toast to the absent cast. 'I bet they enjoyed every minute of it. God, I wish I knew what they were up to. What d'you say we drop in on the way home?'

'You can *not* be serious!' Buchanan choked out, rolling his eyes about like he was looking for somebody to run up with a strait-jacket. 'You're going nowhere on the way home, Fizz. Mark said you could go for a run in the car this afternoon, he didn't say you could do a tour of Scotland till you were dropping on

342

your feet. What do you think he's going to say if he turns up tomorrow to find you've had some sort of a relapse? Huh? For heaven's sake, get some sense! You haven't even had your X-ray yet. There could be something seriously wrong inside you somewhere. Don't even bother to argue with me. You're going straight home and straight to bed.'

'I'll put that down as a 'maybe', then,' Fizz suggested amiably, but he wouldn't look at her.

After a long discussion they came to an equitable agreement. They had a very good meal and a long rest at The Old Mill and only then, when they were both quite rested, proceeded back to Edinburgh and Greenfield House. Why the Arabs and the Israelis couldn't settle their differences with the same proficiency, Fizz couldn't imagine.

It had been a hot day and, the evening being still and pleasant, they expected to find the delinquent oldies in the garden. However, as they got out of the car near the entrance to the block of flats, Paul came out arm in arm with Cheryl. Cheryl saw them instantly and raised a hand to wave, but then she caught sight of Fizz's face and let out a shocked cry, her hand sinking slowly down again as though she had forgotten it.

Paul stopped in his tracks, his head on its

thin neck pecking briefly forward with surprise, and then they both came uncertainly towards them. When they got nearer Fizz could hear Cheryl murmuring, 'Dear me . . . Oh, my goodness . . . '

'My dear Fizz,' Paul said, visibly horrified by what was now The Face Behind The Mask in glorious Technicolor. 'What in heaven's name has happened to you?'

'I was beaten up on my way home last night,' she said, making her voice as severe as she could given present conditions. 'Probably by somebody who knew I was investigating the circumstances surrounding Chick Mathieson's death.'

Cheryl's whole body flinched and her fingers tightened on Paul's arm but she said nothing, and neither — for once — did Paul, who seemed too taken aback to speak.

'You did know that we were acting for the man who has been charged with Mathieson's murder?' Buchanan asked.

'No. No, indeed we didn't.' Paul shook his head vigorously. He was patting Cheryl's arm in a steadying manner but he looked none too steady himself.

'But you did know Chick Mathieson, didn't you?'

Paul was not a good actor and Cheryl wasn't even trying. There was a short silence while they both stared at the ground and then Cheryl lifted her head and looked earnestly into Paul's face. 'Paul — '

'Yes, Cheryl, but just give me a minute . . . I'm thinking.'

'But, Paul — . . . '

'Hush, dear, it's all right.'

'No it isn't,' she said firmly. 'Not when people are being hurt. If we'd trusted these two young people earlier this might not have happened . . . '

Her voice shook on the last word and tears welled in her eyes.

'Don't upset yourself, Cheryl.' Buchanan said in his trust-me-I'm-a-solicitor voice, and gave her his hankie. 'We have a fair idea of the part you and the others played in this business and I suspect Fizz's injuries may have only an indirect connection.' He looked at Paul and said, 'Shall we have a talk about it? All of us . . . including Boston.'

Paul was seriously upset and racked with uncertainty. It took him a moment or two to realise that he had little choice of action. 'Yes . . . I think we must be frank with you. I . . . um . . . ' He turned to look down the garden. 'The others are over there . . . but . . . '

'Miss Moir, Paul,' whispered Cheryl.

'Yes, dear. I'm thinking about Miss Moir.'

He pressed his hands together, probably to stop them trembling, and held Buchanan's eyes for a moment. 'There's no need for Miss Moir to be upset, Tam. She knows nothing about what we did and we wouldn't want her to find out — not like this, at any rate. Will you give us a few minutes to . . . to remove her?'

'Of course,' said Buchanan.

Fizz squinted towards the distant group. 'If that's my grampa with them you could get rid of him too,' she said bluntly. 'If he sees me with a face like a chewed toffee he'll go on all night about how he told me so.'

Paul nodded and led Cheryl away across the grass, both of them looking stooped and unsteady on their feet. Buchanan was transparently consumed with remorse for upsetting them but there were questions that had to be asked and either he and Fizz asked them or the police would.

They watched Paul and Cheryl reach the group and bend over Miss Moir. There was a short conversation, following which both she and Grampa rose, linked arms and started to head back. It wasn't difficult for Fizz and Buchanan to avoid being seen by them, a handy grouping of conifers providing an adequate screen, and as soon as the two old people disappeared into the vestibule Fizz shot off down the garden with an impatient stride. The less time the gerries had to discuss tactics the better and, anyway, she was agog to hear what they had to say.

They were met by a ring of disturbed faces, among them, Fizz was surprised to discover, that of Nigel's daughter, the delectable Lizzie. She had been hidden from sight, as they approached, by an intervening spirea and Buchanan's reaction to seeing her there was really quite funny. Fizz's first thought was that Paul might have had the sense to pack her off with Miss Moir and Grampa. Her second thought was: why hadn't he?

There was a muted outcry from all of them at the sight of Fizz's face. Nigel immediately hauled himself to his feet to offer her his lounger and took an upright chair beside Buchanan.

'Archie is going to ask Boston to join us,' Paul said, sitting on the edge of his seat and rubbing nervous hands up and down his skinny shanks. It was quite sad to see his hitherto irrepressible *joie de vivre* so completely extinguished. 'He shouldn't be more than a couple of minutes but I'd just like to say, on behalf of all of us, that we are very distressed to think we might have caused you to be put in danger. We had absolutely no idea that what we were doing could have serious consequences for anyone else.'

'Absolutely none,' Helen stressed. 'In fact we were quite convinced that none of Mathieson's men knew what had happened. We thought we had got off scot-free. I can't imagine how they could have found out — can you, Lizzie? — but it looks like they'll be coming for us next.'

'No, I don't think that's at all likely, Helen,' Buchanan said soothingly. 'Instant retribution is the rule in Mathieson's organisation. If they'd known about you they wouldn't have waited this long to make an example of you.'

'So, how did you get on to us, Tam?' Lizzie asked, but Boston was, at that point, spotted jogging across the lawn and her question was lost in the general reshuffle to accommodate another chair.

'What's up?' said Boston just as he caught sight of Fizz's face. 'Je-zuz!'

'Yes. That's what's up,' Anthony said gruffly. He was wearing a greenish shirt that brought out the colour of his eyes and a purplish-red silk cravat that brought out the colour of his nose and a yellow straw hat that clashed with both. 'Fizz and Tam are acting for that chap McAuslan who's up for Mathieson's murder. Some thug did this to Fizz last night, maybe to scare her off the investigation. Can't have it. Time we came clean.'

Boston's face was set in a rigid expression of dismay. He closed his eyes for a long second and then muttered hoarsely, 'Be sure your sins will find you out.'

Fizz was inexplicably unsettled by his reaction. He appeared to be taking the news even harder than the gerries, if his clenched face and tightly gripped hands were reliable evidence, and that didn't feel right. He wasn't the nervous type.

'OK. Would someone like to put us in the picture?' Buchanan said. He ran his eyes around the circle of faces but nobody seemed willing to volunteer. 'Paul?'

Paul tried unsuccessfully to pass the buck and then sighed unhappily and ran his tongue round his lips. 'I don't know how much you know about Mathieson, but he was an evil man. A beast.'

Fizz opened her mouth to say they knew that but Buchanan silenced her with a look and that meant they had to sit through the whole story about Boston and his brother.

'And Boston's case was not the only one,' Paul continued earnestly. 'There are other instances of his brutality that Boston could tell you about — horrific beatings, even murders. It has gone on for years — a reign of

349

terror — and the police do nothing.'

He paused and looked at Nigel and Helen but they gave him no support so he rubbed a hand over his bald pate and said, 'February this year he bought the property downstairs from Miss Moir's flat and then set about a campaign to get her — and her two neighbours — to sell their homes to him and move out. I won't go into details but the price he was offering was derisory and would not have been sufficient to allow them to purchase another home in any area other than a slum. Miss Moir was not well-to-do and, although she had planned for some time to move into Greenfield House, she couldn't afford a flat here unless she sold her home at the market value. She was very frightened of Mathieson and desperate to move but no one else would buy the flat — not with Mathieson throwing rubbish and stink bombs into the entry and damaging the door, et cetera — and if she accepted Mathieson's offer she would be eighteen thousand pounds short of the Greenfield asking price.'

'It was insupportable!' Helen burst out, startling everybody. 'The brute had already frightened off both her neighbours — two elderly couples who had no one to back them up — and he was hounding Miss Moir into her grave. Nothing she could prove, of course, but constant harassment. So we decided to take the eighteen-thousand-pound shortfall from Mathieson.'

'Only the eighteen thousand she needed,' Cheryl put in, still sniffling intermittently into Buchanan's hankie. 'That barely brought Mathieson's offer up to the market value but it was all that was necessary.'

No one seemed willing to carry on from there and after a minute Buchanan had to say, 'So, how did you plan to do that?'

Nigel took that one, clearing his throat nervously before he spoke. 'Paul's original plan was to sell him my mobile home — that was the only thing we had that was worth that sort of money — and somehow take it back from him afterwards. We knew how to get false papers from an old van in a breaker's yard — and we were confident that Anthony would be able to do any sleight of hand that was needed to substitute them for the originals if need be — but we couldn't be sure that Mathieson would want to buy the van in the first place. We had to think of a way of making him want it.'

'That's where Boston and I came in,' said Lizzie. She wasn't half as good-looking as she had appeared at the party. She had gone very pale and the blusher under her cheekbones stood out like someone had slapped her

351

round the chops. 'Boston knew Mathieson better than all of us and he knew how his mind worked so, between us we worked out a way to get him hooked.'

She looked across at Boston, giving him the chance to take up the narrative from there, but Boston had his eyes on the ground and didn't raise them. It looked to Fizz as though he was making a determined effort to avoid being drawn into the conversation, which was in direct contrast to the others who were now beginning to perk up.

'It was a brilliant plan,' Helen claimed, her face alight with enthusiasm. 'And Mathieson never suspected a thing. He really wasn't a very intelligent person, you know. Not at all intelligent, I would say. Goodness knows how he came to be such a godfather.'

'So?' said Fizz to the arch-plotter.

'So . . . ' Lizzie said, returning her look with a big helping of ice, 'we worked out a way of making him think he could make a large amount of money virtually overnight. This meant arranging for him to see Boston behind the wheel of a very expensive mobile home. Fortunately, Nigel is well known at Hetherington's, the firm he bought his own vehicle from, and he was able to take one out for a test drive.' She looked again at Boston and when he didn't raise his head, she said, 'I think you should tell this bit, Boston.'

He straightened and lit a cigarette, inhaling deeply before he started to speak. 'OK, so he comes up to me and he says, 'Well now, you've come into money, have you? So you can fork out the rest of the cash you still owe me.' And I says, 'No, Chick, this isn't my van, I'm just doing a job for Hetherington's.' He says, 'What sort of job's that, then?' and I tell him I can't talk about it because it's all very hush-hush, which makes him prick up his ears and come on real heavy. Then I let it out that Mr Hetherington, the managing director, is desperate to get back seven vans that he sold recently and I'm going round, seeing the owners, and repossessing the vans. He wants to know why Hetherington is so keen to get them back and I say I don't know but I'm to tell the owners that there's some suspicion that they might have been stolen and they can have their money back plus a hundred and fifty pounds off a replacement purchase. He also gets it out of me that I'm getting two hundred down plus two hundred for every success.'

He paused to draw on his cigarette but still didn't make eye contact with anyone. None of the others moved. They must all have heard this before but they were still listening as though totally engrossed.

'Mathieson smells a rat, of course. One stolen van is a possibility but not seven of them. So he knows right away that if Hetherington is willing to pay three hundred and fifty a time to get them back there's something wrong with these vans, so he's probably open to blackmail. Mathieson, as long as I knew him, was a greedy bast — beggar. He'd stop to pick up a penny on the pavement, so I knew he'd go for it. Next thing I know he's hopping up into the passenger seat beside me and saying. 'Right, this looks like a two-man job. Let's see that list of names.' I tell him I've already repossessed the ones in Inverleith and Cramond, and that the one we're sitting in is on its way back to Hetherington's from Juniper Green, so there's only four left to do. So he comes with me to Hetherington's to take the van into the forecourt and I try to get him to wait there but he insists on coming in with me, like we knew he would.' He raised his eyes, just for a second. 'Nigel was waiting for us inside.'

'I was, of course, playing the part of Hetherington,' Nigel said, as all eyes swung, as one, in his direction. 'I had been in conversation with the real Mr Hetherington in his office, which was a glass-partitioned area of the salesroom in full view from the doorway. When Cheryl, who was keeping watch, signalled me that Mathieson and Boston were on their way in, I cut short my business with Mr Hetherington and walked to the door with him where we stood chatting long enough for Boston to point us out to Mathieson. Then Cheryl, posing as my secretary, intercepted them.'

Cheryl had been waiting on tenterhooks for her cue. Her tears were gone without trace and her face was alight, and had shed about fifteen years, as she took up the tale.

'I put a blonde rinse in my hair for the part,' she announced. 'And I wore — '

'Never mind what you wore!' Anthony exclaimed. 'That's got nothing to do with it.'

'I am trying, Anthony, to indicate that I looked younger,' Cheryl returned with spirit. 'I would have had to, wouldn't I? Anyway ... I said, 'Mr Hetherington says he'll see you outside, Mr Boston. We've had a terrible time with that reporter from the *Evening News* hanging round again, trying to talk to the mechanics, so he doesn't want to be seen talking to you. If you can wait for him by the van you just brought in, he'll be only a few moments.' Mathieson was pretending he wasn't with Boston at that point. He was standing looking at a display of wing mirrors but I made sure he heard what was said.'

Every head then swung, with Wimbledon precision, back to Boston, who nodded, drew a long sigh and said, 'Chick wants to know what the press are doing, snooping around, but I tell him I haven't a clue. We go back to the mobile home and he hides in the toilet cubicle while Nigel comes out and gives me my two hundred quid and the cheques for the two vendors I've to see that afternoon. He also tells me not to talk to this press reporter who has got his teeth into some rubbish that was in the *Evening News* last Friday and is trying to get evidence for a big exposé in the weekend papers. He says it's all lies and has nothing to do with him but you can't trust the press not to make things up for the sake of a story. He says he's so keen to keep any hint of scandal from damaging the firm's reputation that he's willing to pay whatever it takes to get the vans back. He says that if any of the owners refuse to part with them I can keep upping the discount offer till they cave in. No limit — 'even if it's a free bloody van.' And I say, OK.'

He trod out the stub of his cigarette and lit another one, during which operation Helen lost her patience and continued for him.

'Mathieson knew of course that the answer to the mystery of Hetherington's motive must lie in that evening paper, so he rushed round to the *Scotsman* and *Evening News* office, taking Boston with him, and found the story that had inspired Lizzie to come up with the plan in the first place. This was — '

'The story of an explosion in a camper van in Aberlady,' Fizz suddenly remembered aloud, bringing the eyes swinging round to her in collective surprise. 'Caused by a nonprofessional gas installation, according to the *Evening News*.'

'That's right,' Lizzie said, still eyeing her curiously and getting used to the idea that there might be a brain under all that hair. 'Gas installations in mobile homes and camper vans are supposed to be done by certified fitters but some people who do on-the-cheap conversions employ cowboy fitters who'll do it for a fraction of the price. Of course, if they're found out the penalties are severe and if, for instance, Hetherington had been exposed as someone operating on that level he'd have been out of business.'

Even Fizz, who had never been and never expected to be in the market for a camper van, was familiar with Hetherington's. It wasn't one of your back street, railway arches type of operations. It occupied a prime site close to the centre of the city and its prestigious chrome and glass frontage had been a landmark since Fizz had first come to

357

school in Edinburgh. It was hard to imagine such an established firm being involved in cut-price conversions but if they had been, and were caught out, the effect on business would have been on a devastating scale.

'That explains how both your list and the relevant page of the *Evening News* happened to be in Mathieson's coat pocket,' Buchanan said placidly, any feelings he may have had about the ethics of the scheme hidden behind his usual professional mask. 'So then, I imagine you took Mathieson round the last four people on your list and pretended to repossess vehicles from them. We already know that Paul played Mr C. Charles of Dunfermline, Helen was Dr J. Robinson of Comely Bank, and Anthony was the genial host of The Old Mill at Giffnock Toll. That much we have already established. Which leaves Mrs P. Whittock of Prestonfield, alias . . . you, Lizzie?'

She said nothing, just gulped a bit and made a defeated sort of gesture with her hands. Fizz was inclined to sympathise with her quite a lot. At least she'd had the guts to play an active part in her own battle plan.

Her father gave her a concerned look and said, 'We simply picked a house that was up for sale and currently unoccupied. Most estate agents are perfectly willing to give you a key and let you look the place over by yourself, particularly if you've already viewed it in the company of an employee, as we had. We picked one that was still partly furnished, added a few small items of our own, and had Mathieson in and out again inside half an hour. Boston's pitch was that he had made preliminary calls on the Prestonfield and Comely Bank vendors and explained the problem to them, so it was merely a matter of exchanging the documents and handing over the cheque and discount voucher.'

'Where were you getting the vans?' Fizz asked, since Buchanan was skating around the question like he didn't want to hear the answer.

'Test drives,' Nigel said, smiling a little. 'All of them from Hetherington's. We only needed three of them because the last one, the one we used for the sting, was my own.'

'Ah yes. The sting.' Buchanan smiled back at him encouragingly. 'I'm all ears.'

There was a brief interval while they all looked at one another uncertainly, leading Fizz to suspect that the fun bit was over and the criminal part was about to begin. Finally, Paul appeared to draw the short straw.

'All that action — everything we've told you so far — happened on the Thursday afternoon,' he said in a voice that sounded uncharacteristically flat in the absence of his usual facetiousness. 'The following morning I met Boston and Mathieson outside a house in Dunfermline — you evidently know about that — and our business was completed without a hitch. We had planned the itinerary so that the last call — to The Old Mill — could not be made till quite late on the Friday afternoon and we used Nigel's van, partly because it was the most expensive of the lot — he paid Hetherington's twenty thousand for it — and partly because, if anything went wrong, we actually owned the van and couldn't be accused of anything.'

'You weren't worried that Mathieson might have examined the other documents too closely?' Buchanan asked.

'Mathieson only got a glimpse of the documents,' Boston put in. He had got his head together a bit while the others had been talking and was now at last able to look them in the eye. 'I did all the business, checking the documents, signing exchange papers, handing over the cheques. All Mathieson did was observe the setup — and relieve me of my bonus at the end of the day. He didn't doubt that everything was genuine. He'd seen 'Hetherington' in his office and heard him talking to me and, anyway, he wasn't interested in the actual repossession deals, he had his eye on the big money he would squeeze out of Hetherington once he had his hands on the last vehicle. He knew that Hetherington had to get all the 'dubious' vans back in his possession before the story broke on the Saturday and he knew that he'd be willing to pay big bucks for the last one. He reckoned he could just about ask what he liked — as long as he had the van in his own hands.'

'Anthony had — of all of us — the most difficult part to play,' Helen stated, with such pride that it was clear she'd had a hand in directing him. 'He had to — Well, you tell them, Anthony.'

Anthony, under the unexpected barrage of interest, responded with an aubergine-tinted flush and spent a moment wondering where to start. 'Well, when Boston and Mathieson turned up about four in the afternoon I pretended to be the owner of the place, strutting about and giving orders to the barman, that sort of thing, and took them straight outside to the car park. Cheryl was hiding close by the back door, in a red wig and glasses, so that she could re-establish my identity by shouting across to me that there was a phone call for me and I could say I'd call them back. We needed Mathieson to be confident I was genuine but, in any case, he was too excited to be suspicious. Couldn't get the deal closed fast enough. Went bananas when it turned out that the cheque wasn't signed. Lost the place a bit.'

'The cheque wasn't signed?' Fizz heard herself mutter but nobody took any notice of her.

'Pandemonium. Mathieson cursing and blaming Boston. Ball up on the slates. Too late to drive back to Edinburgh and get another cheque till after the weekend. Then Boston said, would I be happy to accept cash? Certainly would. Boston says to Mathieson he could pay it himself and get the money back from Hetherington on Monday. But Mathieson says he'd have to go to his own bank and there isn't even a branch of it any closer than Falkirk and even that would be closed in another twenty minutes. Paced up and down for a bit, went back to his car and came back with eighteen thousand in cash. Had it on him, by God, like Boston swore he would! Didn't even have to go to the bank for it!'

Anthony's exuberance got the better of him for a moment and induced a bout of wheezy coughing, but he was making too much noise for anyone to seize the baton and he was soon able to say, 'Handed over cash, 'pon which yours truly swopped the genuine papers for the fake ones and off he went in the van, Boston following in the Mercedes.'

Buchanan had been following all this very closely, his chin on his fist and his eyes switching between Anthony and Boston. Now he said, 'Very clever. Well thought out. But how did you get the van back from Mathieson?'

'Simple,' said Boston. 'As soon as he parks it in the forecourt and goes into Hetherington's, which is on the point of closing when we get there, I leave the Merc at the pavement and simply drive the van away using our own set of keys. Mathieson has only an envelope full of dummy papers to prove he'd paid for it, the Mr Hetherington he saw the day before is not the one that's there now, and if he tries to trace Mr Bryce-Cowan or any of the other vendors he'll draw a blank. God, I wish I could have seen his face when he realised he'd been shafted!'

'Meanwhile,' Helen crowed happily, 'or to be accurate, a week before, Miss Moir had sold him her flat and moved to her new home here with us. We made her think the extra money had come from a charity known only to Paul but actually we gambled three thousand pounds each to give her the money in advance. Now we have our money back, our dear Miss Moir is settled and happy, and, quite coincidentally, her persecutor is no longer around to bully anyone else. If that's not a happy ending, I don't know what is!'

Fizz glanced across at Buchanan but his face showed none of the dissatisfaction she herself was feeling. There was something missing, she was sure. Something Boston and Lizzie had omitted to consider. Given peace to think for a couple of minutes she'd pin it down.

Buchanan said, 'That's it, then?' and was answered with a chorus of nods.

Then, into the silence that followed, Boston muttered, 'Um . . . not quite.'

19

Buchanan caught Fizz's bright flash of understanding and gave her a faint nod. The two of them seemed to be the only people not stunned by Boston's remark, which spread alarm and despondency through every one of the conspirators. It was something of a relief to Buchanan to see that Lizzie was just as shocked as the others, since her implication in this crazy plot had been causing him some disquiet.

She at least, however, must have wondered at the dubious promptness with which Mathieson's murder followed on the heels of her carefully orchestrated confidence trick because she said, 'My God, Boston! What have you done?'

'Nothing!' Boston said quickly, jumping up out of his seat as though he felt trapped in it. 'I didn't kill him. I wanted to — I've wanted to see him dead for years — but I didn't kill him.'

He put a hand to his head and jammed the other into his pocket and started to pace up and down, four jerky paces one way and four the other, while his fellow sinners watched him tensely, evidently fearing the worst. After a minute he stopped, lit a cigarette, and gripped the back of his chair.

'I wanted him dead,' he said again, directing his remarks largely towards the gerries. 'I might have had a go at him right after he crippled my brother but I . . . I was crazy then and . . . and anyway he's not easy to get at. Afterwards . . . all I wanted was to find a way to pay him back. I tracked down a few of the other traders he'd been bleeding dry, like I told you, and I talked to people who drank in the Cally Bar, and I made friends in the casino, and I hung around his shop, and I waited my chance.'

He paused to draw on his cigarette and thought for a moment, not looking at anybody. It was so quiet that Buchanan could hear bees buzzing in a lilac bush ten feet away.

'Anyway, I never learned anything I could make use of but, over the years, I started to get a feeling about Mathieson. He was a dark horse. You could never find anybody who knew much about him. It was always Kennedy who did the talking and even he only said what he had to say and then shut up. But I kept my ears open, picked up a crumb here and a crumb there, and after a while the crumbs started to add up and suddenly I'm thinking, this Mathieson — he isn't such a master crook, in fact, some of the things he's done make him look like a bit of a thicko. So after a while I start to think, if he's as dumb as I think he is, how come he's Mr Big? And then, I find out about the shop and the student flats and I think, how come he's wasting his time with tuppenny-ha'penny stuff like that?'

Buchanan already knew how come. He had been edging towards the conclusion for a couple of days but it was only when Boston started talking that the truth hit him smack in mid pupil. He glanced at Fizz, directly across from him, but she was staring at Boston as though she was in a hypnotic trance, her swollen lips apart and her slitted eyes unblinking.

Boston looked at his audience for a long moment. 'After a while I was pretty sure that there had to be a Mr *Bigger* and that Mathieson was nothing but a front man. Somebody had set him up with a fancy house and a fancy car and all the gear to go with it — gold jewellery, cashmere overcoats — but all he did was draw the heat away from his boss — and beat people up. He really liked that.'

A corner of Boston's mouth curled up in a smile. 'Trouble was, he started to believe his own cover story and tried to be a Mr Big in his own right. I reckon he can't have been all that successful because there were stories about him getting credit at the casino, leaning on people for money before it was due, et cetera. All his flashy lifestyle must have been paid for by Mr Bigger because all the signs say the money he gave Miss Moir for her flat just about cleared him out. He'd had a disastrous night at the casino and had another the following week, and it looked to me like he was scared stiff about it. He was trying to sell his shop and his car and he was trying to get in outstanding cash from anyone he could — and we're talking about a hundred quid here and fifty quid there. The guy was desperate. I reckon the casino is another of Mr Bigger's enterprises and Mathieson was scared of getting caught out.'

Lizzie nodded unhappily. 'I see now why you were so confident that Mathieson would go for the blackmail scenario. He must have thought all his prayers had been answered at the eleventh hour.'

'He was very happy the last two days of his life,' Fizz told the congregation, her eyes, what was visible of them, shining with the satisfaction of getting to the truth at last. 'His wife said so, and so did Freddie. Now we know why. All his worries were over. At least he died happy.'

'I doubt that,' Boston said with quiet satisfaction. 'People who rip off Mr Bigger don't usually fade peacefully away.'

'He was ripping off his boss?' Nigel exclaimed 'He must have been mad!'

'No, just desperate.' Boston walked round his seat and sat down. 'You see, what I didn't tell you was that I knew Mathieson didn't *have* the eighteen thousand he needed to buy the van. He didn't have eighteen *hundred*. All he had was the week's takings from Mr Bigger's business interests — the money he was taking, together with what Kennedy had collected, to the bank.'

'*WHAAAT?*' Anthony roared, displaying a large collection of amalgam fillings. 'You made him use his boss's money? He wouldn't dare! He must have known he'd be crucified!'

'Think about the odds,' Boston said, leaning forward with his elbows on his knees. 'He was totally certain that Hetherington would pay whatever he asked for the final van, so in effect, he was only borrowing the cash for about an hour and a half and would still be able to bank the full amount at the usual time. Weigh that against the trouble he'd be in if Mr Bigger found out how deep in debt to the casino he'd got himself. In any case, he was a gambler at heart. He'd have gone for the quick profit even if he hadn't been desperate.'

'So, in fact,' Lizzie said, still looking seriously worried, 'when he realised he'd been set up he had no option but to make a run for it. He had no way of paying back the money to Mr Bigger and he must have known what kind of retribution he was facing.'

'You know what he did, don't you?' Fizz asked Boston, who nodded. The others clearly didn't know, however, so she prattled on, 'He headed for Dunbar because he knew he'd need money to disappear and he knew he could get it — in the form of heroin — from a dealer there. He shot the dealer and was probably planning on stealing his boat to make his getaway but I reckon that's where Mr Bigger's men caught up with him.'

'Unlucky for him they got on to him so quickly,' Paul remarked.

'Well, no,' said Boston. 'Not unlucky.'

Heads turned to him in a taut silence and then Anthony barked, 'Tipped 'em off, did you?'

'Yes.' Boston's eyes locked with Lizzie's and he grimaced in what looked very like apology. 'I had to, Lizzie. I knew it would never have worked the way we planned it. Even if Mathieson had got clean away he'd never have let me live after what I'd done to him. What I said about going to London — I'm sorry but that was never on the cards. I trailed Mathieson till I saw which way he was headed and then phoned the Cally Bar. By that time Mathieson was well overdue at the bank and I knew that Mr Bigger would be looking for him at the Cally, where he and Kennedy met up every Friday evening. Kennedy knew no more than anybody else about any Mr Bigger so all I told him was that Mathieson was heading south on the coast road. He didn't know what to make of the message but, according to some of my friends, he soon found out. He was hustled out by a couple of heavies less than five minutes later, which meant that Mathieson didn't have much of a head start.'

Buchanan found he had slouched down in his chair till his feet were almost in Fizz's lap. He sat up and crossed his legs and said, 'You knew, then, that he was headed for Dunbar?'

'No. I didn't know about the drug dealer,' Boston admitted, intimating with a twisted smile and a nervously waggled hand that he'd made a serious mistake there. 'I knew Chick would need getaway money because there can't have been more than a few grand left of his collection money and I'd expected him to solve that problem by meeting Kennedy and

371

relieving him of his collection as well. I don't know why he didn't — maybe he was after the boat, as Fizz said — maybe he was scared they'd already be looking for him at the pub. It could even be that he'd had that particular bolt hole in mind for a rainy day. But it didn't make a lot of difference in the end. He's dead and Mr Bigger doesn't know he was set up. Mission accomplished.'

What he was failing to take into consideration, Buchanan reflected, was that the con trick that he and his associates had perpetrated was a criminal act, the penalty for which, depending on the mood of the bench, could be extremely severe. Evidently nobody present dreamed for a moment that either Fizz or Buchanan would shop them to the police, and they were right, but it was difficult to see how Freddie could be cleared without some of the story leaking out.

'Thank you for being so frank with us,' he said to all of them. The strain of the conversation was showing on all their faces, and both Cheryl and Anthony looked like they'd taken just about as much as was good for them. 'I'm glad, for the sake of your peace of mind if for nothing else, that we've at least established that your actions weren't to blame for Fizz's beating last night. Evidently we have Mr Bigger to thank for that, so my advice to you is to forget you ever knew Chick Mathieson and put the whole matter behind you. You can rest assured that we'll both do our utmost to keep your story a secret.'

Fizz was positively not wanting to leave and indicated irritably that she had still questions to ask but it was visible to Buchanan that she was as burned out as the rest of them and he let her see there would be no discussion about it. She could come now or walk.

Part of his impatience — a small but insistent part — stemmed from the fact that he didn't know what to say to Lizzie. He was more concerned than he would have expected by the discovery that she was not only implicated in a criminal act, but had actually co-masterminded it. The fact branded her as a loose cannon of an even larger calibre than Fizz, who had certainly broken the law before, but never — thank God! — had she been an accessory to someone's murder and — whatever he had just told them — Lizzie and her little gang of swindlers certainly were.

She came up to him as the others were taking sympathetic leave of Fizz and said quietly, 'I can't tell you how sorry I am that I ever got mixed up in this thing. Paul had already sold my father and the rest of them on the idea of attempting his own wild scheme — which would probably have landed them all in serious trouble — and since they were bent on doing *something* to help Miss Moir, all Boston and I could do was come up with an alternative.'

Buchanan looked away. 'It's a bad business, Lizzie. I can't deny it.'

'Will it . . . will it make a difference to us, Tam?'

He wasn't going to lie to her but when he turned back and saw that her eyes were full of tears he hedged a little. 'I don't know.'

'Will you phone me?'

He touched her cheek. 'Probably not.'

★   ★   ★

'You know, of course, that none of this is going to let Freddie off the hook?' Fizz said as they headed back to the car. 'Even if we go to the CID with the whole story — which is totally unthinkable anyway — we don't have a scrap of proof that Freddie wasn't the hit man. Everybody knows he was working for the organisation — Mr Big or Mr Bigger, it makes no difference.'

Buchanan appeared infinitely depressed. He hadn't been looking wonderfully vivacious all day, now that she came to think of it, but he was definitely pretty pissed off now. He walked on a bit in silence, his eyes on the grass and his hands in his pockets.

'The fact is, Fizz,' he said bitterly, kicking a toadstool into touch, 'we're back at square one. We've wasted too much time on side issues, we haven't a clue who Mr Bigger might be, and we haven't a single lead to work on.'

'Well, we might not have a clue who Mr Bigger is but he sure knows who we are because who else would have arranged to have us beaten up? That must be a clue of sorts, right? How many people knew we were investigating the case?'

'Enough,' he grunted. 'We haven't exactly been keeping a low profile, especially as it turns out that the casino might be owned by Mr Bigger. The place is probably heaving with his subordinates.'

'Well, what about those two geeks who attacked us?' Fizz insisted, unwilling to admit defeat. 'I bet we could track them down — maybe at the casino, maybe at the Cally Bar. I don't know about your one but I reckon it would take more than a touch of make-up to disguise what I did to mine. Any guy over six feet, short of a few front teeth and walking funny would be worth keeping an eye on.'

Buchanan tried to look hopeful but made a hash of it. 'The trouble is, we really have to move more carefully from now on. Hanging around the Cally Bar and the casino would be asking for trouble.'

'OK, so we watch from outside,' Fizz said, with stubborn buoyancy. 'We have to keep moving forward and that's the only line to follow.'

'Maybe Catriona could come up with something.' Buchanan walked round the car to the driver's door and then paused, looking thoughtfully at her across the roof. 'She wasn't aware that Mathieson had a boss. It's possible that, when we tell her there's a Mr Bigger in the background, she could make a guess at putting a name to him or at least pointing us in the right direction. There had to be a fairly regular communication between Mathieson and Mr Bigger. Who did he see or talk to every other day?'

'Kennedy?' Fizz suggested but even she knew that was a daft idea. Mathieson had punched Kennedy at least twice, according to Freddie McAuslan — and lived.

Buchanan sprung the locks on the car and got in. 'I'll have to go and have another word with Catriona. She's the only one who can give us a lead.'

'Not tonight,' Fizz groaned, slumping into

her seat. 'I'm whacked.'

'Not ever, as far as you're concerned,' said Buchanan. 'There's no need for us both to talk to her. You're going to have at least a morning in bed tomorrow and we're both of us going to keep out of the public eye as much as we possibly can. If I can get Mark to come and sit with you for an hour sometime tomorrow I'll pop over and see Catriona by myself; if not, I'll phone her.'

Fizz didn't feel able to argue with that strategy. She was pretty sure that Catriona responded to a woman-to-woman approach better than she responded to Buchanan, who made her skittish, but the thought of a morning in bed outweighed all other considerations. The headache that had troubled her earlier was now beginning to thump again and the thought of climbing the one hundred stairs to her flat was one she didn't care to dwell on at any length.

Buchanan, when it came to the bit, half carried her up to the top landing with an arm around her waist and a constant litany of reproach and self-recrimination for letting her get so tired. He served her a supper of hummus on toast and then dashed out to phone Mark and to arrange for a neighbour to feed Selina.

'If the doorbell rings, don't answer,' he

said, at the door. 'It won't be me — I've got your keys — and it won't be Mark and you're not at home to anybody else. OK?'

'Bet your sweet ass,' said Fizz, turned over, and fell asleep.

20

It was still broad daylight outside, Buchanan noticed as he hurried down the stairs. From the window on the top landing he could see across the rooftops to Calton Hill and, beyond, to small chips of sapphire that were glimpses of the Firth of Forth.

His watch said twenty-five to ten, which meant that he had a long evening ahead of him, with Fizz asleep and neither TV nor reading material in the flat. A newspaper and maybe a bottle of Glenmorangie wouldn't go amiss, he was thinking when he reached the lower door and saw Mark through the glass, just lifting a hand to ring the bell.

'I'm glad to see you,' Buchanan said, grinning, his first thoughts being that he'd at least have some company for an hour or two. 'I was just dashing out to give you a bell.'

'Nothing wrong, I hope?' Mark, as usual, looked as if he'd just been run over by a road sweeper. There was iodine, or something similar, on his shirt, the knot of his tie had slipped down past his collar button, and his hair was well past its cut-by date.

'No, Fizz is fine. She did too much today

— you know what she's like — but she's back in bed now and I think she'll sleep.' Buchanan handed him Fizz's door keys. 'Go on up. I've got a lot to tell you but first I have to phone and get a neighbour to feed Selina, and I may pop into the off licence on my way back. Won't be a minute.'

'So you were just phoning me for a chat?' Mark said, looking at him strangely.

Buchanan had to force himself to stop rushing. 'No . . . I wanted to ask you if you'd sit with Fizz for an hour or so tomorrow so that I can go and question someone.'

'Sorry, tomorrow's out. How about Thursday?'

'Out? You can't be out all day,' Buchanan objected.

'I'm afraid I can, Tam. In-service training. A two-day course in Perth. But I'll be back by late afternoon on Thursday.'

Buchanan slapped the door frame in irritation. There was no way he would leave Fizz on her own but he couldn't think of anyone else he could ask to sit with her. At the same time, the longer this case took him to bring to a conclusion, the longer Fizz — and he — would be in danger. He took another look at his watch. Nine forty. Still not too late to call on Catriona.

'Mark, can you hang around for an hour?

There's someone I really must talk to as soon as possible. I can be back by ten thirty if need be.'

Mark jiggled the door keys. 'OK. Ten thirty. But I can't stay longer than that, Tam. There's a home confinement that could run into trouble and if I'm called out I'll have to go.'

'Ten thirty. You got it.'

Luckily he'd managed to park reasonably close by, for once, so he was in the car and moving in seconds, zigzagging through the sluggish evening traffic in a reckless way that probably didn't save him more than a few seconds overall.

There were lamps glowing in the downstairs rooms of Catriona's house and, as Buchanan pulled into the driveway, he could see Sam's Astra parked down the side of the house. This gave him a moment's pause but he decided not to let it deter him. Catriona had probably told Sam everything that was going on so she wouldn't be inhibited by her presence and, in any case, who could tell what little tidbits of information Sam might be able to offer?

Neither of them appeared at all nettled at having their tête-à-tête interrupted. They cleared a space for him among the magazines and fashion catalogues that littered the couch and tried to insist that he should have something to drink even if it were only a tonic water.

'No, really. Thanks all the same but this is just a flying visit,' Buchanan told them. 'I just wanted to bring you up to speed with what's been happening and see if it might set you thinking along different lines.'

'My goodness, you do keep ferreting away, Tam, I'll say that for you,' Catriona said with a noisy laugh. She had manifestly been drinking quite a bit and her eyes were ever so slightly out of focus. 'What have you turned up now?'

'Just that your husband wasn't Mr Big.' Buchanan said, not wasting any time beating about the bush. 'It appears he was nothing but a front man for someone who had a lot more irons in the fire.'

Catriona and Sam looked at him with identical expressions of astonishment. Catriona's bottom lip drooped lifelessly, giving her a gormless appearance. It took her several seconds to mutter, 'But the police said . . . the CID man told me they'd been on to him for some time.'

Buchanan nodded. 'I dare say they have, but the reason he wasn't arrested was almost certainly that they were hoping he'd lead them to his boss. Chick had one or two little scams of his own but his was a very small operation. His main function — the occupation that paid for your lavish lifestyle — was merely to divert attention from the real Mr Big. Unfortunately, Chick tried to dip his hand in the till and Mr Big had him killed.'

Catriona took that news badly. The hand that held her drink started to shake so much that some of the gin slopped out on to her white skirt. 'I don't understand. First he's a crook . . . then he's working for one . . . How did you find this out?'

'I haven't time to go into all that tonight, Catriona. I have to get back. Fizz was attacked outside her home last night and she was badly beaten up so I want to get back to her as soon as I can.'

'Oh, how dreadful!' One of Sam's hands fluttered upwards as if to ward off the words. 'I hope she wasn't badly hurt?'

Buchanan had to spend a few precious minutes reassuring them that Fizz would pull through, then he got back to business. 'The thing is, Catriona, Chick must have been in regular contact with his boss, either by phone or in person. Can you think of anybody — however unlikely — that he saw every day, or even every other day? Anybody at all.'

Catriona's brain was not at present firing on all cylinders and the large gargle of gin she put away before answering didn't help matters any. 'How do I know who he saw? He was out of here by nine every morning and came back when he felt like it.' She hauled herself out of her chair, walked with careful steps to the drinks table and topped up her glass with neat gin. 'He almost never asked friends here and when he did I was expected to disappear. Business. Nothing to do with me. Phone? Oh, he phoned people all right. He was never off the phone but God knows who he was calling. I never heard him say anything worth remembering. Jesus! I am so sick of this bloody business! I wish I could just turn my back on it and get on with my life!'

Sam looked up at her as she walked back to her seat. Her plump face looked concerned for her friend but she said firmly, 'The sooner they catch who did this to Chick the sooner you can put it all behind you. Try to think, my darling. What about that chap Kennedy? I only saw him once but, I'll be honest with you, I didn't like the look of him.'

'No, not Kennedy,' Buchanan told her. 'We've already eliminated him.'

'Well, what about that man we saw him with a couple of months back — that day we went to the Living Earth exhibition?' Sam leaned across to lay a hand on Catriona's wrist and gave her a little shake, which barely roused her from the alcoholic trance she was slipping into.

'What? Who? I don't remember seeing Chick with anyone.'

'Oh Catriona, don't be provoking, my darling. They were getting into a taxi as we drove into the car park. Surely you remember? A tough-looking man in jeans.'

Catriona blinked dazedly, looking deep into her gin as though it were a crystal ball.

'Any idea who that could have been, Catriona?' Buchanan said crisply, trying to penetrate her awareness. 'A tough-looking man in jeans? Ever seen him before or since?'

Catriona lifted her eyebrows. Her lids didn't come with them, however, but stayed at half-mast over her bleary eyes. 'Search me. I don't even remember the Dynam . . . mammnic earth. Sorry . . . ' A wide grin illuminated her haggard face. 'Sorry . . . I'm pissed.'

Sam and Buchanan exchanged smiles.

'What about you, Sam? Can you remember anything more about this guy? Tall or short? The colour of his hair?'

'Catriona had a better view of him than I did, I'm afraid.' Her brow puckered as she thought back. 'I'd say he was about medium height and quite thickset but — honestly — I couldn't say whether he was dark or fair. All I remember is thinking he was an odd sort of bloke for Chick to be getting into a taxi with.'

'And this was a couple of months back?'

'About that. I'm sorry, but I couldn't even make a guess at the exact date.'

Buchanan's thoughts were irresistibly drawn to Boston but, obviously, the description was much too vague to carry any weight. He checked his watch and got to his feet. 'I'll try to come back tomorrow,' he said, abandoning a lost cause. 'If I can't call round I'll phone sometime in the afternoon.'

Catriona, whose head had now developed an Eeyore-like droop, answered only with a royal wave but Sam stood up and walked with him to the door.

'I'll make sure she gets the message when she's in a more receptive frame of mind,' she said gently, and added, 'You mustn't blame her for drinking a little too much. I know she doesn't like to admit it but she was really crazy about Chick. I always wondered why. He bullied her abominably, you know, but she forgave him. Time after time, she forgave the brute, and now she's devastated, poor darling. Totally wrecked.'

Buchanan muttered something trite and escaped into the blue twilight as fast as he could. He still had fifteen minutes to get back to the High Street, which was plenty as long as he didn't get held up. He could have done it in ten if he hadn't got stuck with a police car on his back bumper all the way to the town centre but, as things turned out, it was dead on ten thirty as he turned into the High Street. Of course, there wasn't a parking place to be seen in either direction and it took him precious minutes before he found a space in a quiet backwater called High School Yards. Parking regulations were tough there, which meant he'd have to move the car before the parking attendants came on duty at eight thirty in the morning or risk having it towed away, but right now that was the least of his worries.

He found Mark waiting for him at Fizz's door, a touch frosty perhaps, but at least not yet summoned to his home confinement. He didn't hang around to hear the latest news, merely suggesting that Fizz should have an X-ray as soon as possible, just to make sure all was well, before clattering away down the concrete stairway like the delivery of a ton of coal.

Buchanan locked the door behind him, latching the Yale, turning the key in the lock and fixing the safety chain. Fizz was sleeping soundly on her back with her arms flung wide so there was nothing to do but to get a blanket out of the airing cupboard, throw the cushions from the armchair on to the floor and try to get some sleep.

When consciousness returned Fizz was sitting at the table in her shorts eating a kiwi fruit with a teaspoon as you'd eat a boiled egg. Her face had gone yellow in patches but the swelling had diminished and she was able to move her lips as she said, 'I was beginning to think you'd died in your sleep.'

Buchanan was incapable of conversation that early in the morning. He put an arm over his eyes and tried to retreat into the warm haze from which he had just emerged, but he couldn't quite make it. Images of Fizz in her shorts kept insinuating themselves between his eyes and his eyelids, and a faint but insistent voice kept asking what it would feel like to wake up every day to the sight of her brown thighs and the sun turning her hair to a golden halo.

Finally he had to get up and go for a slash while he still could and it was only when he was splashing water on his face that it occurred to him to look at his watch.

'Bloody hell!' he yelled, so loud that Fizz ran into the hall to ask what was the matter.

'It's bloody ten to eleven!' He galloped back through to the living room and started throwing his clothes on. 'The bloody car will be gone by this time! How the hell did I sleep so long?'

He took the stairs in a series of suicidal leaps and sprinted the length of Blackfriars Street, running in the gutter to avoid the window shoppers. Fifty paces away from High School Yards he knew he was too late. He could hear the high-pitched peeping of a backing lorry and, as he turned the corner, he saw the Edinburgh Council tow truck just sliding its lifting bars under the Saab.

'*Hey!*' He lifted his arm to wave and had taken two paces forward when there was one godawful explosion and he was flung backwards into the oncoming traffic.

⋆   ⋆   ⋆

Fizz had just sliced the top off her second kiwi fruit when the doorbell rang. She knew perfectly well that it was Buchanan — he had probably forgotten his car keys in all his rush — but she fastened all the door locks before she pressed the button on the entryphone.

'Yo.'

'Fizz? Is that you? It's Catriona.'

'Catriona?' A buzz of alarm and suspicion zipped through Fizz's chest like an electric shock. How did Catriona know where to find her? What the hell did she want? Whose side was she actually on?

'I just met Tam and he said to come on up.'

That seemed possible but Fizz was taking no chances. 'He'll be back in a couple of minutes, Catriona. He's just gone to move the car, he'll let you in when he gets back.'

'Can't *you* let me in, Fizz? I'm really, really scared standing out here.'

She did sound scared, Fizz realised. She also sounded like she was crying.

'Scared of what?'

'I . . . I know who did it, Fizz. I know who Mr Big is and I know why he killed Chick . . . but I think he might be on to me and . . . oh, God, Fizz! . . . please let me in!'

Fizz's head was a battleground of conflicting emotions. She simply could not bring herself to believe that Catriona could be dangerous and she was haunted by the images — from countless B-movies — of the informant being bumped off before managing to pass on the vital information, but she knew it would be silly to let Catriona in. Had her windows faced in the right direction she could have kept an eye on Catriona for the few minutes it would take Buchanan to return but even that would not save her from a hidden gunman.

'Why are you doing this, Fizz?' Catriona was sobbing openly now and the shake in her voice sounded totally genuine. 'For God's sake don't keep me standing out here!'

It suddenly occurred to Fizz that she could let Catriona into the staircase where she would at least have some degree of protection. Even that appeared, in her present state of nervousness, to be taking a bit of a risk but she knew she was just being foolish.

'OK,' she said, pressing the release switch. 'Come in. But I can't let you into the flat until Buchanan comes back.'

She could hear Catriona's steps echoing up the stairwell, interspersed with the sort of racking sobs that are really hard to fake. There was absolutely nothing to be afraid of but all the same she found herself sweating ice cubes while she waited for the steps to reach the top flat. Catriona — or anybody else, for that matter — would have a hard job kicking the door down but, nevertheless, she took the precaution of arming herself with a pair of scissors which happened to be lying on the hall table. What she thought she was going to do with them she'd have found it hard to say but she felt Buchanan would have approved.

As soon as Catriona appeared in the area covered by the fish-eye spyhole she knew the tears were authentic. The woman was not only distressed, she was terrified out of her skull. It was quite spooky to see the well-groomed, composed Catriona standing there with mascara from eyebrow to cheek-bone, mouth contorting, nose running, chin juddering and eyes that stared back at her with naked despair.

'Don't let them get me, Fizz . . . Dear God, I've never been so . . . ' Her lids dropped over her eyes, leaving a narrow white line at the bottom. 'Uh . . . I . . . I'm going to faint . . . '

Her face lurched towards the spyhole till it was all nose and, all at once Fizz realised she was being neurotic. She unlooped the chain, turned the key in the lock and unfastened the Yale.

As she pulled open the door there was a dull popping noise and Catriona fell forward into her arms with such force that Fizz staggered backwards and collapsed, with Catriona on top of her, and only narrowly avoided kebabbing both of them on the scissors.

The impact as her already bruised head hit the floor left her stunned. The first thing to impinge on her awareness was Catriona's face above her, blood dripping from her nose, and two mascara-blotched eyes staring, half-open, into her own. Suddenly, just as she registered what she was looking at, the face disappeared and Catriona rolled off her, falling against the hall table which keeled over on top of them both.

'Get up!' said another face, taking the place of Catriona's. 'Come on, move it.'

Fizz moved it, encouraged by the sight of a pistol aimed at her chest from a range of only a few feet. She was upright and clinging to the wall by the time she grasped that Catriona was dead and the person holding the gun was her pal Sam.

The pistol waved her towards the still open door. 'Let's go.'

'Where — '

'Keep your mouth shut and do exactly what I tell you or you'll get a bullet in the back.' Sam backed out on to the landing and jerked her head at the stairs, indicating that Fizz should precede her. 'Don't think I'm bluffing. There's a silencer on this gun. Now move your arse.'

Fizz stumbled blindly down the stairs, still too stunned to get her head round what was happening. She found the scissors clamped in her hand and had the savvy to hold them under her T-shirt while she tried to think what to do. Buchanan would be back at any second but Sam was setting a brisk pace and there was no certainty that he would be in time to do anything constructive.

'Are you taking me hostage?' she asked at

the foot of the stairs.

'That's right, kid.' Sam's smile glittered like sunlight on broken glass. She looked taller and slimmer than the frumpy housewife in Catriona's back garden and she wasn't nearly so lovable. 'Play your cards right and I might let you live. Now move it.'

They were in the street only for a matter of seconds. Fizz had prepared herself to catch someone's eye and communicate — by facial expression, thought transmission or the sheer force of her desperation — that help was needed. But would a single sod look at her? No way! They stared in shop windows or up at the medieval tenements or downhill to Holyrood House or uphill to the Castle or across to St Giles Cathedral but not for a moment did a single glance drift her way.

Sam halted at the entrance for a good look in both directions and, as she did so, Fizz had the brilliant idea of cutting off a lock of her hair and dropping it unobtrusively at her feet as a message for Buchanan. It wouldn't tell him much, other than that she had been alive and sentient when she left the scene, but it complied with what she thought of as her old family motto: do *something* even if it's *anything*. The idea of leaving a trail of hair clippings held a certain appeal, so she quickly hacked off another lock and held it in her clenched fist while, with the other, she tucked the scissors into the waistband of her shorts and pulled her T-shirt over them.

She had expected to be hustled into a car at the kerb but instead Sam herded her only a few paces along the pavement to the next entry, North Gray's Close, which formed a sloping pedestrian walkway joining the High Street to the street below. At the foot of the close, pulled up on to the pavement inside the lower entry, stood Catriona's blue Toyota.

There was not a single possibility of effecting an escape. On each side of the close, tenement walls towered six storeys above them, and lower down, where the car was parked, scrub bushes and ivy arched across the walkway from a piece of waste ground, forming an effective screen from the windows above.

When Sam unlocked the boot and waved the gun at her Fizz had no option but to climb inside. As she did so she heard the dull thump of an explosion followed by a cacophony of car horns and squealing brakes.

21

It seemed to Buchanan that his legs were running before he even hit the ground. It was certainly true that as he was charging back up to the High Street he could still hear brakes screeching and bumpers clashing and horns blowing behind him. The Saab was a thing of the past, as were the two blokes who had been preparing to tow it away, but he knew, even as he picked himself up, that Fizz was unquestionably next on Mr Bigger's hit list so this was no time to be hanging around.

Blackfriars Street was a torrent of running people, all going in the opposite direction, yelling into mobile phones, brandishing video cameras, and telling each other it was the IRA. Buchanan went through them like he was going for a touchdown at Murrayfield, unaware that it wasn't sweat but blood that was running down the back of his neck and gluing his shirt to his spine. His own injuries were the last thing on his mind but as he slalomed through the High Street traffic he was assailed by a crippling dizziness that made him stagger against the wall at the entrance to Fizz's flat.

For several heartbeats his brain refused to accept the significance of the nine-inch lock of curling gold hair that was lying in the shadows behind the wrought-iron gate. His feet were twitching with the need to keep on running but he stood there stupidly, staring down at it, waiting for what seemed like seconds before his head cleared.

Hair — Fizz's — there where it shouldn't be — where it *wasn't* less than ten minutes ago — Christ! They'd got her!

He knew instantly that he was right and that it would be a waste of time to climb up to the flat. He spun round, looking for her in the throng of people who had congregated at the end of Blackfriars Street, from where a column of black smoke could be seen writhing up between the buildings in High School Yards. She couldn't possibly have been gone for more than three or four minutes, and the traffic was jammed solid, so she was probably not far away.

Pushing himself away from the wall, he bent down and picked up the lock of hair — impossible to leave it lying there in the dust — and started running up and down the lines of trapped cars, checking out the drivers and peering into the back seats. He was too frightened to think. A faint, vulnerable voice somewhere in a detached part of his brain was pleading with the God he didn't believe in, promising any quid pro quo accessible to the imagination if he could just get Fizz out of this alive, but all his concentration was focused like a laser beam on finding some trace of her among the shocked faces that stared back at him.

It must have been barely five minutes after the explosion when he spotted a young constable he knew running up the road through the stationary cars. He didn't know the chap's name but he'd said good morning to him outside the High Court on many an occasion and he felt optimistic that the copper would recognise him.

'Hey! Hang on a sec,' he said, nipping smartly across to get in his way.

'Mr Buchanan! Sorry, sir, but there's — '

'I know, it was my car,' Buchanan told him, taking a firm grip on his arm. 'Two men have been killed and if we want to prevent anybody else biting the dust I've got to speak to DI Ian Fleming of B Division right away. Right away, understand? Can you get him for me?'

The constable swept him with an appraising glance, missing nothing of his unshaven chin, sockless feet, blood-soaked shirt and no doubt crazed expression, and decided that the occasion demanded an unconventional interpretation of the rules.

'Just a moment, sir.'

He tipped his radio and rattled off his request. Buchanan watched him tensely, drumming his fingers on the top of a convenient Mitsubishi whose driver glared at him unnoticed through the side window. He knew that Ian Fleming had not been assigned to Mathieson's murder. However, the murder wasn't the only crime Mr Bigger was wanted for and if Ian got the credit for bringing him to justice the resulting kudos would wipe from his mind any residual bitterness resulting from their last encounter. Finally the constable passed across the mobile.

'Ian?'

'What the hell now, Buchanan? You involved with this exploding car?'

'Yes, but that's not the problem,' Buchanan said tersely. 'I need you to get here right away. Fizz — '

'Not me, Tam. I've got my hands full right now what with — '

'Ian, listen, I've got your Mr Big for you — not Chick Mathieson — his boss. He just had my car blown up and he's probably now making a run for it. He has taken Fizz hostage and — '

'Jesus! I might have guessed it was Fizz!'

Buchanan stuck a finger in his free ear. 'You . . . what?'

'Never mind. I'll tell you when I see you. Where exactly are you? OK, don't move and I'll pick you up in five minutes.'

Buchanan returned the phone to the constable, who resumed his sprint down Blackfriars Street as the wail of fire engines and police cars swelled over the sound of the clearing traffic jam.

Suddenly he found his legs were shaking. He lurched across to a pavement café whose patrons had moved away from the tables for a better view of the disaster area, leaving their fish and chips cooling on the plates, and used some paper napkins moistened with vinegar to remove some of the blood and grime from his person. Two young waitresses watched him, big-eyed, through the plate-glass window and a minute later one of them appeared with a mug of coffee in her hand.

'Were you hurt in the explosion? You look as if you need a hot, sweet drink. That's what the first aid manuals tell you to do for shock.' She took his hand and wrapped his fingers around the mug, staring into his face with real concern. 'Your head is cut open quite deeply at the back. Why don't you sit down and I'll call a doctor?'

Sitting down struck Buchanan as good advice and he took it, refusing medical attention on the grounds that a friend was picking him up, and cradling his warm mug till the girl reminded him to drink the coffee while it was hot. It helped, just a little, to fill the yawning crater just under his ribcage, a crater caused not by hunger but by fear of what might be happening to Fizz. He couldn't begin to think who might have taken her or where they might be going but he knew that the time for individual action was past and he needed help.

Fleming arrived, not in his dirty black Polo but in a police car with a blue light flashing on the roof. That mention of Chick Mathieson's boss had concentrated his mind wonderfully. There was another guy with him, whom he introduced as DC Adams, a freckle-faced redhead with green, accusing eyes. Buchanan disliked him on sight.

'Ian, we have to — '

'Sit down, Tam. There's no place to go right now.' Fleming kicked a chair back from the table and dropped into it and Adams did likewise.

'But Fizz — '

'Yes, we know about Fizz. She was bundled into the boot of a blue Toyota at the foot of North Gray's Close.'

'You know? You knew about it when I phoned you?'

'We didn't know it was Fizz,' Fleming said with an unpleasant smile, 'but who else would it be? If you were to run a poll in Edinburgh on 'Who would you most like to bundle into a car boot?' she'd be number one. I've got the road patrols keeping an eye out for it.'

'How did you find out?' Buchanan had to ask. He wanted to be on his feet, running somewhere, punching somebody, but what happened next was Fleming's call.

'Someone rang the station,' Adams said, in an offensive nasal whine that went with his face. 'One of the waiters in the Carlton Hotel was having a fly smoke in the boiler room in the basement, blowing the smoke out through a grating. He saw the whole thing and phoned 999. Unfortunately, he couldn't make out the licence plate.'

'But she was alive?'

'Yep.'

Buchanan drew the first deep breath he'd taken since his car exploded. 'So he saw the guy who — '

'Not a guy, Mr Buchanan. An ordinary, respectable-looking woman in last year's Festival T-shirt. So you got that wrong, I'm afraid. It wasn't your Mr Big.'

The shock hit Buchanan like a tsunami. Sam? *Sam?* She was the last person he would have suspected . . . but then . . . if she'd been less discreet the CID would have been on to her long ago. No doubt her close friendship with Catriona had been merely a cover for her frequent meetings with Mathieson, and since his death it had made it easier for her to keep track of what Fizz and he had been doing.

'We've known for a long time that Chick Mathieson wasn't the top dog,' Adams said, unable to keep the sneer out of his voice. 'He was only a front man, just one of half a dozen front men the real Mr Big employed: one for the drug business, one for the protection racket; one for the brothels and pornography et cetera. That's why we let him run.'

'Well, now you know who Mr Big really is,' Buchanan told him, smiling very politely. 'Her name is Samantha Phillips. She found out the day before yesterday that Fizz and I were making inquiries pertaining to the murder of Chick Mathieson and she arranged to have us 'discouraged' by a pair of thugs that same night. The blue Toyota you say she's driving is no doubt the one I've seen at Catriona Mathieson's house so you can trace the number that way.'

Adams got on his radio right away, snapping out his request for the number trace with unnecessary rudeness. While they waited Fleming pulled a skipped cap out of

403

his pocket and put it on, probably to protect his balding pate from the sun.

'How sure are you that this woman is the top dog?' he said, the intensity of his stare betraying the fact that he was hoping for the biggest bust of his career.

'I'm certain,' Buchanan told him. 'She was the only person Mathieson was in contact with virtually every day. I couldn't prove that but she knew last night that I was close to it and that's why she decided to disappear for a while till the heat died down like she did after Chick Mathieson's murder. She'd only just returned from that trip when we met her but she must feel more endangered this time because she's taken a hostage.'

He realised abruptly that Fleming wasn't listening to him; his attention appeared to be fixed on another blue-flashing police vehicle that was parked a couple of hundred yards up the road, just — Buchanan realised with a jolt of apprehension — outside the entrance to Fizz's flat.

He leaped to his feet, knocking over an empty chair behind him, but a blinding wave of dizziness made him stagger.

'Find out what's going on there, Adams,' Fleming snapped, grabbing Buchanan by the wrist and pulling him back down. 'For God's sake, Tam, take it easy. You ought to be used to Fizz's débâcles by this time. We'll get her back, don't worry.'

It would have taken more than a few kind words to calm Buchanan down. He felt as though he were clamped in a vice so tightly that every drop of blood was squeezed from his body. This was what it felt like to be a victim: degraded, impotent, a worthless, empty shell. He probably looked pretty rough too, he realised, because the young waitress came out and offered him a clean napkin dampened with hot water and what smelled like Dettol.

Fleming smiled up at her with his usual appreciation of female pulchritude and ordered more coffee and a plateful of sandwiches. As they arrived Adams came loping back down the street, still talking on his radio.

'Got the car number, sir. It's being passed to the patrols. And the incident up at Baillie Fyffe's Close — it's a shooting in the top flat. A tall auburn-haired woman in her forties. Shot in the chest.'

'Catriona,' Buchanan said, beginning to feel he'd had just about as much unwelcome news as he could handle all at once. 'Chick Mathieson's wife.'

'Dead?' Fleming barked.

'No, sir. She's pretty bad but there's a

405

doctor with her now and an ambulance on the way.'

'Well, that's something Ms Sam Phillips will have to answer for, at any rate,' Fleming remarked. 'And, with a bit of luck, Mathieson's widow might help us to pin the other charges on her as well. God knows we've amassed enough evidence against Mr Big over the past couple of years, some of it's got to fit Phillips.'

He opened a sandwich to inspect the filling but just as he lifted it to his mouth his radio said, 'Bravo sierra zero four.'

'Fleming here . . . Yes — oh, bloody great! Where? . . . Uh-huh . . . Yes, I know it . . . Right. Keep me posted.' He was already on his feet and striding towards the car, the sandwich in his free hand. 'Right, let's go. She's swapped cars. Dumped the Toyota just past the Maybury roundabout, which means she's headed west.'

Buchanan staggered after him, weighed down by despair. 'You mean, we've lost them?'

'For the moment,' Fleming said, snapping on his siren and U-turning with comforting speed. 'But we'll pick them up again. All the patrols have their description and Fizz is fairly unmistakable.'

Buchanan tried not to notice it but Fleming's assurances had a hollow sound.

★ ★ ★

When the Toyota swung to an abrupt halt
Fizz was convinced that Sam had heard her
mucking around with the lock of the boot.
She had discovered that she could locate the
screws that held it — by touch, there being
no light at all in there — and had been
working away at them with a blade of the
scissors. She'd hardly made any impression
on them at all, which was just as well because
otherwise Sam might have noticed something
when, after a pause of three or four minutes,
she threw up the door.

'Out!' She was a woman of few words but
her cold eyes didn't invite argument.

Fizz crawled forth, assisted by a painful
yank from bitch-features, and stood there
with her heart going like a Catherine wheel,
rubbing the blood back into her cramped
thighs. The Toyota was parked close to some
bushes by the gateway to a field, only a few
hundred metres from the main Glasgow road.
The Mayfield roundabout was right behind
them, therefore the airport was only a few
minutes' drive away. Fizz had wondered if
Sam was heading for the airport but now she
felt pretty confident she must be going
further than that, otherwise why change cars
now?

'Move!'

Behind the Toyota, only a few paces away, stood a dirty grey car with the engine running. The driver's window was broken and there were deep gouges around the handle of the boot. Evidently Sam was no amateur.

She didn't get near enough for Fizz to swing a kick at her and the muzzle of the gun pointed unwaveringly at the centre of her chest. Obviously, going for the heroic option would not be a good idea, which was just as well because Fizz had never felt less heroic in her life. She'd been shit-scared once or twice before but this was something else. This bitch had no intention of letting her live beyond her use-by date and the only real chance Fizz would have, when it came to the bit, would be to rush her with the scissors. She'd take a bullet somewhere about her body while she did it, of course, but at least she'd have a small chance of surviving, which was better than zilch.

Sam's eyes didn't even flicker as she opened the boot of their new conveyance and chivvied Fizz inside. She could have been looking at an inanimate object instead of at a person.

The interior of the Toyota boot had been cramped and uncomfortable but this one was foul. It smelled of petrol and wet dog, and it was littered with rubbish and bits of clothing and other things Fizz didn't even want to identify. When the car lurched into motion everything hurtled about in a maelstrom that made her feel like a soup ingredient in a food processor.

She tried to follow the swing of the car to left and right in the hope that she could estimate where they were going but it was only when their speed picked up that she began to suspect they had joined on to the motorway. If she was right the chances were they were heading towards Glasgow, which was good news inasmuch as it meant she had another hour to live, there being nothing of interest between here and there.

The car accelerated round a bend, setting everything in motion again, and as she pushed rubbish away from her face Fizz's hand came into contact with something that made her heart flutter. She brought up her other hand and fiddled with it and was rewarded with a blinding beam of light. It was a small black bicycle lamp, something that could easily have passed unnoticed by Sam but, just possibly, could mean the difference between life and death to someone with a pair of scissors and an hour to spare.

An hour later, however, she was still

working on the screws that held the lock of the boot and even an optimistic estimate would have set a completion date of at least another hour, or even sometime next week if some of the screws were jammed.

★ ★ ★

Fleming strolled back from behind the hedge, where he had gone for a slash, and joined the crowd around the Honda. There were now seven of them in the party, including the two policemen whose patrol car had been first on the scene, and Mr and Mrs Kendrick whose Ford Granada had been stolen.

'This country is going straight down the plughole,' Mr Kendrick was telling everybody else. He was a small elderly man with almost no hair and his face was, at present, unhealthily flooded with colour. 'You can't walk on the pavements without treading in dog shit, you can't shut an eye on a Saturday night for students' bloody parties, you can't move in town without being accosted by beggars, you get no service in shops, you can't find a number in the phone book, and you can't even leave your car on a farm track for half an hour to walk the dog without some scum of the earth making off with it! Why doesn't anything *work* any more? Hmm? Can you tell me that? Why is there never a policeman around to hear the racket at three o'clock in the morning? Why isn't something done about dogs? I'd poison the lot of them, I don't mind telling you — not the dogs, the owners. And what — '

Fleming took Buchanan by the arm and drew him back to the police car. 'Take the weight off your feet, Tam. You may feel you're making things move faster by pacing up and down but, take my word for it, all you're doing is wearing yourself out.' He walked round the front of the car and got behind the driving wheel. 'You must have taken quite a whack on the head in that explosion. If you had any sense you'd bugger off back home and leave us to get on with things, you realise that, don't you? It's not as if you're likely to make a lot of difference to the outcome one way or another.'

Nobody knew that better than Buchanan. He felt totally helpless and it was driving him mad. His thoughts were so focused on Fizz that he couldn't speak, couldn't take in what Fleming was saying, couldn't think about anything but how to reach her. They had been stranded there beside the abandoned Toyota for three-quarters of an hour, waiting and praying for a report from one of the road patrols to say they'd sighted the grey

Granada, with two women in it alive and well. Buchanan had been in the position of worrying about Fizz before — and it was vaguely comforting to remember how often and how pointlessly — but this time she was up against real evil, of a calibre that beggared the imagination. There was no way Sam would let her live — she knew too much — and right now nobody could guess where they might be headed.

'Fizz won't be sitting around waiting to be rescued, that's for sure,' Fleming said, fingering the lock of hair he'd found in the boot of the Toyota. 'Say what you like about her, she's as tough as they come and she's got her head screwed on the right way.'

'Yeah, right,' Buchanan returned. 'And who was it blowing his top at her, last Christmas outside the National Gallery? I seem to remember your last words to her being about the high probability of her ending up in a drawer with a label on her toe.'

Fleming looked uncomfortable for a moment, as though sobered by the thought that those words might indeed prove to be his last to Fizz. Then he smiled. 'Well *her* last word to *me* was 'off!'.'

The sound of his call sign on the radio riveted them both.

'Fleming . . . OK . . . Right, I'm with you

412

. . . No, don't intercept till I get there, just stay with them. You've alerted Strathclyde? Right. Keep in contact.'

He started the engine and pulled forward, giving Adams barely time to dive into the back seat. 'The car's been spotted outside Barrhead, travelling south.'

'Is Fizz in it?' Buchanan asked, keeping his voice level.

'If she is, she's in the boot.'

'So where are they headed?' Adams said, leaning an arm on the back of Buchanan's seat and directing his nasal whine straight at his eardrum. 'Prestwick airport? Or the Irish ferry?'

'Could be either,' Fleming supposed, making a beeline for the M6. 'We'll know soon enough. Take a look at the road map, Adams, and see where the roads diverge — it should be somewhere around Irvine.'

'Why would she head for Prestwick airport?' Buchanan objected. 'It's no safer than Edinburgh or Glasgow and it'll take her another hour to get there. She'd just be putting herself in unnecessary danger. The Irish ferry is a different kettle of fish entirely. It's a safer way of getting out of the country and probably worth the longer journey.'

Fleming zapped past a row of stationary cars and took the next roundabout at a speed that tilted all three of them sideways in their seats. 'That's a point. We could alert the RUC but if she has good proof of a fake identity and plenty of time to change her appearance she won't be easy to pick up. Find out when the next ferry leaves, Adams.'

Buchanan had never before travelled at such speed on the public highway and his sense of urgency was appeased, to some extent, by the wail of the siren and the sight of traffic pulling into the side to let them pass. They were south of Glasgow before the radio spoke again.

The grey Ford Granada had left the motorway suddenly and the patrol had lost sight of them in the maze of suburban streets beyond the exit.

★ ★ ★

The temperature inside the boot had been rising steadily for the past hour or more and Fizz now felt that she could fry an egg on her forehead. When they had been speeding down the motorway it had been bad enough but now that they were crawling along at a snail's pace and stopping, presumably at traffic lights, every few minutes, it felt as though she was being roasted alive.

Sweat was sticking her bare legs together

414

and dripping off the end of her nose, and every inch of tubing from her throat to her duodenum was parched to the consistency of Ryvita. Added to that discomfort was a fiendish pain at the nape of her neck caused by the angle at which she had to hold her head to be able to work at the lock. She already had four screws loosened and there were only two more to go but both tips of the scissors blades were getting very blunt and weren't fitting the slots in the screws as well as they'd done at the beginning.

One thing she had plenty of, however, and that was motivation. She had only the vaguest idea of what the time might be — she wasn't even sure what time she'd got up that morning — but she was pretty sure that Buchanan must have returned to the flat a couple of hours ago at least, so surely somebody was looking for her by now. In reality, that wan assurance meant very little because the last place they'd think to look for her was in a car boot. However, it was all she had to hang on to.

The movement of the car told her that Sam was in a hurry. There were long periods when they trundled along, probably doing no more than thirty, but these were followed by short spells of sixty or seventy, during which she was flung from side to side as if Sam were overtaking dangerously or nipping in and out of slow-moving traffic. Fortunately for Fizz's lock breaking activities, the slow spells accounted for at least eighty per cent of their travelling time, making it a little easier to keep the scissors blade fitted in to the screw.

She had the last screw half out when Sam put her foot down and kept it down. After the first couple of minutes a sense of increased urgency transmitted itself to Fizz's brain — something in the sustained speed, the reckless cornering, the tirade of enraged car horns in their wake — and she knew in her bones that it boded her no good. Either Sam knew she was in danger or they were nearing her goal. Possibly both.

All she could do was hold on for dear life, thankful only that her cramped conditions prevented her from being thrown more than a few inches in each direction. When the brakes were suddenly applied, squashing her relentlessly against the boot lid, she knew she had only seconds left to get the boot open.

Unscrewing the final screw that held the boot lock was out of the question so, in a fierce burst of desperation, she wedged it in the V of the scissors and levered with all her strength. She couldn't believe it when it shot out like a bullet, both it and the scissors hitting her in the face, and the boot sprang open. Without giving herself time to bottle out she grabbed the rim of the opening and flipped herself over.

The first thing she saw was that she was in the car park of a ferry terminal, the same one she'd passed through on the way to Arran last year with Buchanan. There was no sign of the Arran boat but there was another white ferry further along the dock that looked as though it was just getting ready to pull out. The rails were lined with brightly dressed passengers watching the casting-off and waving goodbye to people on the wharf, calling to each other over the din of the churning engines.

In the same split second, as she spun round and dived for the sanctuary of the packed rows of vehicles, she saw Sam sprinting away from her, hampered by the weight of a small black suitcase. There was nothing between her and the ferry except a seaman who was cranking the gangway away from the ship's side. As Fizz watched in helpless frustration, the sailor tried to stem Sam's rush but was struck in the chest by the heavy suitcase and thrown to the ground. In seconds she had scrambled to the top of the gangway where, ignoring the shocked stares of the other passengers, she half clambered, half fell across the metal gate at the top and disappeared into the throng.

'*Stop her!*' Fizz knew it was futile to stand there screaming like a banshee. No one could hear her over the sound of the churning engines and by the time she could talk anyone into doing something the ferry would be halfway to Ireland and Sam, if she were as practised a crook as she appeared to be, would be indistinguishable among the hundreds of other passengers. It was five years since Fizz had worked in Northern Ireland but she imagined that it was probably just as easy now for a resourceful criminal to sneak past the RUC as it had been then.

She started, nonetheless, to hobble towards the wharf, totally unable to accept that the whole damn shooting match was going down the loo. Bad enough that neither she nor Buchanan had been able to finger the real Mr Big — or Ms Big, as it turned out — but the sight of Sam getting clean away hurt Fizz like she was trapped in a microwave and cooking from the inside out.

She had something like a hundred yards to run, much of it in the wrong direction because the gate that led from the wire-fenced car park to the boarding area was halfway along the side boundary and the fence was something like twelve feet high. However, before she had taken more than half a dozen painful bounds the sound of a fast-approaching police siren jerked her head round and she was just in time to see, as it whizzed past her, the grim profiles of three men, two of which were Fleming and Buchanan. Late as usual.

They pulled into the car park behind her but the police car was trapped on the far side of the enclosure by the rows of parked cars and the three running figures which emerged from it had the full width of the car park to cover to reach the gateway to the wharf. There was simply no way, Fizz realised as she limped doggedly onwards, that any of them had a chance of catching up with Sam before the boat pulled out.

Behind her she could see Ian Fleming and another guy running along the wrong side of the chain-link fence at right angles to the edge of the wharf and only yards from the gangway. They still had fifty yards to go to reach the gate but Buchanan emerged from behind a Transit van and took a couple of flying leaps, one to the bonnet of a Land Rover and one to the roof, from where he grabbed the top of the fence and swung himself over. He dropped a couple of points on the landing but he was up in a flash and almost at the gangway before Fleming had reached the gate.

Fizz, by that time, had staggered to a halt,

completely blown. She was hanging limply to the fence when Buchanan reached the deck hand who was just scrambling to his feet. Unfortunately, the man had now been joined by a second deck hand and together they looked determined — and able — to block Buchanan's charge.

Buchanan shouted something unintelligible but the other two weren't having any.

One of them spread-eagled his arms across the end of the gangway and bellowed in a voice that carried like a foghorn, 'For fuck's sake, are you all mad or what? We're no' goin' *oot* — we're comin' *in!*'

Buchanan just stood there, panting, his arms hanging by his sides, while the other two caught up with him. After a minute he heard Fizz's hysterical laughter behind him, turned his head, and eventually managed an uncertain grin.

As he walked over to her she could see he had no socks on and that his chin was blue with unshaved beard. There was a lot of blood on his shirt collar and a tear on the knee of his trousers.

'Well,' she said, 'I don't know about you, but I've had a lousy day.'

He nodded. 'Tell me about it.'

'You too?' She started to walk along the fence towards the gate and he went with her, stealing concerned glances at her through the links when he thought she wasn't looking. 'I wonder sometimes if we're in the right business.'

'Yes,' he said gravely. 'I have to say I've been thinking along those lines myself today. Quite a bit, actually.'

'Maybe we're getting past it.'

'We certainly bit off more than we could chew this time.' He met her at the gateway and slipped a supportive arm round her as they turned to walk back to the gangway.

'Well,' Fizz said, 'you win some, you lose some.'

'Makes you think, though. I reckon we'll be leaving things to the boys in blue in future.'

Fizz twisted her head round to see his face.

'You don't really mean that?'

'I really mean it, Fizz. I've made up my mind.'

'So, this is our last case?'

'It's not a job for amateurs. We're lucky to be getting out of this one alive. Now's the time to be hanging up our bloodhounds.'

'You're right, of course,' Fizz said sadly. 'There's no denying it, but I'll miss it all the same.'

She drew a deep sigh and turned her face away so he wouldn't see her smile.

We do hope that you have enjoyed reading this large print book.

Did you know that all of our titles are available for purchase?

We publish a wide range of high quality large print books including:
Romances, Mysteries, Classics
General Fiction
Non Fiction and Westerns

Special interest titles available in large print are:
The Little Oxford Dictionary
Music Book
Song Book
Hymn Book
Service Book

Also available from us courtesy of Oxford University Press:
Young Readers' Dictionary
(large print edition)
Young Readers' Thesaurus
(large print edition)

For further information or a free brochure, please contact us at:
Ulverscroft Large Print Books Ltd.,
The Green, Bradgate Road, Anstey,
Leicester, LE7 7FU, England.
Tel: (00 44) 0116 236 4325
Fax: (00 44) 0116 234 0205

Other titles in the
Ulverscroft Large Print Series:

STRANGER IN THE PLACE

Anne Doughty

Elizabeth Stewart, a Belfast student and only daughter of hardline Protestant parents, sets out on a study visit to the remote west coast of Ireland. Delighted as she is by the beauty of her new surroundings and the small community which welcomes her, she soon discovers she has more to learn than the details of the old country way of life. She comes to reappraise so much that is slighted and dismissed by her family — not least in regard to herself. But it is her relationship with a much older, Catholic man, Patrick Delargy, which compels her to decide what kind of life she really wants.

NOVEMBER TREE

Ann Stevens

Rowena and Phyllida are both sixty-something, and both on their own — so what better than sharing their declining years? They have known each other for fifty years — and there's something to be said for the devil you know. But who said that retirement would be peaceful? Amidst demanding relatives and with a new suitor on the horizon, it looks as though the future is far from predictable, bringing past resentments and a festering secret to the surface. As the tension rises and tolerance falters, the long-suppressed truth threatens to erupt in a most unpredictable way.